Something exploded under La Loma and he rose up in a blast of flame and acrid smoke. He came down and then something blew him up in the air again. Firecrackers. Someone screamed, 'You bastard! What are you –'

It was the Kristo.

It was the smiling, bald headed man.

The Kristo screamed, 'You've got a bet on the winning bird, you –'

The smiling, bald headed man kept on smiling. As the Kristo began climbing into the ring to rescue the birds, the smiling, bald headed man, drawing a large automatic pistol and as the crowd around fled screaming, aiming carefully, still smiling, shot the Kristo once cleanly between the eyes and blew the back of his head out all over the descending La Loma.

The Kristo, dead in the instant the bullet had torn away his face, gouting blood, coming down like a ton of lead – in the very instant of his victory, fell full length on La Loma the moment he landed, and, decisively, ending the match, crushed him completely to. . .

Well, what else?

. . .*to soup.*

MANILA BAY

William Marshall

Mysterious Press books (UK) are published
in association with Arrow Books Limited
62-65 Chandos Place, London WC2N 4NW

An imprint of Century Hutchinson Limited

London Melbourne Sydney Auckland
Johannesburg and agencies throughout
the world

First published in Great Britain
by Martin Secker & Warburg Ltd 1986
Mysterious Press edition 1988

Printed and bound in Great Britain by
Anchor Brendon Limited, Tiptree, Essex

ISBN 0 09 959370 X

MENDEZ

Boy, when you weren't going to get an even break, you just weren't going to get an even break.

'Texas hybrid fighting cock La Loma of Corregidor!'

You weren't going to get an even break. The moment he craned his neck in the center of the Conquistadore Cockpit on India Street to crow, the Sentenciador – the umpire – stuck his finger into his eye.

Texas hybrid fighting cock La Loma of Corregidor fell out of his handler's arm onto the sawdust. His handler stood on his tail.

'Battling Mendez – Mendez The Great of Manila!' No one dropped him or stood on his tail. If they had, the crowd, screaming in outrage, would have torn the dropper limb from limb and then shot him.

Battling Mendez was an ancient, pure black, all muscle, thoroughly evil-looking fighting cock with one eye and one false leg and so famous throughout the Philippines after his thirty-eight clear victories in the last five seasons that he advertised his own brand of Mendez beer on television and opened supermarkets.

Someone picked up La Loma and held him out of the way as Mendez came in with his handler and winked at the crowd. Battling Mendez had on his second-best fighting false leg, his bamboo one. The handler lifted it up and showed the crowd that it was only going to be a short slaughter before Mendez went back to his hens for the rest of the day.

The crowd screamed, 'Ayo!' Someone in the front galleries, looking at La Loma of Corregidor being held upside down by his handler goggling at Battling Mendez, yelled out, 'Ho! Ho!'

When you weren't going to get an even break, you weren't going to get an even break.

His handler was polishing the sheath around Mendez's taped-on steel spur with a silk cloth. The sheath, on Mendez's good leg, was solid silver. The sheath on La Loma's spur was plastic. The way things were going they were going to make him fight with it still on.

La Loma, still upside down, went, 'Siss!' His handler – *his own handler* – said in Philippino, 'Shut up!'

Battling Mendez's single eye glittered. He sighed – almost – with pure boredom. Boy, when you weren't going to get an even break . . .

'*Anim!*' Standing in the center of the glassed-in rectangular cockpit, entreating the front galleries and the second-class wooden benches behind them, the Kristo – the Christ: the odds setter – raising his arm called the odds on the kid from Corregidor. '*Anim!* Sixes! Six to one!'

There was a roar of laughter. Someone in the stalls yelled back, '*Anim?* On La Loma of Corregidor?' It was the ho, ho man. The ho, ho man shrieked down in derision, '*Dalawampu't anim!* Twenty-six.' The ho, ho man yelled down, '*Sandaan dalawampu't anim!* Maybe *a hundred* and twenty-six to one!' The kid from Corregidor was going back to Corregidor across Manila Bay in a soup tin.

'*Siyam!* Nines!'

The crowd screamed back, 'Ninety-nines!'

The Kristo, outstretching his arms, begging the crowd, shouted, '*Dalawampu!* Twenties!' He looked at Battling Mendez's second-best bamboo fighting leg and Battling Mendez's single glittering eye and he looked at Battling Mendez's adversary looking at Battling Mendez. The Kristo shouted, 'Mendez has won thirty-eight battles over five seasons – no cock before him has ever won more than eight fights in succession! He's not a real cock anymore – he opens supermarkets!' The Kristo said with a smirk, 'He's a television personality!'

Someone yelled back, 'Mendez Beer Makes Men With Hearts Of Steel!'

The Kristo shouted back, 'He's only got one eye and he's eight years old! He's got a wooden leg!' On the other, the right leg, the gaffer was removing the silver sheath covering the taped-on fighting spur. It was a number three curved spur honed razor-sharp, by special arrangement with the Philippines Razor Blade Company. Its edge glittered under the neon lights. The Kristo yelled, 'OK, I'll bankrupt the bookies – twenty-five to one on the other bird!' He had forgotten the other bird's name. 'On La Loma of Corregidor!' It was a little after ten in the morning on a Sunday, the day you pleaded with God for a few favors. The Kristo said finally, 'Give me a bet on the other bird or the match is off!' There was a smooth faced bald headed man wearing an expensive shirt in the front row of the gallery and the Kristo leaping down from the ring and perching on the wooden railing directly above him, shouted, 'Ten pesos – cigarette money! If I can't get a bet on the other bird, then if you've come a long way to see Mendez slaughter something, you've come for nothing!'

Someone behind the gallery – the peasants in the gods, the hecklers, the no-money men – yelled, 'You bet on him! I'll give you two thousand to one!'

'I can't bet on him! It's against the rules!' In the pit he was ready to go. The most famous fighting cock in the entire country, in the world, was ready to go. Held back by their handlers the cocks were getting ready to fight. The Kristo yelled in a desperate final appeal to macho, 'Isn't there anyone here man enough to believe that a champion can be toppled?' Maybe there were a few discontents in the audience. The Kristo, raising his arms in crucifixion – if there was anyone from Counter Subversion listening he was going to need the practice – shrieked, 'The Old Guard can be replaced!'

Mendez's handler was putting the sheath back on the spur. In his handler's arms it looked as if Mendez was going to sleep.

A hand went up in the stalls. It held up two fingers.

The Kristo said, 'Twenty! Twenty pesos at – ' La Loma didn't have a hope in Hell. The Kristo said munificently, 'Two hundred! Two hundred at – *At two hundred and fifty to one!*'

He saw another hand raised. It held up five fingers. Fifty pesos. The place was full of pikers. The Kristo said, 'Fifty at – ' He was going to say one hundred and fifty. Maybe the man was poor. Maybe it was all he had. The widow's mite. The Kristo, like all Manilans, was a good Catholic. The Kristo said, 'At eighty to one!' The man didn't look poor. He looked like a Communist. He was wild-eyed. The Old Guard might be going to be replaced but there was no point in giving the New Guard the funds to do it with overnight. The Kristo yelled, 'Any more?'

'Five hundred.' It was the bald headed man at his feet. Without making a gesture with his hand, the bald headed man said in English, *'Five hundred.'*

The Kristo said, 'What?'

The bald headed man was smiling. The bald headed man said, 'At even money.'

The Kristo said, 'What?'

The bald headed man said, *'Five hundred on the bird from Corregidor at even money.'*

'Five hundred pesos?'

The bald headed man, shaking his head said, still smiling, 'No, dollars.' He asked, 'Yes or no?'

The Kristo said, 'Aye?' He looked back at Mendez and La Loma. The sheaths were off and the handlers had the two birds facing each other on the sawdust. He looked at La Loma. He saw his eye bright with spirit. He saw – He saw the soup tin going back on the hydrofoil to the Corregidor Poultry Restaurant. He saw the bald headed man ending up in the Pasig River with a knife between his shoulderblades if he welched. The Kristo said, 'Yes! Yes! OK? Sure! *Yes!*' The Kristo nodding, remembering the bet, wondering why the bald headed man, who didn't look mentally incompetent, kept smiling, said with enthusiasm, 'All bets closed!' He saw the Philippines Razor Blade Company's work on Mendez's spur flash in the light. The Kristo yelled to the white-shirted Sentenciador in the center of the ring, 'Let the battle begin!' He

4

looked at La Loma and felt better. The Kristo said softly to himself as he took up a position between the bald headed man and the way out, 'Heh, heh, heh!'

The Republic of the Philippines lies in the South China Sea midway between the north coast of Australia, where there is a population density of approximately one human being per ten thousand square miles, and the south coast of China where the statistics are reversed. After four hundred years of colonial rule by Spain and fifty years in the American Commonwealth it is the only Asian country to be almost totally Christian, to use the Western music scale, to speak English as a first language, and to bear no colonial grudges. The country is composed of some seven thousand volcanic islands – more or less, depending on the earth's daily activity – of which Luzon in the north and Mindanao in the south are where most people live.

The capital is Manila in the north island of Luzon where the main interests of the people are cockfighting, basketball and chess, a combination within the same national psyche which has been known to send sociologists fresh from Western universities back to those Western universities gibbering.

The climate is tropical with a wet and a dry season, the people brown and almond-eyed with a propensity for romance and arson. Presently, the going rate for bribing a parking policeman in the poorer areas is approximately seven pesos or fifty-three cents.

Manila's sunsets are justifiably famous if you can see them for the high rise buildings or the fires.

There are almost no tourists in Metro Manila these days and if you do go there, everyone – especially the Foreign Currency Deficit Department – is very glad to see you coming.

Each morning, standing on the balcony of his first floor apartment in Paranaque south of the city center, Lieutenant Felix Elizalde of the Western District Detective Bureau craned to see the sunrise. Each morning, because of the buildings in the way, he could see nothing.

Some mornings, because of the smog, or in the wet season from July to September, he could not even see the buildings.

Each morning, without fail, smelling Manila, hearing it, knowing it was there, he couldn't wait to begin the day.

He went up. He saw, for an instant, Mendez's gut exposed, the bamboo leg flailing in mid-air as they clashed six feet from the floor of the cockpit, and La Loma, slashing, got a lick in with his blunt spur that bounced off the bamboo, split it, careered off the ball on the end where the foot should have been, and coming down, got tangled up in Mendez's feathers. Mendez was a ground fighter, La Loma a wing fighter. On the sawdust, Mendez, turning over to get his spur back for the cut, rolled as La Loma still caught up in him, shoved with all his strength and lifted the bastard up again for a second bout in mid-air.

He had him. Mendez was off line, twisting in the air with his spur in the wrong direction and La Loma, thrusting hard put the spur in at the base of the tail feathers and chopped away half of his rear assembly. The feathers came down like snow. La Loma, turning, getting Mendez's bad eye facing him, hitting the ground, catching him up again and lifting, dragged him up for a third time. He saw feathers. He hadn't been touched. He saw something glitter and Mendez's spur was slashing air and missing him. La Loma, half a second left in the air, somersaulting, exposing for a second his vitals, short-stabbed with the spur and felt it hit. He felt Mendez tremble. He felt . . .

He was winning. He felt Mendez shudder. They were going down. Mendez, on the ground, turning over, slashing, caught him a glancing blow on the crop and staggering, getting up, feeling himself being propelled in the air, went, 'Siss!' He didn't look bored anymore. The kid from Corregidor wasn't going back to Corregidor in the soup tin, he was going back in glory. Mendez, in flight, got in a slash that only took off feathers and, exposed, caught the point of the spur at the top of his bamboo leg and went down towards the sawdust losing slivers.

'Ayo! Ayo!' The crowd, on its feet, shrieked, 'Loma! Loma!'

He was in the air again, not so high, but in the air. La Loma with his last strength, colliding against Mendez, slashing, spinning, his wings out and flapping, drew back his spur for

6

the death blow. The crowd shrieked, 'Ayo! Ayo! AYO!'

He was down. Mendez was down. He was on the sawdust, rolling around, one of his wings loose and useless. La Loma, for an instant, saw the fear in the one black eye. It was as if Mendez was in a shallow hole in the sawdust, rolling around. All he needed was to smother him in sharpened steel.

'Siss!'

He was on him. He saw Mendez jerk his head to keep his eye clear. He saw . . . The spur came back. All it was going to take . . . La Loma, advancing on him, his hackles up, tensed to rise in the air and come down on him like a sack of rice. He rose, he flew, he leapt, he became airborne, he described a graceful parabola, he . . .

Something exploded under him and he rose up again in a blast of flame and acrid smoke. He came down again and then something blew him up in the air again. Firecrackers. Someone screamed, 'You bastard! What are you – '

It was the Kristo.

It was the smiling, bald headed man.

The Kristo screamed, 'You've got a bet on the winning bird, you – '

The smiling, bald headed man kept on smiling. As the Kristo began climbing into the ring to rescue the birds, the smiling, bald headed man, drawing a large automatic pistol and as the crowd around fled screaming, aiming carefully, still smiling, shot the Kristo once cleanly between the eyes and blew the back of his head out all over the descending La Loma.

Mendez was down. He was down. Some days . . .

Some days you . . .

Some days you had a chance of . . .

Boy, when you weren't going to get an even break, you just weren't going to get an even break.

The Kristo, dead in the instant the bullet had torn away his face, gouting blood, coming down like a ton of lead – in the very instant of his victory, fell full length on La Loma the moment he landed, and, decisively, ending the match, crushed him completely to . . .

Well, what else?

. . . *to soup.*

7

I

In downtown Manila on a Sunday morning there may not have been fairies at the bottom of the garden, but there was as sure as hell a headhunter in the dinosaur park.

There were also – in theory at least – Japanese bonehunters, so, altogether in that part of the world – with the possible exception of your shoes – very few parts of you were safe.

The bonehunters were after Japanese bones, the headhunter was after Japanese heads, the stone dinosaurs and pterodactyls and giant lizards, being long extinct and of stone were merely *after*, and the gardener in the Children's Stone Dinosaur Park in Luneta off Taft Avenue had begun to sigh a lot.

In the lair of a stone sabre-toothed tiger the gardener said to Detective Sergeant Baptiste Bontoc, 'That's not a real axe, is it?' He looked at Bontoc down on all fours in the lair, his headhunter's shell necklace hanging out from his T-shirt and his Walther PPK showing in its ankle holster above his sock and, shaking his head, said firmly, 'No, it's just rubber or plastic or something, isn't it?'

Bontoc was gazing out from the lair looking for Japanese. His eyes glittered. About five foot one and a half inches in his running shoes, the necklace clanked as he moved.

The gardener, a slight, begrimed man in his early fifties, wearing his CHIEF GARDENER RAMIREZ, PARKS DEPARTMENT badge proudly on his white coveralls, said, still shaking his head and still sighing, 'No, I can tell, it's just wood or plastic or rubber or – ' The curved neck-shaped axe glinted in a shaft of light from a crack in the cement lair. The gardener said in horror, 'A souvenir axe made of aluminium?'

Bontoc said, 'What?' He had been educated like all the headhunting Bontoc tribe of northern Luzon by American Protestant missionaries and he could only understand basic headhunter and best Minnesota accented English. Philippino as it was murdered in Manila was a complete mystery to him.

The gardener, like all Manilan Philippinos, spoke perfect English with a Spanish accent so thick you could cleave it. He looked at the cleaver.

The gardener said in English, wringing his hands together, still looking at the axe, 'They were here again during the night. They won't come during the day.' Everywhere in his beautiful nurtured and cared for garden there were holes where the Japanese, looking for the bones of their fathers and grand-fathers killed during the Second World War, had attacked the landscape like moles. The gardener said, 'How many bones can there be in one little park? They must have them all by now.' The gardener said encouragingly, 'The Bontocs gave up headhunting centuries ago, didn't they?' He looked at Bontoc's eyes and the edge of the tattooing on his chest he could see behind the shell necklace at the top of his T-shirt. The gardener said, ' – decades ago – ' The gardener said, 'Years ago – ' The gardener said, 'No one still – ' The gardener said nervously, 'Do they?'

'The weekly plane to Tokyo doesn't leave until Tuesday morning.' Bontoc, fingering his axe, said firmly, 'They'll come.' He peered out from his den at the park. Everywhere, between the flowers and trees, rising out of the painted concrete primeval mud there were painted concrete primeval beasts. Bontoc said, 'The great minds at Police Headquarters have thought it all through, picked the best man for the job, made a game plan that has a one hundred per cent chance of success, consulted the airline timetables, cast their bones and they'll come.' There was a speck of dirt on the short narra-wood handle of his head-axe and he flicked it away with a manicured fingernail. Apart from the fingernails he looked like

9

a man who knew how to use a head-axe. Bontoc said, 'Don't worry. All I'm going to do is scare them off.' He said softly, 'We don't want to cause an incident.'

Maybe it was decades since the Bontocs had taken heads. The gardener, nodding, said, 'Right.' The gardener, nodding, said, 'I've got a lot of time for cultural minorities like the Bontocs and the mountain people. I think it's a good thing that people like you – ' He looked at the axe and tried to think of something polite, ' – that people like you are integrating themselves into the cities and bringing the best of your – ' He again tried to think of something polite, ' – of your life-ways to Manila to enrich us.'

'Sure.' He touched his shell necklace.

The gardener said, 'Um . . .' He glanced back at his pock-marked garden and looked worried. The gardener said, 'Look, I know that things are different up in the mountains and that – '

Bontoc said darkly, 'No one in the Bontoc tribe has taken a head for weeks.'

The gardener said, 'Ha, ha, ha!' The gardener said, 'Oh.' If you looked hard at the man – with him on all fours like the mad beast of Borneo you had to twist your neck to do it – you could tell that he was a person of reason. The gardener said, 'Right.' The gardener said, 'I think we in the New Society should encourage our cultural minorities to experience every facet of metropolitan life.' The gardener said, 'I wouldn't be the one to – ' The gardener said, 'I saw a documentary about the primitive tribes on Channel Four once and I – ' He wasn't vicious or tough or decapitory at all. You could tell. Someone in his police headquarters was merely giving him the opportunity to –

The gardener said desperately, 'Please, for the love of God and all my hard work over the years, if you get hungry, please don't start eating the trees!'

'*Durian* bombs? He throws *durian bombs*? No one told me that.' In United Nations Avenue, a little down from Western District Police Headquarters, Fidel Manuel Antonio Martinez (it was on his ID taxi card), looking horrified, said, 'No.

Absolutely not. No way, never! Forget it!' Hand grenades would have been OK, maybe even the odd Claymore mine or dynamite stick taped with four-inch nails, but *durian bombs*? Martinez, putting his hand protectively on the bonnet of his taxi and shaking his head said, 'Durian bombs? No! Forget it!'

Detective Sergeant Jesus-Vincente Ambrosio merely smiled. He was Mr Cool. He was fresh from his Detective Sergeant's Course. The course was called the Socio-Public Relationship Officers' Orientation Group (SPROOG)/Intermediate General Leadership Level (IGLL). Ambrosio said unperturbed (after SPROOG and IGLL you took on a mantle of imperturbability), 'He doesn't throw in durians, he only throws in a glass vial containing – '

Martinez said, 'What? Fruit of the durian?' The durian was the vilest fruit on the face of the Earth. Closed, on the tree, a member of the jackfruit family, it resembled a spiky melon. Open, cut into slices for the enjoyment of its connoisseurs, it still resembled a melon. It smelled, however, like a year-old sewer after a herd of water buffalos had used it as a rutting hole and then, getting sick of it, had pissed all over it, and then – Martinez said, 'What? *Pulp* of the durian?'

With SPROOG and IGLL you were on your way UP (Urban Promotions). NSC (Next Stop Commissioner). Ambrosio – SPROOG-IGLL-NSC-UP – all that, said calmly, 'No, essence of durian. Durian juice.'

'He stops cabs in the middle of Roxas Boulevard and throws in – !'

Ambrosio said, 'They're already stopped at traffic lights or – '

'He stops cabs in the middle of the street – airconditioned cabs – and he gets the passenger in the back to wind down his window and then he throws in – ' The smell around him in United Nations Avenue, the usual level of near fatal carbon monoxide and exhaust fumes was as nothing – 'He throws in a glass vial of durian juice?' Martinez, his voice rising, said, '*Into my airconditioned cab?*' Martinez said, 'Are you *mad*?' He had thought when he had first seen the man flagging him down that he was a rich bugger off to the races. The expensive, embroidered long sleeved barong tagalog shirt and the pressed trousers – even the glowing, scrubbed face – had made him think –

Instead, what he had got was a crazed cop. Martinez, glancing at the date on his calendar watch to make sure it wasn't April the First, said, 'You want me to drive you up and down Roxas Boulevard so you can pass as a rich person so some maniac, when we're stopped at a traffic light, can get you to wind down the window so he can throw into my cab – into my airconditioning system, into my livelihood – *a durian bomb?*' Martinez said, 'What's in it for me?'

The course had taught you to keep calm, to weather the storm, to let the civilian have his say and then, when he had done, when he gasped for breath or went red in the face with exasperation, to simply state to him in clear terms what it was you wanted. Ambrosio said, 'Full insurance cover and one hundred pesos an hour.' It always worked.

Martinez said, 'No.'

'And the chance to have your licence endorsed as a friend of the police.'

Martinez said, 'No.'

'And the opportunity to help in the apprehension of a criminal preying on the poor.'

Martinez said, 'I thought you said it was the rich. If the people he hits with the bomb in the back of airconditioned cabs are so poor what are they doing riding around in airconditioned cabs?'

Appeal to the civilian's self-esteem, his *amor propio*. Ambrosio said, 'The rich are people too.'

Martinez said, 'No, they're not.'

Don't lose your cool. Ambrosio said, 'And also you'll have the opportunity to participate in an exciting adventure on the roads.' He was a born-again middle manager. The course had taught him to manage. Ambrosio said, 'And to get your parking tickets fixed for a month!'

'I won't have any parking tickets! My cab will be in the fumigation station at Customs!'

The course had taught him never to need his fist. He was kneading his fist. Ambrosio said, 'And – and to have my undying gratitude!'

'Who the hell are you?'

'One day I'll be Commissioner!'

'One day I'll be able to fumigate my cab!'

Appeal to the civilian's sense of womb-like security. Ambrosio said encouragingly, 'I've got a gun.'

It didn't encourage. 'A what? I thought you said he threw in durian bombs!' Martinez, stepping backwards into the traffic, beginning to think of suicide, said, aghast, 'You didn't say he had a gun!'

'He hasn't got a gun!'

'Then why did you tell me you had a gun?' Martinez, looking him up and down, trying to work out where the diabolical thing was strapped to his anatomy said, 'All cops carry guns. Why did you make it a point to tell me you've got a gun?'

'I was trying to reassure you!' That was part of the course, reassurance. He thought he had done all right in it in the classroom. Ambrosio said, 'Look! Look at me: I'm young and fit and I can fight off anyone without even *using* my gun.' Confuse the civilian.

He wasn't that sort of civilian. Martinez, looking him up and down, said, 'Who told you you were fit?' He looked weedy.

'The Police Board!'

'Did the Police Board tell you to tell people that you carried a gun when you didn't have to tell them you were carrying a gun?' Martinez, backing away, said, 'These rich people riding around in airconditioned cabs, after he throws in his durian bomb on them – what does he do then?'

Ambrosio said, 'He robs them.'

'Of what?' On the sidewalk behind him there were bags and packages from Bloomingdale's meant to look as if they contained expensive and exclusive shopping. They looked as if they contained bricks. People were walking around them; no one needed any bricks. Martinez said, 'In airconditioned cabs, people keep the windows closed. How does he throw a bomb in through a closed window?'

'He gets them to wind their window down.'

'How?'

Leave them guessing. Ambrosio said, 'If you won't help me I

can't tell you that.' He smiled his secret smile.

Martinez said, 'Good.' He turned to get into his cab. Martinez said, 'Nice talking to you. Enjoy yourself. If I see you in trouble on the street you can rely on me to drive straight past you.'

'He offers to sell them something and they wind down the window to buy it!'

'What?'

Ambrosio said, 'Look, please, as a favor to me . . .'

'What does he offer to sell them?'

'Will you do it if I tell you?'

'Maybe.'

Ambrosio said, 'We don't know! The six people who have been robbed so far in the last two days – to a man – won't say!'

Martinez said, 'Dirty books – '

Ambrosio said, 'Three of the victims were women.'

Martinez said, 'Ahh . . .'

'Elderly women.' He was on his way UP. He was on his way down. He was weedy. Ambrosio, starting to hop on the sidewalk said, 'Look, you'll be insured, you'll be covered. If anything happens to your cab or to you you'll be covered by insurance.' It wasn't working. It had all worked in the classroom when he had practised with other cops, but it wasn't working in United Nations Avenue. Keep the steady gaze on the civilian and state firmly what you want. If all else fails, give him a direct order in an authoritative voice that will chill him into obedience by its officialdom. Ambrosio said, 'Christ in Heaven, you're the third cab driver this morning who's said no to me! If I don't get someone soon I'll be ruined!' The working stiff appeal, the fellow laborers in the vineyard of civilisation approach. The desperate, soon to be demoted to patrolman, non-SPROOG, non-IGLL falling on the knees and grovelling touch . . .

Ambrosio, no longer smiling, no longer firm, no longer on his way UP, said in utter total desperation, pleading, 'Please, oh please, I'll even pay you extra out of my own pocket!'

Such was ambition.

Ambrosio said, 'Well? Please? What do you think? Will you do it?'

*

1 There are descendants (sons and grandsons) of Japanese
   soldiers who fought in the Philippines in the Second
   World War (1941-1945) digging in the enclosed
   Children's Stone Dinosaur Section of the Luneta Parks
   Complex for the bones of their ancestors (fathers and
   grandfathers) who were killed in the Second World War
   (1941-1945) in the area of Manila.

In his tiger's den, Bontoc read the carefully typed sheet of
paper with its Instructions For Cultural Minority Morons laid
out line by line.

2 This practice (the things they are doing: digging up the
   public parks) is illegal.

He was surprised they hadn't added '(Against The Law)'.

3 Japanese visitors to the Republic Of The Philippines are a
   valuable currency earner and it would be wrong to arrest
   them.
4 They should be frightened off.

It was obviously composed by someone in Headquarters
with a mind so advanced he had no trouble making the most
complicated instructions sound like they came straight from
the mouth of a child.

5 You will frighten them off.
6 You will appear, with your cultural background and
   primitive life-way-experience (headhunting and massacres), to be a frightening, uncontrollable figure loose in
   the area of the park (Children's Stone Dinosaur Section).
   You will appear to be aggressive and angry.

No trouble at all. After all, he had only spent fifteen years of
his life in grade and high school, four years studying Business
Administration at Minnesota University and two years working on his Master's at night from Harvard.
Loyal to his superiors' every command, squatting in his lair,

15

fingering his axe and rattling his beads, Bontoc said with no difficulty at all, '*Grrrr!*'

Ambrosio said, 'And you can – ' He was grovelling. He was grovelling to a mere Manila taxi driver. Ambrosio said in one last, final, humiliating, non-SPROOG, non-IGLL gasp (all that was over: he was going to spend his life forever as nothing more than a Sergeant to Elizalde's Lieutenant and – the sum total of his achievement – as a person of average height to Bontoc's pygmysm), 'And you can – '

Where were the hopes of yesteryear? Or even two hours ago?

Ambrosio, crushed, broken, finished, done, the epitome of the rotten cop, said as that worst incitement to crime in the entire history and entity of Asia, 'And – and – '

Martinez said, 'Yes?' His eyes glittered.

Ambrosio said, 'And you can – '

Ambrosio said, 'And you can *speed!*'

He took the insurance papers.

He took the pay chits.

He took the Bloomingdale's bricks and put them on the back seat.

He took Ambrosio gently by the hand and led him to the open rear door.

He took all his hopes and dreams and SPROOG and IGLL and UP and NSC.

Like all Manila taxi drivers, faced with clear, pure logic and a calm, cool demeanour and months of detailed, reasoned sociological learning, he took everything you had.

He took no time thinking about it at all.

His eyes glittered. He was convinced.

Martinez said as an order, '*Get in!*'

7 The bonehunters appear to have maps of the sites of the bones of their dead ancestors.

In his tiger's den, Bontoc, crouching to relieve the strain on his calves, resting his family headhunter's axe that he had bought in an antique shop on Roxas Boulevard that morning carefully against a stone tiger's turd, looked at that one intently.

Maps of the exact area of Luneta Park where their fathers and grandfathers had fallen during the war.

Maps.

He wondered where they had got them.

'Oh Christ! Oh, Christ! Oh CHRIST!'

In the back of the cab, as Martinez went straight through a red light and almost collided with, in turn, a horse drawn calesa, two buses with people hanging off them, a motorcycle, a party of schoolgirls on their way to their devotions, three barrio council trucks carrying full loads of coughing human beings in the rear passenger areas, one dog, three pedestrians and a fire engine, Ambrosio, riveted to the seat, shrieked, 'Slow down! *Slow down!*' No one could hear him above the sound of the traffic and the screams of barely-missed pedestrians, 'Slow down! Take it easy! Slow – ' The speedometer was up to a hundred and eighty kilometers an hour. The cab, weaving in and out of the worst traffic in the world and drivers who always drove on a six-lane highway when there wasn't a highway wider than three lanes anywhere in the country, lifted one wheel off the ground as it turned into Chicago Street, then, running another red light, swerving to avoid workmen carrying spades, made a roaring sound, passed cleanly across three lanes on the airport side of Roxas Boulevard, almost ran down a party of art lovers crossing from the Art Gallery and, making a screeching sound, turned into Roxas Boulevard going towards the docks.

On the far side of Rizal Park there was Manila Bay where you watched the sun go down. You didn't have to go that far. It was going down in the back of the cab.

Martinez, your average Manilan taxi driver, shrieked, 'El Tigre *rides!*'

In the back, Ambrosio, looking for something to hold on to – your average Manilan – in abject, complete, helpless terror, screamed, 'Oh, God! Oh, God! OH . . . *GOD!*'

*

17

11 a.m. on a bright, clear Sunday morning. Everyone was out, all the shops were open, far out on the southern approaches from the airport a couple of suburbs were still smouldering and on TV the government was blaming subversives and people who smoked in bed and seriously considering re-imposing martial law.

But at least it wasn't raining.

2

'He almost won.' In the Conquistadore Cockpit on India Street, the Sentenciador, looking at the remains of La Loma in the center of the ring as Lieutenant Elizalde of the Western District Police turned the Kristo's body slightly on its side to check the pockets, said with admiration, 'Maybe another second . . . But Mendez had Saint Peter on his side.' Elizalde was a mestizo: a mixture of Spanish and Philippino blood with, judging by his face, some American thrown in somewhere back during the days of the Commonwealth. The Sentenciador changing from Philippino to English said to make it clear, 'The patron saint of cockfighters.'

As usual, when there was a crime in Manila, the least interesting part was the crime. The fascination was how witnesses, the moment it happened, disappeared completely into thin air and were never heard of again. In the rows and galleries of perhaps a thousand seats there were left to be counted only three human souls and they were all uniformed cops looking for the fired cartridge case in the front rows. With the body on its side, Elizalde, reaching down and hauling out what was left of La Loma by one of its legs, said, 'Here, take this.' The spur on the right leg was covered in blood. All around it, the sawdust was spotted with little bits of bone and matted hair from the back of the Kristo's head. Elizalde said to the Police Pathologist gathering other little bits of skull from

19

the sawdust at the side of the ring, 'There's nothing here.' He took the Kristo's wallet from his side trouser pocket and flipped it open to look at his ID card. He asked the Sentenciador, 'Royares. Was that his name?'

'Francisco Royares.' The Sentenciador wore very worn leather shoes. They were the sort of shoes men with money had hand made and then wore for years. Even when they were old they were a badge of wealth. To some minds they were even more of a badge of wealth when they were old. The Sentenciador said, looking at the dead cock, 'He was fighting Battling Mendez of Manila. He had spirit.'

Once, the Kristo had had life. Elizalde, glancing at the Police Pathologist Doctor Watanabe as he bent down in his checked golf trousers to collect another piece of skull, said evenly, 'Who shot him?' Cockers were a breed apart. You saw them in the barrios carrying their cocks in the crook of their arms, their hands constantly stroking their birds' heads and talking to them. You never seemed to see their wives and children. Elizalde said, 'Royares.' He spoke Philippino to make it clear: 'Royares. You must have seen who it was. Was it anybody you knew?'

Hideki Watanabe was a Japanese-Philippino who always looked like he was on his way to a golf open. At the side of the ring he said, 'Ah!' He had found something.

The Sentenciador said, 'No.' He was still looking at La Loma and shaking his head.

Elizalde said suddenly, 'Look at me!'

'No! All I saw was a bald headed man who had made a big bet with the Kristo on La Loma – '

'Forget La Loma!'

' – who had made a big bet and then – '

'Where are the betting slips?'

'There aren't any. The Kristo in a cockfight always remembers the bets.' He looked at Elizalde with contempt. He wasn't an aficionado. The Sentenciador said, 'All I know is that I heard a couple of bangs and then Royares fell over and stopped the fight.' If he wasn't a cocker to hell with him. He didn't take orders from Spanish-looking cops. He looked hard at La Loma and gave its corpse a salute. The Sentenciador said,

20

'Think of it: a rank outsider from Corregidor, maybe here today, could have toppled – '

Elizalde was still going through the dead man's pockets and transferring the contents into a glassine envelope in the pocket of his cotton hang-out safari shirt. Drawing a breath, he called out to Patrolman Innocente bending down in the front gallery, 'Anything?'

Innocente stood up. He had something stuck on the end of a pencil. Innocente, touching at the ivory butted .357 magnum he wore in a thumb break holster on his Sam Browne belt called back, 'A cartridge case. It's a case from a .45 automatic.' He turned the case on the end of the pencil and cast his expert eye over the markings, 'Hardball, US issue for a Government Model Colt, very common.' He looked directly to where the Kristo had been standing when the gun had gone off. Innocente said with admiration, 'That bastard could really shoot! Where did he get him? In the head?'

The trouble with Manila was that, by and large, in their own way, everyone was mad about something. Elizalde said, 'Yes, he got him in the head.' He said in case there might have been some small clue where Innocente stood to make sense of it, 'He threw two firecrackers into the ring and then he shot from where you're standing.'

There wasn't anything there where Innocente stood that might have made sense of it. Or, if there was, Innocente wasn't looking for it. Innocente, putting his hand on his gunbutt and looking significantly at Patrolman Pineda, said with enthusiasm, 'Wow!' It was Spanish Catholicism. If you couldn't enjoy sex without guilt you turned to guns. Innocente said in Pineda's direction, 'Maybe if you carried a decent gun like mine you could shoot like that too, Pineda!'

Maybe if they both carried decent guns they could shoot each other. Elizalde, looking over at Patrolman Gil moving up one of the aisles, asked, 'Anything?'

Gil shook his head.

Watanabe said, 'Here.' He had something in a glassine envelope. He saw Elizalde still gazing to Gil as the man went up the aisle looking at the floor. Watanabe said, 'Felix – ' He held out the envelope. 'Chinese firecracker paper.' There was even part of the manufacturer's name on the burned brown fragment. Watanabe said, 'The Chien Lung Firecracker Company, Taipei. It's something left over from Chinese New Year.' He was a pure Japanese who spent his entire life trying to look Philippino. It was a hopeless task. Brushing at his checked golf trousers and seeing memories of the Second World War in the Sentenciador's eyes that simply weren't there, Watanabe said to curry acceptance, 'I see the ads on television Battling Mendez does.' He was trying to think of a way of suggesting that he didn't have a Japanese-made television set to watch it on, but since there were no other television sets in the entire world anymore he wasn't going to make it, 'I follow the cockfights. I'm married to a Philippina from Cebu. We've been here in Manila now for years. I love it. I follow the fights. Mendez is some bird, huh?' He was speaking Philippino. It sounded like Japanese. He saw it in the Sentenciador's eyes. 'Do you think if the bird here hadn't been killed – ?'

Elizalde said, 'Where is the other bird?'

Watanabe, still looking at the Sentenciador's face said quickly in English, 'Mendez. The other bird was the famous Battling Mendez – '

'And his handler?'

'They left.'

Elizalde said, 'And La Loma's handler?'

'They all left.' The Sentenciador, stepping back as Elizalde, still checking the pockets, moved the body a little too far and the dead eyes glared up at him, said, 'They left before the Kristo died. They left when he was only dying.'

'He died instantly.'

'No.' The Sentenciador, shaking his head, said firmly, 'No. I saw him hit the ground and he was still moving and they left with Mendez before he became still.' The Sentenciador wringing his hands and looking down at his expensive shoes, said without doubt, 'When they carried Mendez out to the Cock Hospital to have his wounds seen to, this man was still alive. I saw him move.'

He had had his head blown into fragments by a single smashing bullet moving at fifteen hundred feet a second. In the hole in the back of the head, mixed in with what was left of his brains, you could actually see where the crushed, metal-clad slug had lodged. Elizalde said, 'He was dead the moment he was shot.'

'No! No bird can fight again for a month if it's been present at the death of a cocker in the cockpit!' The Sentenciador was stepping backwards, shaking his head. His expensive shoes were picking up feathers on the sawdust from the battle. He rubbed his shoes together to get the feathers off, 'No! Mendez is owned by rich men! No!' The Sentenciador said, 'No, Mendez's handlers took him straight out of the pit before the Kristo died so the curse isn't on him.' He was echoing something he had already said that morning to someone on the phone, 'Mendez still has the protection of Saint Peter and there's no curse on his luck at all!' He said before Elizalde could argue with him, 'No! That's definite – finished!' He said in Philippino, shaking his head once to end the matter, '*Hindi tama*, this is correct!' He was very badly frightened, '*Hindi tama!*'

Watanabe the Philippino said slowly, 'Well, it's possible . . .'

Elizalde said, 'It *isn't* possible!' There was more than just dead cocks and guns and firecrackers and great shots in the cockpit, there was a dead human being. Elizalde said, 'Where is the Cock Hospital?'

'On Pasig Street.' The Sentenciador, still shaking his head, disappointing Watanabe by taking no notice of him at all, said to make it clear, 'Anyone would have done the same. We have a code here. The bird comes first.' He looked down at the dead Kristo, 'And he believed in it!' He was beginning to shake. He was very frightened. 'And he would have done the same! Mendez was his bird too – Mendez is owned by –' He changed his mind, 'It's a valuable bird! It brings in money!' He looked at Elizalde's face, 'You won't understand this, but the bird has spirit, luck, fortune – *power!*' He saw the two cops with the big guns were listening: he could tell from their faces they understood. The Sentenciador said, 'Anyone who loved gamebirds would have done it.' He looked down at what was left of La Loma, 'If he could speak he would have told them to

23

take his enemy away to save him too!' He was losing control. He was talking to some sort of mixed-blood Western educated liberal. The Sentenciador said, 'When Mendez was taken away from the cockpit Royares was still alive!' He said, 'The Cock Hospital on Pasig Street! If you've got any questions ask them there.' The Sentenciador said, 'Ask for Paulo.'

'Paulo what?'

'Royares!' He looked down at the Kristo. The Sentenciador said angrily, 'Yes! That's right! His brother!' His eyes were filled with hate.

The Sentenciador, kicking feathers and blood and bits of white bone in the sawdust with his shoe, not caring what it did to the wonderful worn-in leather, said with real, undiluted hatred, 'You. It's people like you, one day, when this country finally goes to hell, who are going to get the cockfights banned!' He said with his mouth twitching with reined-in emotion, 'That day – that day, Lieutenant Elizalde of the Metro Manila Police – I . . . *I leave!*'

'*Hey!*' From his lair, as the gardener went by mowing with a petrol mower in the main park on the other side of the fence to make grass to pad one of the stone cells, Bontoc called out, 'Hey! That's the Tasaday tribe who eat foliage, not the Bontocs!' The Tasadays, all twenty-five of them, according to an article he had read recently in *Anthropology Today* spent their entire time standing around under trees munching on orchid petals. Bontoc, shrieking above the noise, yelled, 'We Bontocs are educated!' All the seven gates of the six and a half acre dog-leg Stone Dinosaur Park were locked. If the Japanese were going to come they were going to have to come over the fences. That meant they would be young and fit. Bontoc shouted, 'Just so you know that if I call for help you're dealing with an educated man who can tell real danger from hysteria!' The gardener, mowing happily, a handkerchief over his mouth and nose to protect his sinuses, couldn't hear him. 'We Bontocs come from a long line of missionary-educated thoughtful men.' He shrieked out above the noise, 'We don't eat trees! We realize their value in the ecological scheme of things!'

He fingered his axe. From what he had seen on television, what the Japanese did was finger swords.

'OK?' He just didn't want the gardener to get the wrong idea.

The gardener hadn't heard a word he said.

Just for a moment there, the thought of the sword-carrying Yellow Hordes coming over the fences had worried him.

He felt better making it clear just who they were dealing with here.

He nodded to himself.

There was a dried twig in the lair next to him to represent something the sabre-toothed tiger had dragged in along with its last victim and, listening to the sound of the mower going up and down, feeling more confident, he put it thoughtfully into his mouth and began chewing on it.

'*Kristo!*'

'*Sandaan!* One hundred.'

'*Kristo!*'

'*Dalawang – dalawang daan!* Two – two hundred.'

In the rear passenger section of the jeepney – one of the converted Toyota Landcruisers painted up like a Surrealist's nightmare that plied the street as private buses in Manila – the bald headed man, holding the earplug from his miniature businessman's personal dictaphone hard in his ear, listened to the playback.

'*Kristo!*' He had held the microphone up a little under the long sleeve of his left arm and it had picked up, closer, some of the betting in the galleries.

'*Siyam!*'

'*Sampu!*'

'*Siyam! Siyam!*'

'*Sampu!*'

They were people betting not in multiples of hundreds or even tens but in single pesos or centavos.

'KRISTO!' He heard a big better. He heard the roar drown out the reply as Mendez was brought in.

He ran the tape forward.

'Two hundred! Two hundred at – *At two hundred and fifty to one!*'

He heard a muffled roar of derision. He heard – 'Fifty at – '
He touched at the baseball cap he had pulled down over his
bald head. It read MENDEZ BEER MAKES MEN!

He heard a click on the tape, as under his shirt, he had
slipped the safety catch off his automatic.

Opposite him on the other seat there was a sixteen- or
seventeen-year-old girl watching him. Like all Philippinas she
took your breath away.

'At eighty to one! Any more?'

'Five hundred . . .' Without making a gesture with his hand,
the bald headed man had said in English, '*Five hundred.*' He
heard his own voice. He looked at the girl watching him. She
was coveting his tape recorder. He looked with interest at the
way she sat in her short office girl's skirt and she looked away.

'What?'

'At even money.'

'What?'

'*Five hundred on the bird from Corregidor at even money.*'

The jeepney turned suddenly and without warning into
Roxas Boulevard and he almost tipped over with the sudden-
ness of it.

'*Five hundred on the bird from Corregidor at even money!*'
He played it back to hear his own voice again. It was in
English. His accent sounded educated, American, expensive.
He pushed the plug harder against his ear and reached down to
settle his worn and ripped cloth airline-style bag between his
legs. The girl thought it was a ploy to look up her skirt. The
bald headed man saw her look away and snap her knees
together.

'Five hundred pesos?'

He liked wearing the MENDEZ cap. He thought it showed
a bit of macho.

'No, dollars. Yes or no?'

'Aye? Yes! Yes! OK! Sure! *Yes!*'

The bald headed man smiled to himself and touched the
forward button again. He could hear nothing for the shouting
as the battle was fought. He heard the urging and barracking,
the yells and sighs as the birds fought in mid-air tearing at each
other. He heard what sounded like a giant thudding pulse on

the tape – the potency of the crowd – the death in the air – his own heartbeat. He heard, clearly – there – a fizzing sound.

He heard the two firecrackers go off.

He heard, for an instant, silence.

He heard himself stand up: his body rustle, move, stiffen, get ready –

He heard . . .

In the jeepney, terrifying the girl, the bald headed man said suddenly, 'Ahhhh . . .!'

He heard the gun go off and kill the Kristo instantly in the ring where he stood.

He heard the screaming, the terror. He heard people running.

He heard –

It was all, every word and sound of it, on the tape.

The bald headed man, his eyes closed in the back of the jeepney, said softly to himself, 'Ahhh . . .'

He liked killing. It was what he did best.

He opened his eyes and, a moment before he banged on the roof of the jeepney with his fist to signal to the driver that he wanted to get off, he looked directly into the girl's face and, with something in his eyes that terrified her, smiled at her and turned off the tape.

In the deaf and dumb café off Rizal Park, Luneta, Elizalde wrote on a scrap of notepaper, *One Alhambra cigar and may I use the telephone in the kitchen?* He put a five peso coin on the waitress's tray and waited for her to read the note.

The waitress, a lined woman in her fifties – the manageress of the place – nodded. She wrote, as she always did, *The phone is in the kitchen, Mr Elizalde.* She smiled at him, a warm smile, and indicated with her hand, as she always did, the direction to the kitchen door.

Above the honor roll outside the Western District Police Headquarters on United Nations Avenue there was a plaque which read, in bold carved script to commemorate all the dead officers; 'Go Spread The Word, Tell The Passers-By,/That In This Little World Men Knew How To Die.' It had above it, with the Metro Manila Police Crest, the demands Merit. Patriotism. Dignity.

If he could possibly avoid it, he never went there. It frightened him. Elizalde, taking a cigar from the box the woman proffered, mouthed Thank you. He smiled at her. He wondered, as he always did, what possible use a cooperative of deaf and dumb people could have for a telephone – not for their customers outside in the restaurant – but for themselves in the kitchen. It had only been put in when he had started coming there.

He wondered.

He wondered if they had put it in for him.

He looked at the woman's face smiling at him and almost took up the pencil and paper again to ask her.

Taking his cigar, reaching into his pocket for change to leave on the phone to pay for the call, he went into the kitchens, into voicelessness, to use the telephone to ring the dead Kristo's brother at the Cock Hospital.

Walking, the bald headed man reached the Manila Hotel. With the cap and the torn airline bag, none of the taxi drivers or the grovellers outside waiting for the rich people thought to bother with him and he went undisturbed to the main entrance and, proffering not the usual sort of tip the rich people gave, but only a one peso coin, the bald headed man handed the doorman an envelope containing the tiny tape from his recorder.

He said nothing to the white uniformed and starched man. He did not move as the doorman stepped in front of him to cut off his view of the great reception room in the hotel with its chandeliers and wealth. The doorman, six foot one if he was an inch and pale faced as if there was American blood in him somewhere along with the Malay, said, 'Hmm.'

The legend on the envelope read *Room 333*. The doorman felt at it to check it was not a bomb. He looked down at the one peso coin with contempt.

The doorman said in Philippino, looking only at the baseball cap and the torn airline bag, 'Right. Clear the area.'

In the torn airline bag was a Colt Government Model .45 automatic in a padded post office bag.

The bald headed man hefted the bag slightly and felt its weight.

The padded post office bag was already stamped and sealed, ready to be posted.

The doorman said irritably, looking over him, 'Well, didn't you hear me? *Out!*'

There was a taxi coming from the airport with guests in it, and the doorman, giving the bald headed man a shove that apparently was nothing more than a gentle pat, but in fact, almost knocked him off his feet, said as he pocketed the coin, 'Go on! Get out of here!' He stepped forward towards the stopping taxi putting on his warmest smile.

The doorman said between clenched teeth over his shoulder, 'Now! Go! Your little envelope will be delivered! *Go!*'

He couldn't believe it. They had stopped. He had actually obeyed a red light.

For an instant, he saw someone cross between the cars by the Cultural Center and, ducking down, go straight for the median strip in the road. He thought he saw, for an instant in his hand, something black and rectangular. He thought he saw, between a jeepney and a gaggle of cars, between the fumes and the shouting and the abuse and the maneuvring, a cab with the legend AIRCONDITIONED COMFORT on it. He thought he saw –

He saw the figure stop in the central reservation. Ahead, the lights to allow the pedestrians to get across had changed to amber.

He saw a hand come out of a back window of the airconditioned cab as it was wound down. He saw –

The vehicle was less than fifty feet away.

He thought he saw –

He saw the figure with the rectangular package draw back his hand.

He heard the mighty engine of El Tigre roar as Martinez revved it up to full power as the pedestrian lights changed back without warning to red.

He saw –

He shouted, 'There! There! That's him!' He pummeled Martinez hard on the back of the shoulder.

Ambrosio in a frenzy of excitement, yelled, 'There! That's

him! Go! *GO!!*'

He heard the engine of El Tigre die.

Ambrosio said, 'Oh no!'

Martinez said, 'Oops.'

He couldn't get the door of the cab open! It was bent, buckled, fiberglassed, panel-beaten, ill-fitting. Beneath its glossy potent coat El Tigre was a tabby cat.

Wrenching, pulling at the door to get out before the durian bombs started flying with him only fifty feet away, Ambrosio, pulling, yanking, hauling at the door, yelled to Martinez trying to start his engine, 'Open this door! Get this door open or I'll make you suffer!'

Martinez said, 'No!'

'Open this door!'

'Never!'

'Then I'll kick it open!' The brutal approach.

Lying full-length on the seat, pulling at anything he could get his hands on for purchase – in this case, the driver's neck – Ambrosio began kicking maniacally in a frenzy of renewed hope at the door of the cab.

'They have credit cards! The Bontocs, these days, have credit cards!'

No one was listening.

It was the Tasadays who ate flowers and trees and grass.

It was the Tasadays.

It was.

Bontoc said in Bontoc, '*Tufo!*' It was a vile Bontoc swearword. It meant a small container about three by three inches woven from sugar cane leaves used for storing un-cooked rice.

Like the man himself, it lost something in translation.

It was definitely not, in the long and noble history of the race, the best day the Bontocs had ever known . . .

3

MENDEZ BEER FOR LIFE'S HARD STRUGGLE!

Standing rampant and invincible on his polished narra-wood false leg, he was even in the kitchen of the deaf and dumb café on a cardboard poster above the charcoal ovens. It was the essence of the Philippino spirit, a reflection of life. Even if you had a defect, a malformation, some terrible strike against you from birth – even poverty – all you needed to succeed was strength, a little luck, God and maybe some capital you could save up to start with.

Below the poster the waitress manageress of the place and her daughter, both small, scrupulously clean and neat and hope-eyed, were making bibingkang malagkit mix for their patrons' morning snack and pouring it directly into little earthenware bowls on the charcoal to cook. Merienda – the mid-morning meal or mid-afternoon, or mid-evening meal – was taken all the time: the café, run on the capital of the cooperative, stayed open from before dawn until after mid-night. The malagkit as it cooked smelled wonderful. A sort of golden crusted pudding served in a bowl on a wooden platter lined with a banana leaf, it was a combination of coconut milk, brown sugar and aniseed mixed in with rice soaked overnight. It was the café's specialty. No one else in Manila could put the golden crust on it the way they could. It was their specialty. Everyone, to survive, had to have one. At the phone Elizalde

31

took out the glassine envelope from his pocket containing the dead Kristo's wallet and maneuvred it open to read the address on its identity card.

Royares, Francisco X. PO Box forty-five, Mabine Post Office, Metro Manila. There was nothing else. His specialty had been odds-setting. Elizalde looked at the wallet. It was empty except for perhaps a hundred and fifty pesos and the ID card. His specialty had been avoiding getting robbed of everything he had. The wallet itself was old, creased; a second-best wallet, or, if he was exactly what he had seemed to be, his only one.

He remembered the expensive shoes of the Sentenciador and looked again at the billfold. It was old but not that used for its age. It was a second-best wallet. He saw the manageress at the charcoal look over at him and he mouthed, nodding at the steaming bowls in the fire, 'Wonderful.' He still had the cellophane-wrapped cigar in his hand. He put it in the top pocket of his light safari-style shirt and turned to the phone.

The Philippines and the Philippinos: they existed on posters and religion and hope. In the absence of power they existed on a system of elaborate politeness and grace until, when they finally got power and wealth and position . . .

Not that many of them ever got it so it was a moot point.

They had put the phone in for him: he was sure.

He was equally sure that unless he put the cigar in his mouth and began smoking it either the woman or the daughter would offer him a bowl of their specialty and refuse payment for it.

The smell was wonderful. He touched at the cigar in his pocket.

He seemed deep in thought – on business. At the charcoal, the manageress, catching the look in her daughter's eyes, shook her head for her not to disturb him with an offer of food.

The daughter, perhaps eighteen years old and, like all the members of the cooperative who had founded the café, deaf and dumb from birth, shrugged. She saw Elizalde at the phone take the paid-for cigar from his pocket and begin to unwrap it. She thought him a handsome, tall man who was probably married, with children.

He had strong, powerful hands, but his fingers were long

and sensitive and scrupulously clean and cared-for.

She saw him begin to dial a number.

She felt her mother suddenly dig her elbow in her side and looking down, she saved the bowls of golden crusted malagkit from the fire at exactly the right moment and, scurrying out with them on a tray, smiling secretly to herself, went to serve her customers waiting in the café.

It was rumored that Mendez even had a carved ivory leg set with jewels for Presidential and diplomatic occasions.

It was said . . .

The number of the Cock Hospital in Pasig Street was engaged.

In the empty kitchen with the smell of the charcoal and the malagkit in his nose, Elizalde stood gazing at the poster above the glowing ovens, smoking his cigar.

He had made it, Mendez. He was a fighting cock: his trade was killing.

He had made it.

His specialty, on the other hand, was survival.

MENDEZ BEER FOR LIFE'S HARD STRUGGLE!

In the kitchen, Elizalde thought he would wait five minutes and then try the number again.

'*Manggagamot?*'

In the Cock Hospital treatment room on Pasig Street Nitz said in Philippino, 'Yes.' The way the man on the phone had said the word for 'cockdoctor' sounded a little wrong. It sounded as if he had learned his Philippino not in Manila in the northern island of Luzon as Nitz had, but in the south, on the island of Mindanao. Nitz said, 'This is his assistant Nitz.' He was answering the phone in a corner of the treatment room under a framed copy of Lansang's *Rules Of The Pit*. Angel Lansang had been the father of modern cockfighting. He had raised it into a respectable pursuit for the educated. Nitz, twenty-one years old and completing his education at night, had read Lansang's book. In his book, Lansang had said that whatever else a follower of the cockfight was he was a man of respect. Nitz, glancing across the room past the little steel table in the center, past the rows of bottles of penicillin and potions, the suture needles and unguents, said softly in what he hoped was something resembling the same accent as the caller's, 'There has been a loss.' He saw Doctor Paulo in the next room in the cock morgue hanging dead and gutted birds up on hooks, 'Mang Paulo's brother, Mr Francisco Royares, the Kristo at the Conquistadore Cockpit has, sadly, lost his life.' If the man was from Mindanao it was possible he was an Arab. Nitz did not say, 'God rest his soul.' Nitz said, 'We are heartbroken.'

'I will speak to Mang Paulo.' It was an order. The accent changed. It was pure Manila. The man was not a cocker. The only reason he had mispronounced the word for cockdoctor was that he did not use it.

Nitz said plainly, 'He cannot be disturbed.' Jobs were hard to come by. Before the brothers Francisco and Paulo had offered him the job he had been yet another unemployed student. Nitz said, 'It would have to be extremely important for him to come to the phone.' He saw Mang Paulo come out from the cock mortuary and glance in his direction. Of the two brothers, Paulo was the one Nitz had always liked. Nitz, cupping his hand over the mouthpiece of the phone, said, 'It's someone who wants to talk to you. I've told him about the Kristo, but he – ' He saw Paulo try to take in what he said. His eyes were wet with tears. Nitz said, 'He isn't a cocker.'

'Who is he?'

Nitz said into the phone, 'Who are you?'

'Put Paulo Royares on.'

Nitz said, 'He won't say.'

Paulo said, 'Tell him to go to Hell!'

The voice on the other end of the phone said, 'Tell him it's . . .' He seemed to pause, 'Tell him it's . . .'

Paulo said, 'Give me the phone.' He took it from the boy's hand. Paulo said, 'This is a hard time. If you were a friend you would not ring now. If you were someone I wanted to talk to I would ring you!' Paulo said a moment before he drew back the receiver to slam it down, 'Who are you? You bastard!' He said suddenly, hearing the reply, 'Oh, Madre – oh, oh my God!' Mang Paulo, glancing at the boy, said quickly in English, 'I can't talk on this line.'

'You have a private line. In your office.' The voice said, 'The number isn't listed.' He said, 'Give me the number.'

Paulo said without hesitation, '59-54-44.'

The voice said, 'Good.' The voice said, 'I'll ring you back in fifteen minutes exactly.' The voice said, 'Be there. We have an arrangement to come to.' The voice, cold and hard, speaking English with the faintest trace of an American accent said, 'Is that understood?' The voice said, '59-54-44. In fifteen minutes exactly.' The voice said with a trace of anger, 'And make sure that smart-arsed kid is well out of earshot. What I've got isn't for him.' He almost yelled, '*All right?*'

'Yes.' The line went dead. He still had tears in his eyes for his dead brother. He was the one Nitz had always liked, the one who had given him the job.

Nitz said solicitously, 'Sir? Paulo . . .? Mr Royares . . .?' He went to lay his hand gently on the man's arm to comfort him.

Paulo said, 'Don't touch me.' He wore a white apron over his clothes. He felt in his pocket and then in the pockets of his shirt but he could not find his cigarettes. He saw the boy take one of his own cheap Hope brand cigarettes out of his pocket and offer it to him and he took it with a shaking hand and tried to keep steady as the boy lit it for him. Paulo, putting his hand on the boy's shoulder and patting it, said, nodding, trembling, shaking, the cigarette still in his mouth, 'It's all right. It's all right.' He took the cigarette out of his mouth and his hand was wet with perspiration.

Mang Paulo, nodding, trying to smile, shaking with fear, said, 'It's all right. There's always a way.' He was a short, lined man with thinning hair. He ran his wet hand through his hair and, briefly, held himself by the nape of the neck to steady himself, 'At least he rang first.' He nodded hard to the boy. 'At least he rang first.' He was sure. He was certain. Paulo said, 'See? It's all right.' He said, still nodding, 'No, it'll be all right. He rang first. He's a man, like me – and you.' He saw the boy smile at him, trying to encourage him, 'No, *it'll be all right.*'

He said softly to himself in Philippino, 'Oh, God in Heaven . . . Oh, Jesus . . .'

He went quickly into his private office where the other phone was and, standing above the desk, still smoking the cheap cigarette, rubbing his hand on his bloodstained cock-doctor's apron, glancing constantly at his watch, he began waiting for the call.

There was a wrenching noise, a cloud of powdered fiberglass filler, nuts, bolts and bits of paintwork and the rear cab door was open. In the front Martinez made no protest. He couldn't. He had been half-throttled. Black faced, he sank down somewhere in the lower recesses of his seat making gurgling noises. Fifty feet ahead the cab window was down, the black-sleeved hand coming out to get something in the durian bomb thrower's hand. The durian bomb thrower had his other hand in his pocket, feeling around for his durian bomb. Ambrosio running, hopping, cursing, reaching for his PPK in its ankle holster, missing its butt and tearing all the hair from his leg as the Velcro retaining straps came off and the gun came out still in its holster, yelled, 'Police! Stop! *Police!*' He had his MANILA POLICE baseball cap in his other hand. He had to get it on to calm the onlookers.

'Hold it!' He was yelling in English. The durian bomb thrower turned to look at him. You could tell he was evil. He just stood there and gaped. Ambrosio pointing the holstered gun down range, shrieked, 'Freeze!' It always worked on TV. It worked in the streets. There were crashing noises as drivers complied instantly. He saw the passenger get out of the car to thank him. Ambrosio yelled, 'Stay in the cab! Stay in the cab!' You could tell he was frightened. He was a priest. He put his hands together in an attitude of prayer. The black rectangular object in the durian thrower's hand was a book. You could tell he was a bad person. He, like the man in the cab, was a priest. They were well-known bad people. There were a lot of them around. Ambrosio, pointing the holster, yelled, 'Halt or die!' He knew. He knew before anyone spoke that the package-carrying priest had chased the cab to return a book to the cab-riding priest. The book was a Bible. He knew. God, he knew . . . Ambrosio, slowing down, his face falling, wanting to go backwards, said sadly, 'Police officer, stop or . . .' He came to a stop. Ambrosio said sadly, 'I thought . . .' Two priests. He could have done with a blessing. They weren't going to give

36

him one. Ambrosio said like a record being played at the wrong speed, 'I . . . thought . . . it . . . was . . . a . . .'

He said softly to himself, 'Oh – '

He stopped, wringing his holster in his hands.

He looked at the traffic, at the crashed and stalled cars. They all looked empty -- all the drivers and passengers were full-length on their floors, praying.

Ambrosio said, 'You can come out now . . .'

He turned back to his own cab and saw a black faced man fall out of the driver's door onto the center reservation, clutching at his throat. Ambrosio said . . .

Ambrosio said brightly to the two priests, to anyone who might listen, 'I'm a cop!'

'*I'm a cop!*'

Ambrosio said to the two priests waiting expectantly for him to say something to them, 'Oh . . .'

Ambrosio said at the top of his voice, 'Sabbath Squad!' He turned and yelled to the appearing motorists, still waving the holstered gun, 'It's Sunday! *Why aren't you people all in church?*'

'Pasig Street Jewellers.'

In the little alcove in the kitchen of the deaf and dumb café Elizalde glanced quickly down at the number he had written in his notepad. He had taken it directly from the phone book. It was correct. Elizalde said, 'Pasig Street Cock Hospital?'

'I'll put you through.'

Elizalde said, 'I want to speak to Paulo Royares . . . Mang Paulo, one of the cockdoctors.'

There was a pause. The girl's voice said a little urgently, 'Could you hold a moment, please?' There was a click.

The girl's voice said, 'Yes, he's waiting for your call. Hold, please, I'll put you through to his private number . . .'

After he had spoken to Royares he had rung Room 333 at the Manila Hotel. The man in Room 333 had listened to the tape of the cockfight. The man in Room 333 was convinced.

In Pasig Lane, the bald headed man, still wearing the MENDEZ BEER baseball cap, dressed in coveralls, hefted his brown paper wrapped racing bicycle onto his shoulder and touched at something in his pocket to check it was still there. The lane was a cul-de-sac off Macarthur Street, running parallel with Pasig Street. For the sake of anyone looking, he reached into the top pocket of his coveralls and took out a scrap of paper as if to check an address.

The bicycle, wrapped in sheets of heavy paper and tied carefully with string looked brand new. After he had stolen it he had cleaned the tyres carefully in the back of his four-wheeled drive Toyota Landcruiser, and overly oiled the hubs so the oil would show through on the wrapping paper. Pasig Lane was empty except for a few kids playing outside a back doorway to one of the shops. He saw them look, not at him or his face, but at the brand new bicycle he was delivering. He saw them look down the lane to the iron stairs to the front building and wonder who had had a windfall and bought it – not for their children: that was impossible and only happened on American TV – but for themselves.

The bald headed man touched again at his pocket surreptitiously glancing at his watch. He reached the end of the lane and hefting the bicycle, the great gift, began carrying it up the stairs into the last building.

It was a fire escape, exactly the way a man who had made a purchase, would order a delivery man to come in order to keep his possession from the eyes of thieves and coveters. After he had cleaned the tyres and oiled the wheels he had bought a brand new chrome-plated racer's water bottle in a bicycle shop and made sure that the paper was ripped where it lay clipped on the handlebars of the wonderful machine. As he climbed the stairs the bottle glittered with newness.

Ten minutes. He entered the building, glanced up the darkened corridor and, seeing no one, opened the steel fire door and went up towards the roof.

KISS. Keep It Simple, Stupid. It was an American Army term.

He was keeping it simple.

He reached the fire door and, maneuvring the bicycle in the narrow passageway, he got the door open and went out onto the roof.

Keeping the wrapped bicycle down, he glanced at his watch and then across the street to the Pasig Street Jewellers shop.

The shop was on the ground floor. Above it – directly opposite and slightly below the level of the roof – there were the barred windows of another establishment which, because it was known to those who would use it and therefore required no advertising, had no business name written on it.

He counted one, two, three windows and, reading from left to right, placed them as the mortuary, treatment room and, last, the private office.

It was the Pasig Street Cock Hospital. He saw, for an instant, behind the bars in the last – office – window the shadow of a man waiting for a telephone call.

Nine minutes.

Taking the two Chien Lung number eight large size Chinese firecrackers from his pocket and putting them carefully on the little wall at the edge of the building that protected him from view, the bald headed man, setting his cap firmly on his head, took out a little pocket knife and began cutting the string and paper from the bicycle to unwrap it.

He heard a rustling. The lawn mower stopped for a moment and there, somewhere in the trees at the fence, he heard a rustle.

They were coming. In his lair Bontoc heard the bonehunters coming.

The Bontocs might have credit cards, but there were times when an axe was better. This was one of them.

He felt a strange, atavistic calmness come over him. He felt his mouth draw back of its own accord and bare his teeth. He felt his axe in his hand. He heard the enemy rustle in the jungle. He smelled the smell of earth and trees and rocks. He was a man of wide and exhaustive education. He felt his eyes narrow. He heard himself say in a whisper, 'Agggghhhh . . .' He tasted blood.

He was a headhunter.

Crawling, making no sound as he made his way through the impenetrable snake and disease infested rain forest jungle of the Children's Stone Dinosaur Park, touching at his shell necklace to stop its jangling, he went to get a head.

*

By the sounds in the earpiece, they were cutting the call into a direct number.

In the kitchen Elizalde looked at his watch.

11.40 a.m.

He waited for the connection to be made and Mang Paulo, the dead Kristo's brother, to come on the line.

What hurt most was that Martinez, driving El Tigre carefully, slowly, legally and, glancing only occasionally into the rear view mirror, with his eyes full of tears, said not one single, solitary word.

Nothing.

The rear door, shoved back into place – never to be the same again – banged as he drove.

What hurt most was the silence and the grace with which he suffered.

He had even turned the airconditioning up to the rear of the cab to increase his passenger's comfort.

El Tigre rode.

In the back, in the silence, El Finko, trying not to notice the thumb prints on the driver's neck where he had tried to strangle him, *withered*.

11.40. Eight minutes.

Behind the barred windows of the first floor Cock Hospital twenty yards across the street, the bald headed man, folding the last of the brown paper and string into a neat square and stuffing it down the front of his coveralls, saw the shadow of a man waiting for a telephone call.

The two firecrackers were in front of him on the parapet of the roof. The unwrapped bicycle and the rifle that had been taped to it under the paper lay ready on the ground in front of him.

It was a short-barrelled, five groove, left hand twist weapon in .303 caliber fitted with a flash eliminator he had filed off from its original funnel shape to a flattened cup.

11.41. The bald headed man took his wind proof Zippo lighter out from his pocket and put it close to the two firecrackers. He reached out and straightened one of the fuses.

He saw the shadow in the office behind the bars. From his position to the shadow was no more than – tops – sixty-five feet. No need to bother about sights.

Reaching into his top pocket where the blank scrap of paper was, he took out a single blank cartridge and, smearing his fingers on the case and the gun's receiver as he did it to avoid fingerprints, he fitted it into the breech and, pushing the bolt closed, again smearing his fingers, he cocked the weapon with a single click.

4

He swallowed hard. He was prepared to negotiate. On the
phone Royares said, 'Yes, sir?' He was nervous. Elizalde heard
him giggle.

'This is Felix Elizalde of the Metro Manila – '

'I know who you are.' Royares said, 'At the cockpit it was – '
Elizalde said formally, 'I'm sorry about your brother.'

'I was there when it happened.' Royares, kneading his hand
against his side, his voice low, said, 'I'm in my office. I'm alone.
No one can hear what we say. We can talk.'

There was a silence.

Royares said anxiously, 'Hullo, are you there?'

'Yes.'

He thought he was someone else. Out in the café the
manageress and her daughter were serving customers. In the
kitchen there was only the hissing of the charcoal on the fires.
Elizalde said, 'I heard you were a rich man.' He waited.

'I can negotiate.'

'I heard your brother Francisco – the Kristo – was a rich
man. I heard that the money he made from the bookies – '

'He made nothing from the bookies.' The boy had said the
man wasn't a cocker. He understood nothing. Royares said,
'That wasn't his job, that was his vocation!' His hands were
sweating. 'He was – he was like me! He was – '

'I heard he lived in a big house in Forbes Park – '

'No.'

'Are you saying he had no money? Are you saying you have no money?' He thought he was someone else. Elizalde said, risking it, 'All right, if that's the position you're taking then there's no point in continuing this conversation.' He said, taking the phone a little away from his mouth, 'In that case, I'll – '

'Don't hang up!' He was breathing hard, gasping, trying to think. Royares said, 'We were both – we both – we both lived for the cockfights – I – he – we. *I'm sorry I shouted!*' He asked abruptly, suddenly, in a whisper, 'Was it you? Were you the one who – '

'Who killed him?' It was going too far. If, later, he had to face the man, it had gone too far. Elizalde said, 'Maybe.'

'You have to agree that he wasn't dead when I took Mendez out.' He wasn't a cocker: he wouldn't understand. Royares said, 'No one will ask. No one will ever ask you, but in case anyone does you have to agree that – '

'I don't think you're in a position to – '

'It isn't much! It doesn't affect our negotiations!'

'Are we negotiating?'

'Yes! It isn't some sort of fixed price! I'm prepared to negotiate!' Royares asked suddenly, 'You were the one who shot him at the pit, weren't you?'

There was a silence.

'Were you the one who shot him?'

What the hell had he gotten himself into? 'I was at the pit, yes. Later.'

'*Were you the one?*'

There was a silence. In the alcove of the kitchen, Elizalde, with his forehead pressed up against the wall, somehow trying to shut out anything extraneous, anything that, for even an instant, might distract him, said quietly, menacingly, 'You know what I want.' He risked it all. Elizalde said, 'I want Mendez.'

'*You can't be serious!*' On the phone, all the anger there and naked in an instant, Royares shouted, 'You rang me! You wanted to negotiate! Negotiate seriously! We both know what you know and what you want and I'm prepared to negotiate!

In the name of God, fix a price and if I can meet it – '

'What are we negotiating about? Exactly?'

'*Don't play with me!* Who do you think you're talking to? You know all about me – ' The voice went suddenly cold. Royares said, 'I'm fifty-one years old. I've lived a hard, healthy life. I'm a cocker. I deal in death. Don't think you're talking to someone's grandmother. Don't think I can't still – '

'Tell that to your brother.'

'What do you want? *Exactly?*'

'Whatever you've got to give.'

'How much do you know?'

'All of it.'

There was a silence. He knew. He had guessed. It was there: the doubt in his voice

Elizalde said hopelessly, 'I know everything.'

There was a silence.

Elizalde put his hand to the wall by his forehead and pressed. Elizalde said, 'I know everything.'

Royares said tightly, in a voice so low Elizalde had to strain to catch it, 'Like what?'

'Like your brother. Like – '

Royares, emotionless, waiting, said, 'Go on.'

'You know why I rang!'

It was not the same voice. Moment by moment, he was realizing it was not the same voice. They were both speaking English. It was the American accent. Royares, changing to Philippino, said softly, lethally, 'This man, Paulo Royares, you're talking to – what do you know about him?'

He knew. He was testing. He knew. Elizalde said, 'I've told you.' He said wildly, 'Mendez. I want Mendez.'

'Oh my God!' He knew. He knew. Royares said in a panic, 'Oh my God, *you're a cop!*' He shouted down the line, 'Who is this? *Who is this?*'

'Elizalde. Police.' It was gone. The one chance. In the silent kitchen, the moment flown, gone, vaporised to nothing, Elizalde commanded the man, 'This is Lieutenant Elizalde of the Metro Manila Police, don't hang up! That's an order! Don't hang up! *Stay on this line!*'

*

He touched at the short-barrelled rifle and then smeared his fingertips. Both the firecrackers were ready on the parapet, their fuses straightened and, where they terminated, opened a little to expose the grains of FFFg grade gunpowder for a quick ignition. It was no more than sixty-five feet to the barred window across the street. Bald Head, on his knees, leaned over the edge for a moment and looked down into the street below. There were people moving about: he saw shoppers and traders, hawkers, and, here and there, the odd raddled, ring-eyed hooker out before business for her late-rising first cup of coffee of the day. Below the Cock Hospital, there were people looking in the window of the Pasig Street Jewellers and shaking their heads at the goods there and the prices that went with them. He saw a young man in a formal, embroidered, long sleeved barong tagalog shirt and his fiancée, also well dressed, looking in the window for engagement rings. She was slight. She held her fiancé's hand hard and kept looking around nervously for muggers.

Perfect.

She would be a screamer.

It was perfect.

Moving back from the parapet, Bald Head looked at his watch.

The time was up.

In the third room of the Cock Hospital, as a shadow, he saw Royares standing by the phone. He seemed to have it in his hand as if he was testing to see the line still worked. Perfect. Moving back to the bicycle the bald headed man unclipped the chrome-plated racer's water bottle on its handlebars.

Perfect.

He unscrewed the water bottle into two halves and took something from it.

His Zippo lighter was on the parapet next to the two firecrackers. The ads said it would stay alight in anything short of a hurricane.

Today, this morning, there was no wind at all.

No one on Earth could put a killing shot through a misted up glass window between iron bars and make sure the shot killed without error.

No one on Earth, this morning, had to.

The blank round was in the chamber of the rifle, ready.

The racer's water bottle from the bike glittered in the light.

Before he finished with it and clipped it back into place on the handlebars, taking his time, he wiped off all his fingerprints with the palm of his hand and then, to be sure, rubbed the sleeve of his coveralls against it until it shone.

'Your brother's full name was Francisco,' he looked down at the name on the ID card, 'Xavier Royares?'

The voice was shaking. 'I don't know anything.'

Elizalde said, 'Xavier. Is that what the X. stands for?' Elizalde said, 'What else?' The cigar was in his pocket. He needed desperately to light it up, not for the smoke but for the calmness of mind that went with it. 'I wonder if bringing Catholicism to the Far East was the wisest move the – '

Royares said like stone, 'I don't know anything about my brother's death.' He said menacingly, 'You lied to me. You misrepresented yourself and you lied to me – ' He also, was trying to think. Royares said, 'There are Complaints Boards that even Police Lieutenants – '

'The only address I have on him is a box number.'

'He lived here, with me! Here. At the Cock Hospital!'

'Maybe he even had a wife and children. I don't know. All I have is his ID card. It doesn't even have his middle name, only an initial.'

'He lived here with me! He wasn't married!' Royares said, 'Look, listen – listen to me – '

'I am. You're telling me about your brother.'

'I don't know anything! It was a mistake! I thought you were someone else – '

'Who?'

'No one!'

'I see.'

'My feelings about my brother are my own concern! I don't have to prove to you that I loved him! I don't have to prove anything!' Royares, losing control, shouted down the line, 'You lied to me! You told me you were someone else!'

'Then make a complaint.'

'I will!'

'I'll write the details down now. Tell me who I told you I was.' Elizalde said, 'For my report.' Elizalde said, 'Name of this person I claimed to be?' Elizalde said, 'You didn't know the name because I told you mine and you accepted it. You even heard me say *Metro Manila*. You thought I was going to say something other than *Police*. You thought I was going to say some other official department. What other official department did you think I was going to say?'

Royares said, 'Police! I thought you were going to say Police!'

'No, otherwise you wouldn't have been so horrified when you realised I was a cop. What department did you think I was going to say?'

Royares said, 'The Gaming Department!'

'There is no Gaming Department!'

'*I don't know anything!*'

'Your brother's *dead*.'

'It was a gambling killing! A gang thing, a –' Royares, weeping, his voice out of control, shrieked, '*I don't know!*'

'What did the two firecrackers mean? Is that some symbol in cockfighting?'

'I don't know!'

'You do know! Yes or no?'

'No.'

'He was your own brother!' Elizalde, desperate, trying anything, yelled in Philippino, 'What sort of man are you? I read somewhere that cockers were the last twentieth-century epitome of honor and manliness!' He had read it in Lansang's book on cockfighting after he had found in America that everyone had wanted to ask him about a sport about which he knew nothing, 'He was your own brother! Your responsibility! What sort of a man are you to lie about him now that he's dead?'

'*I'm a man who wants to stay alive!*'

'You're a liar and a coward and a traitor to your brother's memory! That's what sort of a man you are!' He had him. He could sense it. Elizalde, dropping his voice, said, simply, 'Tell me. Tell me what you know.'

He was ready.

At the parapet, using the Zippo lighter, he lit both the fuses on the firecrackers.

He had time. The fuses were each five second delay.

He had timed it.

Stepping back, slipping the Zippo into his top pocket along with the blank scrap of paper, Bald Head, moving smoothly took up the rifle and, bringing it up to his shoulder, aimed it, not at the barred window, but at the solid brick wall two feet to one side of it.

The gun was barrel heavy.

He heard the fuses fizz.

He waited.

He felt a single drop of perspiration on his trigger finger.

He waited.

The gun had a long trigger pull.

He began to take it up.

'*Tell me what you know!*'

'I – ' Royares said, 'I – ' He was going, losing. All there was was the voice on the line. His throat was tight. He felt tears and pain and all the horror of the day coming up, unstoppably. There was only the voice on the line. Royares said, 'I – I – '

'Who killed him? Who did you think I was?' Elizalde said, 'Whoever you thought I was – that was the man who killed him! *Wasn't it?*'

'*I don't know!*'

'Who else?'

'*I don't know!*' Royares said, 'Yes. Yes. It was him!' It was true. It was. He had been too afraid, but it was true. It had to be. Royares said, 'Yes, it was him!'

'Didn't you have any affection for your brother at all?' Elizalde said gently, 'Paulo, didn't you have – '

'Yes!'

'Then tell me what you know.'

'Mendez – '

'Fuck Mendez! Mendez is a bird! An animal! A creature without a soul! Your brother was – '

48

'ALL RIGHT!' He heard it: he heard the simultaneous explosions. They came as one single pop a long way off, like shots. Royares said, 'What was – ' He had moved towards the window. Through the greyness of the frosted glass, through the lines of the bars, he saw, for an instant . . . He saw . . . Royares shrieked, '*Oh my God!*'

'Royares!' In the kitchen of the deaf and dumb café as the manageress and her daughter stared at him in incomprehension, Elizalde, shouting at the top of his voice, almost tearing the telephone from the wall, shrieked, '*Royares!*'

It was the man on the roof with a rifle grenade. At the window of the treatment room, Nitz, looking out, saw it. He had served in the Army on counter-insurgency duty in Mindanao and he had seen them used. He saw the long rocket-like projectile at the barrel of the weapon. He saw it come up. He saw the man behind it in the smoke from the exploded firecrackers turn it towards the window of the office. He saw the long teat-like primary charge on the tip of the weapon. An anti-tank grenade. He saw it. He saw the sudden recoil – heard nothing of the noise as the blank round in the chamber of the gun fired it – saw only for an instant a blur as it made the distance across the rooftop and the street in a millisecond, heard – actually heard – the primary charge punch a hole through the brick wall of the office section and then, as the main bursting charge, two inches and an eyeblink behind the teat in time and distance went off, his eardrums burst and he was in a hurricane of flying glass and brick and metal and everything in the room was turning over and over and he was awash, drowning, all the breath gone from his body, choking.

'*Paulo* – ' He hit the ground trying to call for Mang Paulo. Mang Paulo, in the next room, was no longer there. The room was gone. As he fell, he saw – he thought, for an instant, the last thing he would ever see – that the room, the office was no longer there and he was looking straight through the treatment room out onto the sky.

He thought he was dead. He was turning over and over. He knew the glass in the room was going to cut him to pieces and kill him. He thought it would never come. He was turning over and over. He called, 'Paulo! Mang Paulo!' but there was no breath in his body and, in mid-air, never going to hit the floor, no words came.

'Royares! ROYARES!' The line was dead. He was shouting into nothingness.

He turned and, for some reason, staring at the look on his face, the café manageress's daughter was weeping, as if seeing him, somehow, forever, she had lost something.

'*Royares!*'

The line was dead. There was only, in his ear, a long, uninterrupted buzzing.

In the street, the young girl, full of hopes for her marriage, afraid, after a sheltered convent-school life, of almost everything, began screaming.

5

On with life's struggle.

In the back of the cab Ambrosio said, 'I'm sorry about your door.' They were parked up by the main rear gate to Intramuros, the old Spanish walled city. There were no cabs there, only calesa horse drawn carriages and hand pushed wagons with wooden wheels. Up there, in the nineteenth-century nobody knew El Tigre's name. Martinez, sitting in the front seat filling in an insurance form, said without turning around, 'I'm humiliated.'

'I'm sorry.'

He wasn't only humiliated, he was pouting. Martinez, still not turning around, said, 'You made me fall out of my cab onto the roadway.'

'I'm sorry.' Ambrosio, trying to lean forward and then leaning back as Martinez cringed, said, 'Look, I've had a bad day!'

'I don't mind being strangled but I object to being strangled so badly that I fall out of my cab onto the roadway!' He stopped filling in the form and fixed his eyes out onto the mini-golf park that surrounded the walls. Out there, there were people playing mini-golf without a care in the world or a cop in their back seat. Martinez said, 'Even muggers don't do that! Muggers are men too! They half strangle you to a point where you black out and you can slump there looking

51

dramatic, but they don't half strangle you to a point where you slump out in the roadway like a sack of dried out goddamned coconuts!' Martinez said, 'I'm very angry about it!'

'I'm sorry! Take it or leave it.'

'Always with the macho!' He was in tears. 'You think because you've got police insurance and a gun you don't have to consider anyone!' He was seriously thinking of joining some subversive organisation as their get-away man. Martinez said, 'You're an extremely bad tempered person and you've got no respect for the feelings of others!' He wasn't finished. Martinez said, 'I'm just your driver, I'm no one! I fell out in the roadway in front of half the taxi drivers in Manila and two priests!' He didn't care about El Tigre's door. Oh, yes, he did. 'And you kicked my brand new door to pieces because you couldn't be bothered trying to open it properly!'

'The door was locked! You locked it! And it wasn't brand new! It was filled with fiberglass!'

'The fiberglass was brand new!'

Ambrosio said abruptly, 'I'm sorry. You're right.' He hated to see people cry. Ambrosio said, 'It was all my fault. Everything! I was dumb. Anyone with half a brain could have seen that they were two priests and that what the priest on foot had in his hand was a Bible and I – '

Martinez said gently, 'Don't abase yourself. After all, who am I? No one.'

'You're a human being! You're a – ' Ambrosio said, 'You're the finest damn cab driver I've ever ridden with!' He hoped God would forgive him. Ambrosio said, 'I was jealous! I was jealous of your driving ability and I wanted to humiliate you to make myself feel better about my inadequacies!'

There was a silence. A calesa was going by, clip-clopping along with its driver half asleep on the box, the back of the galvanised iron framed and leather topped vehicle full to brimming with parcels and packages for delivery. Martinez said softly, 'It takes a real man to admit it when he's wrong.'

Ambrosio said, 'Thanks very much.'

Martinez said, 'Maybe I was wrong about you.'

'I'm really sorry about your neck.' He was. Ambrosio said, 'It's just that I haven't got the remotest idea what it is the mugger offers his victims to get them to wind their window down.' He touched at the door. It was no longer a door. It was wired shut. It was a barricade. Ambrosio said, 'Could we try again?' Ambrosio, leaning forward and clasping his hands together in an attitude of prayer, said winningly, 'El Tigre rides – ?'

Martinez, still rubbing his neck, said, 'Hmm.' He felt his foot on the gas pedal. He was insured.

Ambrosio said, 'Together, we can get him.'

Martinez said, 'Hmm.' El Tigre, at the command of his foot, went, 'Mmm, mmm . . .!'

Brrm . . . brrm . . . ROAR! BRRMM!

He was the finest damn cab driver he had ever ridden with.

He was a cop.

He knew.

Martinez, shoving his foot to the floor, his eyes blazing as the calesa and its driver swerved for dear life, yelled, 'Right! OK!' He shrieked as the cab did a one hundred and eighty degree turn and almost took out the seventh hole on the mini-golf course and the golfer putting into it, 'El Tigre *rides!*' He screamed above the din, 'On!' He had heard the line recently in a tank attack movie. They, for some reason, were his favorite movies. Martinez yelled in total, full, complete forgiveness, 'On! On together to *victory!*'

He even understood Japanese. *Sensei o-hayo gozaimasu. Kore wa pen desu ka? Hai, kore wan pen desu.* Good morning, Teacher. Is this a pen? Yes, this is a pen. Well, it was more than most people knew. Crawling through the foliage at the feet of a stone tyrannosaurus Rex, Bontoc practised it. With the axe clenched firmly between his teeth, it came out as grr, mm, bah, grr, moomphzah . . . Perfect. If anything was going to frighten off a few Japanese bonehunters that was it. He looked up. The park had been conceived as a learning experience for children: the tyrannosaurus had no genitals. It didn't need them. At over thirty feet tall and eight foot long from tail to sternum it probably bred by intimidation.

He heard the rustling. He stopped. He listened. He took a piece of banana palm out of his ear.

He touched at his shell necklace. It made a rattling sound.

He heard digging, the rustling of shoes on soil. He was down with the roaches and the ants moving through a tropical jungle. He, as an atavistic headhunter, a man of the wilds, loved it. That was the theory. Bontocs, these days, had credit cards. He saw something black and many-legged scuttle away in front of him and he shivered.

Sensei o-hayo – grr, bah, grr, moomphzah – it was going to work. He saw ahead of him shadows, movements. He heard the sound of digging. Standing up, getting to his feet, taking the axe from his mouth, Bontoc said –

'*Yaaa!*'

Bontoc said, 'Oh my God!'

'*Yaa –!*'

It moved. Above him, the tyrannosaurus moved. Bontoc said –

'YAAA!' He saw in the foliage, spades, earth, maps, bits of paper and two masked Japaneses go skywards. He heard them running. It moved. The tyrannosaurus moved. Bontoc said –

Bontoc said – He heard them go over the fence, still running. He heard one of them shout in Japanese, receding at the speed of light, 'Ayo! Ayo! The fucking thing moved!' He didn't understand that much Japanese. The fleeing Japanese bone-hunter was shouting in Philippino. Bontoc, chasing after him, yelled –

It moved. It went for him. Behind him, as he passed over the broken soil where the Japanese had been digging, as he saw their torn and ragged map and their two miniature entrenching tools, the tyrannosaurus, all twenty-seven tons of it, solid stone, ball-less for the non-edification of children, in a single, crashing explosion of trees and bamboo, leaves, earth, foliage and anything else in the park that didn't extend straight down to the magma of the Earth, went for him. He was a man of education. He could think logically.

Running backwards through the muck as the sky darkened above him with the toppling monster, all his worst fears realised, Bontoc, reaching the tiger's lair and falling straight down into a hole that had not been there five minutes before, yelled, 'Shit! Oh, shit!' The missionaries had not taught him that one. He had picked it up all by himself. He got out of the hole and straight into another. He was a cop, a man of iron and learning, back, far in his bloodline, the nemesis of flower-eaters like the Tasadays. He saw the great shadow of the tyrannosaurus still falling. Summoning up his last ounce of energy a second before it hit the ground and lifted everything in the park, including the park, a full three inches off the surface of the world in a shattering thump, Bontoc yelled at the top of his lungs, 'Anyone – *anyone* – HELP!'

They almost hit a jeepney.

They missed three schoolgirls on the pavement by inches. They rose up onto two wheels at a corner and emptied a pothole of mud and rubble and bitumen, and emptied the two pothole fillers of every nerve in their bodies.

They –

Martinez, his teeth drawn back in triumph, yelled, 'The finest damn driver you've ever ridden with – right?'

Ambrosio shouted back, 'Right! Right!' He tried hard not to cower. Ambrosio shouted, 'El Tigre rides!' It was tough being forgiven.

'This is the life, right?'

'Right!'

Short but sweet.

He wondered who the State was going to pay his death benefit to.

He had disposed of the wrapping paper in the first refuse bin he had come to after he had left Pasig Lane. In Cebu Street, cycling, going south, Bald Head, still wearing his coveralls and baseball cap, felt at his top pocket for his Zippo lighter and the scrap of paper. They were there. He had the first three metal snap-on buttons of the coveralls open at his neck and, steering the bicycle carefully through the traffic he reached in and put the lighter safely into the pocket of his short-sleeved polo tagalog shirt and snapped the buttons closed on the overalls. He patted at his trousers pockets under the coveralls and checked that his keys and money were still in place.

He glanced at his watch. He had time. Reaching the end of

Cebu Street and standing with the bicycle as the traffic lights stayed on red for the turn into Harrison Street, he looked around and back behind him.

Cebu Street was a minor feeder road, full mainly of antique shops selling wooden santos – carved saints – of the Spanish colonial period and brassware from the Muslims in Mindanao and, at that time of day, on a Sunday morning – in deference to both religions they profited from – the shops were all closed and shuttered.

Far off, coming from the Western District Police Head-quarters on United Nations Avenue, he could hear sirens.

The light changed and he remounted the cycle and went slowly and carefully east onto Vito Cruz Street and, to disguise the wealth of the glittering cycle, got in behind an airport courtesy bus going to the Sheraton Hotel with its cargo of rich people and stayed with it.

He did not hurry. At the corner of Vito Cruz Street by the Old Mill restaurant, he made a left turn into the parking area of the Harrison Plaza shopping complex and, leaving his bicycle against a banyan tree left growing there to give the area shade, went into the complex through a side door directly to the toilets.

He had time.

In the toilets he stripped off his coveralls and tied the sleeves together at the wrists with a reef knot.

He had only the bicycle to dispose of.

In the toilets, he rolled the coveralls up into a small bundle and put them under his arm.

He glanced at himself in the mirrors and touched at his hairless head and face before putting his baseball cap into the litter bin provided and taking from the hip pocket of his trousers another, finer, more expensive soft brimmed, cloth golfer's hat that matched his tailored fawn colored trousers.

He drew a breath and looked at himself in the mirror. Perfect. He had only the bicycle to dispose of.

Leaving the toilets he went across the mezzanine floor of the half-empty complex and went to the Harrison Plaza Hardware store looking like a man who, after a hard week of middle to high executive level work, was on his way to a friend's house to do a little do-it-yourself helping out.

In the store he bought two mousetraps – presumably the friend's house was a weekender a little way out in the provinces undergoing renovation – a small tack hammer and a packet of fifty one-eighth inch thick, three-eighths inch long round-headed joiner's nails.

He had only the bicycle to dispose of.

He had time.

He went back out to the side entrance of the Plaza and there, gazing out onto the parking lot, he smiled to himself.

The bicycle, of course, within no more than the first ten minutes after he had left it there, had been stolen.

KISS. Keep it simple, stupid.

He looked like a successful middle to high level executive out shopping on a Sunday for a few recreational items to help pass the weekend.

In a sense, he was.

Settling the soft hat firmly on his head to cover his baldness, the coveralls and small packages of hardware items held loosely under his arm, he went out of the front entrance of the complex, turned left, and walked up Vito Cruz Avenue to the Sheraton where, his face bland and pleasant and confident, he hailed a taxi to take him to church.

It was 12.23 p.m.

In the back of the taxi, speaking not at all to the driver, the bald headed man, still wearing the new hat, lit a long, imported Pall Mall cigarette and blew the smoke thoughtfully out of the open rear window.

The taxi was not airconditioned. It was unimportant.

As usual – even in the fiercest heat of the tropics – he sweated hardly at all.

6

There had been a momentary silence, and then, as the girl had begun screaming, the entire floor had collapsed into the shop below. They were all dead, the girl and her fiancé, the shop assistant who had answered the phone, and Royares. Nitz, on the floor of the shop with his legs and pelvis cut to pieces, lay quietly staring up at where the roof had been, at the sky through the holes and shattered ceiling and roof. He was in no pain. His back was broken from the fall: he too, soon, would also be dead.

He had the boy's bloodstained ID card in his hand. He was only twenty-one years old. Elizalde, kneeling beside him, said softly, 'Nitz . . . Nitz Alvina . . . can you hear me?'

He had the beatific waxen sadness about his face of someone whose life was ebbing away from him without pain. On the street the patrolmen were looking in. The fire brigade had arrived. There was no fire. They, like everyone else, waiting for the ambulances, also watched in silence.

Nitz said softly, 'Yes.'

There was nothing to be done. There was only surface blood from the legs and pelvis and nothing to be done. Something secret and hidden was flowing away from him inside his body and there was nothing to be done. Elizalde said, 'Mang Paulo . . .' The boy must have been his apprentice. The apron twisted around his waist had once been clean and laundered like a nurse's or an orderly's. Elizalde said, 'He isn't here any more.' If he had been in the room upstairs when whatever had happened, he had been literally blown to pieces. Elizalde said, touching at the boy's hand, 'He's gone.'

He felt the hand. His fingers closed around it. It felt warm and soft. Nitz said, 'Yes.' He didn't need to ask if he was dead. He knew he was. Nitz said, 'He gave me a chance.' He looked up into Elizalde's face and tried to work out who he was. Nitz said softly, 'He never did anything wrong.' He saw the man nod. Nitz said, 'He didn't have to. He could have taken someone who could have paid him to teach them, but he didn't: he took me.' It was private, the duration of all his life, and he could not make it clear. Nitz said, 'There was nothing I could do.' His eyes kept rolling back to white. In the street, the ambulances still had not come. Moving slightly, Nitz saw all the faces at the ruin of the shopfront looking in at him. He held the hand and hid in it. Nitz said in a whisper, 'I've got no one.'

'Did you see what happened?' The hand in his was soft, losing strength. Elizalde wanted to squeeze it. Elizalde, not knowing where to look, said quietly, 'Did you . . .'

'I heard the bangs and I – '

'Firecrackers?'

'. . . from across the street and then he stood up.' Nitz said, 'I was in the Army – ' He said, thinking of something else, 'Mindanao – and I – ' He wanted to weep, but there was no connection between what he wanted and what his body would do. He was sinking somehow into the floor, becoming part of it. There were bits and pieces of ruined carpet by his head. Nitz said – He looked up and saw the sky. He had last seen it from the treatment room. Nitz said, 'I don't – '

Behind him, in the street, there was silence. It was as if he was on an altar in a church performing some silent ceremony and, behind him, hushed and breathless, the congregation waited for the miracle. There was going to be no miracle. Elizalde said, 'Was it a grenade?'

'Yes.' Nitz said, 'I was in the Army.'

'Did you see the man who threw it?' Across the street, on the roof where the grenade had come from Ballistics would probably already have the answers. Elizalde, already guessing, asked, 'Did he throw it or did he – '

He was drifting away. His eyes had rolled back and then come down again and when they had come down again they no longer looked like his eyes. What they were seeing was happening somewhere else. Nitz said suddenly, 'Who are you?'

'Felix Eli – ' Elizalde said, 'Felix Elizalde.'

'Felix?'

'Yes.'

Nitz said sadly, 'The Spanish here . . . the rich . . . I – '

'I'm not rich.'

He smiled at him. The eyes flickered back for a moment and then were gone again. Nitz said, 'Paulo – '

Elizalde said, 'Yes?'

'I'm sorry, Paulo.' His hand had no strength in it. He felt only the warmth against it. Nitz said, 'Please forgive me, Paulo. I never would have let it happen if I'd known.'

'I forgive you.'

Nitz said, 'I'm sorry, Paulo.' He asked, 'Are you all right?'

Out in the street there were dead bodies. Behind one of the smashed glass display cases he could see the body of the shop assistant. She was long dead, decapitated by the glass. By him, as he knelt, there was someone still alive. Elizalde said, 'Yes, we're both all right, Nitz.'

'Oh good.' Nitz said, 'I knew he couldn't be a cocker like us, Paulo, when he said *Manggagamot* the wrong way as if he'd read it somewhere. I knew he couldn't – ' Nitz said, 'I'm sorry about your brother, Paulo.' He looked up – it seemed, for an instant he felt the pressure of Elizalde's hand – 'He was never good to me, Paulo, like you, but I felt for your pain.' He said suddenly as if he was trying to understand the word, 'Felix . . .?'

'I'm here.'

Nitz said, 'Oh,' as he thought of something that saddened him and now he could do nothing to change, 'There's no one. If I could have become someone then there would have been . . .' He said, 'Paulo . . . ?'

'You'll become someone.'

He was weeping. Nitz said, 'I never told you how much it

meant to me.' He said suddenly, urgently, as if something inside him was happening or starting to happen, 'Paulo, I'm afraid!'

There was no ambulance, no priest, *nothing*. Elizalde, pressing at his hand, said urgently, tightly, 'Hold on. Hold on!'

'Paulo . . .'

He turned to look at the shop front, but there were only people watching. He read their faces. He saw it in their faces. They shared the moment with him. They could not be sent away. Elizalde, raising the boy's hand in his, said softly, 'Nitz . . . Nitz . . .' He saw the eyes going. They were going away forever. Elizalde said, 'Nitz . . .'

'I love you, Paulo. Thank you for what you did.'

He had the hand in his. It was like a child's. It had no resistance to it. Elizalde said, 'Everything is all all right.' He felt the taste of salt on his mouth. 'Everything . . .' Elizalde said, 'I love you too, Nitz.'

'Thank God, Paulo . . . thank God, Mendez was taken away before it happened!' Nitz said suddenly – it had begun to happen – 'Oh, Paulo, Paulo – ' He felt his body for the last time. He felt it change. Nitz said, 'Paulo! Help me!' He was dying. The moment had come. Nitz, afraid, pushing his hand into Elizalde's, said in fear, 'Oh . . . oh . . .' He said, his eyes glazing, wandering, no longer seeing, 'Paulo, is that . . .?' He felt his hand, being taken up, resting against someone's face. Nitz said, 'Paulo . . . Paulo . . .' He felt Paulo take his hand and gently kiss it. Nitz said softly, still weeping, his eyes blank and gone, 'Paulo, thank you. Thank you for what you did for me . . .'

He knelt there, the hand against his mouth. He felt the taste of salt on his face and mouth. Elizalde, kneeling in silence with a dead man, said softly, 'OK.'

He could think of nothing else to say.

Elizalde said softly to the dead man, 'OK.' He still held the hand in his. There were people behind him, watching. They, and what he knew they were thinking, did not embarrass him.

He sat still for a very long time without turning around until Patrolman Innocente – for some reason coming in unarmed, without his ubiquitous plastic butted .357 revolver – came and gently taking Nitz's hand from his, helped him up and led him silently out through the smashed and ruined shopfront into the street.

He had his hand on Elizalde's shoulder.

For a long time, as they waited for the ambulance, in silence he kept it there as the other watchers stood back, to protect him.

The State wasn't going to have to pay his death benefit because the State would never be able to recover his body from the mud at the bottom of the Pasig River.

The durian bomb thrower had hit on the richest brothel owner in Manila, Fat Adelaide Asagundo. All two hundred and eighty pounds and twenty-two carats of her, she stood at the open door of her stopped cab on the central reservation median strip dripping stench and screaming. The line of cars and jeepneys which had stopped behind the cab honked and tooted and revved their engines – she shrieked, 'Shut up!' and they shut up. The cab driver, gasping for air on the bonnet of the cab, raised a single quivering finger to make a comment about his airconditioning and his ruined upholstery – she shot him a look and he fell back onto the bonnet and even stopped gasping.

Ever-Loving Adelaide shouted at top volume, 'He took all my shopping – everything!' Someone in a bus shouted something at her, grinning. That was a mistake. The single, short, earsplitting truth about his parents and how they had begotten him sent him reeling back in his seat.

Ambrosio said, 'Are you all right?' Her long, filmy Scarlett O'Hara dress smelled the way Scarlett O'Hara's stables must have smelled three days after the burning of Atlanta on a rainy Wednesday.

'Someone is going to suffer for this!' She looked around for a victim.

Ambrosio looked around for Martinez. Martinez had shrunk away. Ambrosio, trembling as her little eyes lit on him, said with his hands in an attitude of prayer, 'I saw you get out of the car clutching your throat and my naturally chivalrous nature – ' He touched at his head to check he wasn't wearing his cap. He wasn't. He quivered. Ambrosio, inching forward, said, 'Are you all right?'

The stink of the durian juice was appalling. A truck load of farmers on their way to market all went together, 'Aggh!' and held their noses. A single glance from the woman rotted all their crops. Fat Adelaide said gently, 'Yes, thank you.' She believed in love. Fat Adelaide, taking Ambrosio by the arm and feeling grateful that a poor cripple – his legs had given way and she had to hold him – had taken the time to inquire after the fate of a poor old woman alone in the world, said with tears in her eyes, 'The National Bookstore keep all the American *True Romance* magazines for me. He took them all – three months' worth.' The diamonds on her fingers could have run the Philippines drill bit industry for a year. Fat Adelaide, holding his arm in her dainty grip and failing to notice his elbow and hand turning black with lack of blood, said, sniffing, 'I smell.' The cab driver got his head up from the bonnet and sucked in some pure, clean Manila carbon-monoxide smog. There was a miasma of stink hovering about him. He looked at Fat Adelaide's diamonds and let it hover.

'What happened?'

'Out of the goodness of my heart, I wound down the window to speak to the poor man – to offer him a little charity – and he threw in a glass vial of durian juice and then reached in, pulled the door open and took all my shopping!' Fat Adelaide said, 'I had swooned.' Lucky for the durian bomb thrower. Fat Adelaide said, 'He took everything – all my shopping!' She looked around at the traffic. Fat Adelaide said, 'Someone is going to suffer for this.'

'Which way did he go?'

Fat Adelaide said, 'It doesn't matter which way he went.' She had plans of her own. Those plans would terminate for someone taking a quick cement flipper swimming lesson in the river. She looked around in the direction of the Silahis Hotel and the Playboy Club, 'That way. Up there.' Towards Ermita. The Red Light District. Towards the cement flipper factory. Fat Adelaide, gazing in the general direction of Heaven said in a voice that made Ambrosio go pale, 'Up there.'

'What did he look like?'

Adelaide said quietly, 'Doomed.'

He had offered to sell her something or he had shown her something. The rectangular parcel the other victims had seen. Ambrosio, steeling himself, said, 'What did he offer to sell you?'

The eyes were gazing up towards Ermita. Behind the eyes fiendish fantasies were forming. Ambrosio, gagging on the stench as, still held by the mighty grip, he moved in closer to the woman, said smiling, 'People . . . people . . . of your station don't wind down windows for any piece of crap that importunes you – what did he offer to sell you?' He tried to grin. He tried to look casually interested. He tried to sound like a good Samaritan. He felt the coiled springs in the mighty, smelly body turn into switchblades.

'Nothing.' They had all said that, each of the victims. Fat Adelaide said, looking at the cab driver on the bonnet, 'And he didn't see anything either.' The piggy eyes turned on him, 'Why do you ask?'

Ambrosio meant to say, 'Well . . .' What he said was, 'Heh . . .' Ambrosio said, 'Just curious . . .' Ambrosio said, 'Do you want a cop?'

'Yes! I want a cop! I pay protection to the cops and I want a cop!'

'Right!' Ambrosio, releasing himself firmly from the grip, said victoriously, 'I am – ' A bicycle went by with a sixteen-year-old schoolgirl on it giggling with pleasure at the scene. Adelaide's face dried up her womb, made her sterile and sentenced her to a life of failure and kitchen scrubbing with a single curse. Ambrosio said, 'Cop – right!' He saw Martinez twenty yards back cowering behind his steering wheel.

Ambrosio running back towards the cab shouted over his shoulder in solemn promise, 'Right! I'll see if I can find one for you somewhere!'

He smiled. He nodded. He grinned . . .

He *fled*.

On the roof of the building opposite the Pasig Street Jewellers and the Cock Hospital, Technical Sergeant Jorge Gomez, bending down over the abandoned rifle, said, 'I found a few fragments and part of the fusing mechanism in with the rubble over there – it was an early model French made STRIM light anti-tank grenade.' He wore a grey dustcoat over his yellow METRO MANILA AIDE T-shirt – the sort street sweepers wore – 'It's a sort of rocket-like thing in appearance with a teat on the end and fins to stabilise it in flight.' The pockets on his dustcoat had tiny padlocks on them. He was with Ballistics. The things he carried in his pockets were things people wanted. All the pockets looked full and heavy. God only knew what he had in there. He smelled of Alox, the groove lubricant reloaders use to grease their bullets. Gomez, looking hard at Elizalde, said, 'The teat is the percussion fuse of the first charge in the projectile: it hits something – in this case a wall – and the hollow-shaped charge behind it punches a hole straight through it to let the projectile itself in and then, once it's through, the main charge goes off and fills whatever enclosed space it finds itself in – a tank, armored car, or a room – with red-hot shrapnel and burning gases.' He was a small, gamin-like man with a nervous smile. So was Billy the Kid. 'If it's a tank or an armored car the armor contains the blast. If it isn't – if it's a room . . .' He looked over towards where the room the projectile had hit had been. It wasn't there anymore. Gomez said, shrugging, 'Well . . .'

'What about the gun?'

'It's an Australian-made Lee-Enfield Jungle carbine, .303 caliber with the flash hider filed off and modified to take the rifle grenade.' Gomez, his eyes more on Elizalde than on the weapon, bent down and, with his knuckle, flipped open the bolt. He had no need to extract the fired cartridge case: he glanced only at the head stamp. 'Blank round to discharge the grenade.' He said before Elizalde could ask, 'It's an old weapon, Felix, made sometime in the late forties or early fifties, probably Malayan Emergency issue.'

'Fingerprints?'

'I doubt it. Scientific haven't arrived yet but even I with my brutal basic approach to life can see where he smeared his hand across any part of the weapon he touched.' He saw Elizalde go to the edge of the roof and look down at something Gomez had wedged against the side of the parapet in a glassine envelope. Gomez said, 'Firecracker debris. Bits and pieces of burned red paper from Chinese firecrackers.' He said, coming over, 'I don't know if they had anything to do with it. I just found them and bagged them.' He asked, 'Do they have anything to do with it?'

'Yes.'

Gomez said, 'Felix, are you all right?'

'Yes.' Gomez had the right idea: you immersed yourself in the technical and the inanimate and your world was fixed, certain, catalogued and classified into mathematical data and the identification of that mathematical data and you were all right. Elizalde asked, 'Anything on the fired .45 case from the cockpit?'

'Standard US hardball issue, recent vintage – that's to say, within the last twenty years – some primer degeneration from poor storage, but apart from that –'

'Nothing?'

'It's only a cartridge case.' He stood up and looked down at the rifle. 'The firing pin mark might suggest that the pistol had seen heavy use like the rifle here, but in the absence of – '

'What about the rifle?'

'Untraceable.' Gomez, touching at one of his locked pockets, shaking his head a little sadly, said to explain, 'No military disposal stamps. It's something that was either lost or captured or traded maybe thirty years ago and smuggled into Manila God knows when.'

'The grenade?'

'The grenade is in a thousand pieces.' Gomez, going to the parapet with Elizalde and looking over, said sympathetically, 'Whoever owns the jeweller's shop isn't going to be amused when he discovers that the paupers in the Cock Hospital upstairs got it blown to pieces for him.' He said, still on cosy technical ground, 'I saw what was left of a Mercedes 280S parked in the lane over there. I know what they cost, one million pesos. Whoever owns that . . .'

Elizalde said tightly, 'They did.'

'Who?'

'The Royares brothers. It's on the registration slip in the car.' He nodded across in the general direction of the shop,

'And that too. The jeweller's shop. It's above what's left of the door and on the shop registration framed above one of the counters.' Elizalde said, 'They owned that too. They owned the entire building.'

'I thought you said they were just – ' Gomez, glancing over the parapet with an incredulous look on his face, said, 'Two cockers? Two cockers owned that car and – and the entire building?' Gomez asked, 'They were rich?'

'It looks that way.'

'How? Where did they make their money?' He looked again at the ruined Mercedes. 'Where did they live – Forbes Park?'

'No, they lived up there. In two rooms at the back of the Cock Hospital.' Elizalde said, thinking of the Kristo's wallet, 'They didn't advertise their wealth.' Elizalde said quietly, gazing down, 'There are five people dead down there.' That was another statistic. 'Three of them not even twenty-five years of age.'

Gomez said softly, 'Yeah.' He glanced back to the rifle lying on its side behind him and then across to where the anti-tank grenade had hit. Grenades, modified military-issue rifles fired .45 caliber government issue cartridge cases: they were all parts of another mathematical equation. It only needed to be identified. Two rich men dead. The equation only needed to be added up to be identified. He identified it. Gomez said quietly, 'Felix, I think we may be dealing with subversives, some sort of heavily armed – ' He put his hand to one of his pockets and somehow, with a movement of his fingers, undid the lock. Gomez said, 'Here.' He handed Elizalde a small silver hip flask. It was eighty-six per cent proof Tondena dark rum. As he drank, it burned Elizalde's mouth. He knew Elizalde. He knew how he worked. Gomez, looking suddenly worried, taking a steadying drink himself and holding the silver flask in his hand as he gazed with Elizalde out over the street, said very firmly, 'Felix, I think – if I was you – I'd get Headquarters on the line. Right now!'

No need. Headquarters was already on the line.

In the kitchen of the deaf and dumb café off Rizal Park, at the number Elizalde had given when he had called in for help, the phone went on ringing and ringing and ringing.

By it, at the charcoal fires, the manageress and her daughter were still preparing their bibingkang malagkit and their customers outside, a special breed of thoughtful people, and hungry, had decided tacitly as one man not to embarrass them unnecessarily by going into the kitchens to mention it to them.

It was 1.05 in the afternoon.

After a while, the phone stopped ringing and, in the deaf and dumb café, again, there was silence.

Gomez said quietly, 'Felix?' He saw the man looking down into the street as the Scientific truck arrived with the finger-print and forensic gear with Doctor Watanabe a little behind in his car.

Gomez said, 'Here.' He handed over the hip flask with the rum in it.

With all his equations and sure and certain knowledge, he could not read the look on Elizalde's face as he watched. He saw Elizalde's smile as he handed back the flask and nodded for Gomez to finish it himelf. Gomez said, 'Well, of course it's not up to me to second guess my superiors or make reports where reports shouldn't be made by me . . .'

He said, shrugging, watching as Elizalde's gaze stayed fixed on the street, 'No, it isn't. That's right.' Dealing with guns, carrying guns, storing guns, transporting guns, he was con-stantly afraid of what someone might do to him to get them. He touched at his disguise, his METRO MANILA AIDE streetsweeper's T-shirt.

Lately, he had been drinking more and more.

Gomez said quietly, solving the equation, 'Right.'

He put the hip flask to his lips and, gratefully, feeling the dark, calming liquid burn all the way down to his stomach, drained it off.

7

Some people had their mothers, others their wives or psychiatrists, some people even had God (so did the Bontocs, but as Intutungtso: the General Idea Above . . . up there . . . somewhere . . . kind of . . . more or less . . . he was the sort of deity you talked about the weather with more than your problems) – but everybody, everybody had to have somebody.

In the Romans' case they were called alter egos. In Bontoc's they were called Uncle Apo Bontoc and Miss Thomasina Landsborough. They were his spirits. In most theologies spirits were required to be dead. Uncle Apo Bontoc certainly was – or by now he would have been a hundred and twenty-seven years old, but he wasn't certain about Miss Thomasina who could still be nipping about at a sprightly ninety-three.

Still, it was the thought that counted.

Up a tree, he wasn't panicking. Bontoc said, panicking, 'And then it moved! And then . . . and then . . . there were holes everywhere! And then . . . and then . . . *And then the thing toppled over on me!*'

'Shhh . . . shhh . . .' He had loved her voice. When she had taught him in the Episcopalian Mission School in Bontoc between the ages of eight to fifteen, he had loved her. Miss Thomasina said, 'Dear, dear Baptiste, all is understandable by reason . . .'

Uncle Apo Bontoc said, 'Kill!' He had the biggest collection

69

of heads in the district. Uncle Apo said, 'Bontoc *kill* enemy!' He spoke broken English and, for that matter, broken Bontoc. Uncle Apo said, 'Find enemy. Take head. Head on pile. Problem gone. Much honor. Huh!'

Miss Thomasina said quietly, 'Well, Baptiste, that certainly is one way of looking at it' – she was nothing if not a real Christian – 'But will it bring lasting happiness in the end?'

He had loved her. Bontoc said, nodding, 'You're right.'

Uncle Apo fell silent. When Uncle Apo fell silent bodies fell headless.

Bontoc said quickly, ' – probably!' Bontoc steadying himself on the tree and grasping his axe in his hand to keep Uncle happy said, 'I'm a *ukom*, Uncle – a white collar worker – I can't go around chopping people's heads off!' He heard Uncle Apo there in his head go 'Hrrmm!' – 'even as much as I might want to . . .' He sought Miss Thomasina's help, 'And apart from that, it's illegal!' Bontoc said, 'Right, Miss Thomasina?'

'And also against God's law, Baptiste.'

Bontoc said, 'And the government's!' With Uncle Apo you didn't reason, you ducked. Bontoc said, grovelling, 'The government – because they know I'm a Bontoc and so ferocious and so feared by all men – want me merely to show myself to frighten off its enemies – well, not enemies exactly, more minor inconveniences, and they –' Bontoc said in desperation, 'Miss Thomasina, there are people digging holes all over the place looking for the bones of dead Japanese soldiers and they –'

That was a mistake.

'HUH! MACARTHUR SAYS JAP HEADS GOOD!' As well as God and Intutungtso there had been General Macarthur. After him, God and Intutungtso ranked a low fourth and fifth. Uncle Apo, thundering in Bontoc's head, yelled, 'GOT JAP HEADS MANY! GOT HEAD WITH GOLD SPECTACLES! SHOW MACARTHUR! MACARTHUR TALK ME! MACARTHUR SAY *GOOD!* MACARTHUR GOOD FELLOW!'

'And then one of the dinosaurs fell over . . .'

'MACARTHUR MAN OF WORD. MACARTHUR SAY I RETURN. MACARTHUR RETURN. GOOD FELLOW. HEAD-TAKER. MAN TO TRUST.' Uncle Apo say – *said* –

70

'TRACK JAP. FIND JAP. CHOP JAP. I RETURN. GOOD MAN MACARTHUR!' Uncle Apo, taking over, feeling the edge of the head-axe through Bontoc's fingers, said in horror, 'Axe not sharp! Not real axe! Tourist axe!'

Miss Thomasina, feeling for him, said quietly, 'Sharpen your wits, dear Baptiste . . .'

Uncle Apo shouted, 'Sharpen axe!'

Bontoc said, 'They've even got maps. I've seen one of them. The Department thinks I'm an idiot. They don't think I'm educated at all.' He got in before Uncle Apo did, 'Education good. They slink around and dig their holes and get their bones and the only thing so far that's frightened them off hasn't been me but a dinosaur falling over almost on top of them.' Bontoc said, 'The gardener thinks I'm an idiot. Everyone thinks I'm an idiot.' Bontoc said, 'I am an idiot!'

'We are all fools for God, dear Baptiste. Perhaps if you had the appropriate department close off the park . . .'

'The appropriate department has already closed off the park!' Bontoc said, 'I'm a minority group. The Ministry of Public Works is going to have my balls for this!'

'*Bap-tiste!*'

Baptiste said, 'Oh . . .'

Uncle Apo said, 'Track Japs!'

'I can't track Japs! I can't even see them when they get in! They get in through gates they don't have keys for or they climb over fences or they – ' Bontoc, chopping the axe against a branch of the tree, said in total desperation, 'And they're not even Japs at all – they're local Philippinos!' Philippino, Schmilippino. Bontoc yelled at Uncle Apo, 'I can't go around chopping my own countrymen!' If they were Philippinos what the hell were they doing digging up Japanese bones? He was astride his tree gazing out across the heavily wooded dinosaur park. Forty years ago at the time the Japanese soldiers in the place had been turned into bones the dinosaur park had been nothing but a giant bomb hole in the ground. Before that it had been prehistory. It still was. Full circle. He saw the head of a brontosaurus poking out through a stand of bamboo. It was a stone brontosaurus. Bontoc said, hurt, 'They've set me some sort of involved problem to get rid of me. They think I'm just a savage.'

'Dear, dear . . .' Miss Thomasina said, smelling of her wonderful talc, 'Oh, no, no, no . . . oh dear bright Baptiste, my best pupil . . .'

Uncle Apo said quietly, 'What wrong with savagery?'

Bontoc said quietly, '*I just can't fucking work out what's happening!* I am a fucking savage! Hitler was right! There is a racial basis to intelligence!'

Uncle Apo said, 'Uh?'

Miss Thomasina said, 'No!'

Bontoc said in tears, 'Yes.'

The axe in his hand on the branch went tap, tap, tap. Bontoc said, 'I'm so unhappy.'

Tap, tap, tap.

Bontoc said, 'Oh Miss Thomasina, why didn't you let me play happily in the mud piles?' He wished he had his flute. Playing sad songs on his flute would have made him happy. Tap, tap, tap. Bontoc said, 'Oh . . .'

He heard the tap. It wasn't a tap, it was a click. It wasn't Uncle Apo in his bones. Bontoc said sadly, 'Oh, Miss Thomasina . . .'

It was underneath, on the ground at the base of his tree.

Bontoc said, 'Oh . . .'

It was them. It was the Philippinos! It was the Japanese! They were digging! They were digging at the roots of his tree! The had sacks in their hands and spades. They were – Bontoc said, 'Oh!'

He felt the tree move. Bontoc said, 'Oh – '

It didn't move: it shook – it wavered.

'Oh, God!'

It staggered, it faltered, it failed. It was coming down!

Bontoc said, 'Oh – ' Bontoc shrieked, '*Not my own tree!*' Bontoc yelled, 'Oh, no!'

He saw them look up and start running. He saw the empty sacks in their hands. He saw –

He felt the tree fall. It began, slowly, with a cracking, grinding noise to come down.

Oh, Miss Thomasina!

Oh, Uncle Apo!

Oh, Intutungtso!

He felt the tree begin to fall. He felt himself going. He felt –

He grabbed for the branch, for anything – for anything at all, anything to hold onto – anything – anything at all. Bontoc, falling, going over with the tree, in last final appeal to anyone, anywhere, anything, anyhow, yelled at the top of his voice to the lawnmowing gardener far out in the main park looking in his direction not at all, 'Oh . . . Oh . . . Oh, *SHIT!*'

'No, there aren't any bones in the holes! The holes are empty!'

'So were their sacks!'

'Then they stuffed the bones of their dead ancestors in their pockets and they – '

'They were Philippinos!'

The gardener said, 'Sure!' He hadn't said anything about the fallen tyrannosaurus Rex and – even if it had killed him – he wasn't going to say anything about the fallen tree. The gardener said tightly, patting dimwit on the shoulder and making his beads rattle, 'Sure they were.'

'I saw them!'

'Sure you did.'

Bontoc said, 'I'm an educated man, I know a Philippino when I see one!' He was limping. He limped back past the fallen tree, hobbled over the roots and pointed in the general direction of the stand of bamboo and the brontosaurus. Bontoc said, 'They went thataway! They get in thataway! Thataway there's a locked gate and they've got a key for it!' He was standing on the tree root shaking his axe. Bontoc said, 'I was chosen for this job because of my superior brainpower and the fact that I can bestraddle both the primitive and the civilised world' – that was what he had been doing on the tree: bestraddling – 'I know you don't think much of me, but – '

The gardener said in a strangled sound, 'Mzzph!'

' – but I'm going to solve this and when I do – '

The gardener said, 'Yes?'

Bontoc said –

The gardener waited.

Bontoc said – His bruises hurt and he had chipped his axe. Bontoc said –

The gardener said, 'Yes?'

'. . . when I do . . . When I do . . .'

He was a civilised man. Holding his axe in both hands and

pointing it on high to God, to Intutungtso, to Uncle Apo, to Miss Thomasina – to anyone who might listen – in heartfelt, final rendition of his intention, Bontoc said, '*AAAA-GGGHHHHH!!!*'

'We praise thee, O God: we acknowledge thee to be the Lord. All the earth doth worship thee: the Father ever-lasting. To thee all Angels cry aloud: the Heavens, and all the powers therein.
To thee Cherubin, and Seraphim – '
In the nave of the San Augustin Church in Barrio St Luis inside the walled city of Intramuros, the congregation was singing the *Te Deum Laudamus* of Saint Ambrosio.

In the San Pedro chapel of the great church and monastery built by the Spanish Augustinians in the sixteenth century, the Sentenciador stopped for a moment to listen. The church had been built around the Latin Cross plan, its fourteen chapels and libraries reached by long stone colonnaded walks en-closing a central lawn and gardens.

'Praise be to God for Thy flowers in the field.
Praise be to God for Thy trees.
Praise be to God for Thy stillness at night.'
There was a sandalled and straw-hatted monk kneeling at a corner of the deserted stone-vaulted chapel, wearing what looked like a thick cotton apron over his shirt and trousers, tied at the back in a knot. He had evidently discarded his cassock somewhere to do his work and say his Office while he did it. The Sentenciador, seeing what he worked at on the floor, said respectfully to his back, '*Fraile Ratonera. . .*' He was the Brother Mousetrapper.

The monk was setting his little traps and placing them carefully in the dust against the stone walls. He did not look up nor stop in his monotonous muttered Office. The monk, without turning around, said only, 'Hmm.'

'The noble army of Martyrs: praise Thee.
The holy Church throughout all the world: doth acknow-ledge Thee.'
The lovely, far off, Gregorian chant of the congregation and the monks and the mutterings of the Brother about his work slowed the Sentenciador's step. In the vaulted, leadlight

windowed chapel, he paused and crossed himself piously. He had two chains of sampaguita flowers in his hand. He stopped and asked a blessing on them. He walked on worn, ancient flagstones brought as ballast on the great Spanish galleons. He walked beneath wonderful painted scenes of Heaven and Hell on the ceiling. He stopped and took his rosary beads from his pocket and, working them in his fingers, softly, so as not to disturb the monk at his work and his Office, said ten Hail Marys and one Our Father.

The carved wooden santo of San Pedro – Saint Peter – was a little to one side in the ancient room. Bending his head, he went to it and knelt at it, still working the beads through his fingers. Softer now, brought across the lawns and cloisters and colonnades through the closed soda-glass leadlight windows, he heard the lovely calming sound of the chant. The monotone of the mousetrapping monk was a soft steady buzzing. The Sentenciador, rising to stand before the life-sized carved and painted wooden saint, said softly as a plea for intercession, 'San Pedro, look kindly upon my prayer.'

He bowed his head and stood in silence before the saint with his hands clasped together over the two chains of tiny white flowers and the dark beads of his rosary.

Praise be to God for Thy fish in the sea.
Praise be to God for . . .'

He heard a gentle click as the straw-hatted monk set a mousetrap. The Sentenciador, going forward, placed a ring of the flowers around the painted saint's neck. It had been carved hundreds of years ago. The polychrome paint was flaking and it smelled of age and prayer. The Sentenciador said softly, 'Intercede for protection now in these times of danger.' The Sentenciador, stepping back, said, 'Ave Maria, full of grace . . .'

Make them to be numbered with Thy Saints:
In glory everlasting . . .'

He heard the little monk of the mousetraps at his Office.

He heard a gentle shuffling sound as the monk, on his knees, moved, still saying his orisons.

'O Lord, save Thy people: and bless thine heritage . . .'

He was the patron saint of cockers, Saint Peter. The Sentenciador, bowing his head, placed the second chain of white flowers around the neck and, repeating his rosary, put his hands together and prayed.

The Sentenciador said, 'Protect him and keep him safe from all harm . . .' The Sentenciador said, 'Ave Maria, full of grace, blessed among women . . .'

He heard a click.

The Sentenciador, going forward and taking a candle from the little wooden box at the saint's painted feet, said as he lit it carefully and placed it in its holder, 'San Pedro, you alone . . .'

The Sentenciador, working his beads, said, 'San Pedro, friend of all my life . . .' He had a little photograph of the soul to be protected in his palm against the beads and he leant forward and placed it a little in front of the candle. The Sentenciador said softly, changing from Spanish to English, 'San Pedro . . . Saint Peter . . .'

He heard a click.

The little photograph was of one of God's poor creatures in peril. The Sentenciador said –

The Office behind him stopped.

The orison far off in the great chapel had come to an end.

The Sentenciador, turning, seeing the straw-hatted monk standing a little behind him smiling at him, said, '*Fraile Ratonera* . . . Brother . . .'

The monk had both his mousetraps in his hands. He was offering them to the Sentenciador, palm upwards. They were both set. Both of them glittered briefly in the light from the windows.

The Sentenciador saw something bright on them: nickel, or chrome or plating. The Sentenciador said –

They were percussion caps; primers from rifle cartridges. They rested on hammered-in tacks. The monk coming towards him in his apron – in his knotted coveralls – said in a hiss, still smiling, 'Here . . .' The little monk said suddenly, 'Here! *Catch!* Catch – Here . . . *Catch!*'

He saw it. He saw it all happening from everywhere, from all points in the chapel. He saw himself. He saw himself as the saint saw him. He saw the mousetraps flying through the air, turning over and over. He saw it as the monk saw it: he saw them going towards him. He saw them hit his chest. He saw himself. He looked down and the caps had gone off in two flashes of brilliant flame. He heard the two detonations. He heard it from every point in the chapel, from the vaulted, painted ceiling, from the corners of the room. He saw the candle flicker with the force.

He heard nothing.

He heard them.

The two charges shattered at his eardrums. He saw the straw hat on the bald man's head. He was dead. He was at the moment of death and he was everywhere in the place he was going to die. He saw —

He saw —

He saw the long sharp, butterfly knife in the man's hand come up and, as he flicked it, the twin folding handles fly apart and reveal the blade. He saw the edge burn white in the light. He saw — He felt —

The knife, ripping across the Sentenciador's throat, released, with his soul, a gout, a flood, a torrent of blood. That was what the coveralls had been for: the apron. Kicking him, shoving him out and away as the blood came out in a geyser, Bald Head's clothes – the ones he would wear back out into the street with his straw hat and sandals – were marked not at all.

San Pedro —

'Praise be to God for Thy flowers in the fields.

Praise be to God for Thy trees and Thy stillness of night . . .'

The photograph for the saint's divine protection was of a cockbird.

It was a photograph of Battling Mendez.

Bald Head, glancing at it, left it where it was.

His coveralls were soaked in blood.

Unknotting them at the back and slipping them over his head, he dropped them onto the stone floor together with the wiped clean butterfly knife and, his sandals making only a slight slapping sound as he walked, carrying the straw hat for safe disposal out in the street, he left the chapel and, going unhurriedly down the great colonnaded walkways towards the main door of the place, smiled to himself in satisfaction.

It was a little after 4.15 p.m.

As he walked he glanced across at the long shadows forming in the gardens and on the lawns and thought, without great interest in the fact one way or the other, that, in less than two hours, it would be night.

8

In the cab – in the last Ride Of The Valkyries of the day –
Martinez yelled back over the seat, 'I've been thinking about
your troubles.' (Ambrosio's troubles were that God was
dealing him a series of unfair blows solely for His own
amusement.) 'And I've got a book for you! I studied it myself. I
think it could help you too!' They were going the wrong way
down a one-way street. The one-way street was up for repairs.
It was a no-way street. Martinez, tossing it over, said, 'Here!
Look at it!' He asked eagerly, 'What do you think? I keep it in
my glove-box to swot flies!'

It was a locally printed, badly glued, dog-eared, stained with
God knows what, copy of *Socio-Public Relationship Officers'
Orientation Group Papers*.

SPROOG.

Martinez, gazing at him in the rearview mirror, shouted,
'Well, what do you think?' He gave Ambrosio a comradely
grin.

He shouted above the sound of workmen shouting at him
and of the suspension as it crashed over a road that looked
only fit for Patton's tanks or Hannibal's elephants, 'Well, open
your eyes and look at it at least! You never know – it worked
for me!'

Martinez said, 'You know, before I made something of myself
– before I became a taxi driver – I was a cop for a while too.'

*

In Room 333 of the Manila Hotel, the phone rang. It was a little after 7 p.m. and on television the news had just finished.

On the phone, Bald Head said, 'All right?'

There was silence. The man in Room 333, standing by the big Spanish-style four-poster bed in the room gazed out through the big picture window south-west towards Bataan and the island of Corregidor. In the bay there was a cruise ship coming in for an overnight stay: he saw its lights and its gentle movement through the darkness. The man in Room 333 said, deciding, 'All right.'

They had said on television that the dead Sentenciador's name had been Tolentino. It was a name that, up until a week ago, had meant nothing to him at all.

The man in Room 333, hanging up, touched the button on the phone to get the hotel switchboard.

He had a call booked to America for 7.15 and, still gazing thoughtfully at the lights of the ship as she docked, he asked the switchboard not to wait, but – if they could – to put it through now.

He watched the lights of the ship.

Tolentino, the two Royares brothers, the rest of them . . .

He had all their names fixed firmly in his mind.

He had nothing written down at all.

Standing, watching, thinking his own thoughts, sure of what to say, he waited patiently for the connection to be made.

9

Ang Pasiyang Tagahatol ay Pangwakas.
EL FALLO DEL JUEZ ES INAPELABLE.
The Referee's Decision Is Final.
Far below the glass fronted Sky Room Restaurant on the
third floor of the Jai Alai fronton on Taft Street, the referee's
whistle blew and Felicidario executed the *saque* – the serve –
and, his scooped Jai Alai racket cutting through the air in a
downward swoop, sent the first ball of the practice match high
against the wall at an impossible angle and, confounding his
opponent Natividad completely, yelled, 'Ayo!' The Jai Alai
fronton – a closed in amphitheater of seats and bleachers on
two floors safe behind glass from the fastest ball game in the
world – was empty. Tonight both Felicidario and Natividad
would be playing Oyarzabal, the reigning champion. They had
been practising in the giant, side-on style squash court of the
fronton since dawn.

The referee's decision was final. So was his fate if one of the
balls, traveling at a hundred and fifty miles an hour from one
of the scoops hit him. Using the tennis racket he carried to
protect his face, the referee stopped the rolling ball and tossed
it back to Felicidario for his second rally. In the Sky Room
Restaurant sitting at the bar that ran along the length of the
glass, looking down as Felicidario took the ball, Lieutenant
Ernesto Yun of the Metro Manila Gambling Squad made a

note on an open scratch pad with a silver Sheaffer fountain pen. The mark was a single Chinese character Elizalde could not read. It was some sort of handicapping symbol. The ink was green, an accountant's color. Yun, glancing down at the character for a moment and then back to the practice match below, shook his head. He put the cap back on the pen, thought for a moment to put it back in the top pocket of his plain white open-neck shirt and then, seeing Natividad, this time, send back the serve with a sizzling shot that came off the wall like a bullet, put it down by his calculators and open ledgers and drummed his fingers.

He had known Elizalde for a long time. The restaurant was closed for the practice session but he had been able to get one of the fronton staff who waited around while he did his monthly audit session to make coffee for him. With one eye still on the practice match, still drumming his fingers, he waited while Elizalde took a sip of it. Yun said, 'I'm just a bureaucrat, Felix. The only things I might know about the Royares brothers or the Sentenciador Tolentino I'd know from auditing their betting books for the Squad. And even then, all I'd know would be that, maybe some of the betting practices or the odds offered were dubious or, on the other hand, they weren't.' He was Chinese, from his slight, high cheekboned appearance, probably Cantonese. Once, his family had owned half of Chinatown. They had all been ruined by gambling and even the family tombs in the City of the Dead beyond Tondo had had to be emptied and sold off to pay their debts. Yun said, 'All I know about the Royares brothers – '

'Did you know they were rich?'

Even in a practice match the referee carried his tennis racket to protect himself. On the open ledger Yun had two pocket calculators, one solar powered for outside work and the other a government issue clunker that made a clicking noise when he touched it. Yun, playing with it with his long, thin fingers, said cautiously, 'I believe they were well off.' He asked, 'Why don't you look them up in Records?' He glanced suddenly behind him as if he was afraid there might be somebody listening. 'Look them up in Records, Felix.'

'They don't have records.' Elizalde glanced at his watch. It was 7.15 a.m. on a Monday morning. In the closed-in empty restaurant it was cold and quiet. 'What they had was a jewellery business, a Mercedes car, and God only knows how much salted away all over Asia.' Elizalde said, 'And now they're dead. Someone shot the first one, the Kristo at the cockpit with a .45 automatic in plain view of hundreds of people and put a rifle grenade through the second one's window and killed at least three other innocent people.' When they found the Sentenciador, his blood had stopped flowing from his severed neck and they had literally to wade through puddles of it to get to his body. Elizalde said, 'Tolentino had some sort of home-made Special Forces alarm device thrown at him and then his head was almost severed from his body by a folding butterfly knife with an eight-inch blade.' They had found the Sentenciador's identity card. They might as well have found nothing. Elizalde said, 'The only address we have on Tolentino is the cockpit and the cockpit staff say he didn't live there. And the cockpit staff say they thought he was rich too.' Elizalde said before Yun could side-step him, 'Sentenciadors, like Jai Alai referees, aren't allowed to bet on matches and neither are cockdoctors – they're rules you people enforce – so don't tell me that he got rich by gambling.'

'Nobody gets rich by gambling. I don't want any trouble, Felix.'

'I'm not making any, Ernesto.'

Yun, touching at his government issue calculator, said firmly, 'In Manila, if you haven't got a job, you die.' Down in the court, the players had stopped for a moment and were discussing tactics. In the restaurant there was no sound at all. Yun, leaning a little closer said softly, 'I can't afford any trouble.' He shrugged. He smiled. Yun said nervously, 'I'm so poor, I'm honest.'

'I'm not asking you to be dishonest – '

'You're asking me to tell you things that I don't want to know!'

'I'm only asking you for information. I'm asking you as one cop to another – '

'Then put in a request through the Department.'

'If I did that I'd never hear about it again!'

Yun, smiling tightly, said, 'Still playing street cop are you, Felix? How do they pay you these days – by monthly check care of Poste Restante?'

'If I tell Headquarters anything they'll take one look at the rifle grenade and the Special Forces style booby trap and before they've finished screaming Subversives we'll have the Army out on the streets arresting people and firing tear gas.'

The Referee's Decision Is Final. In the old days in China – in the days of the landlords and then later during the Revolution when his family had fled – the referee's decision had always been final too. Usually, it meant you ended up in a ditch somewhere with a bullet in the back of your neck. Yun, deciding, shaking his head, tapping at his calculator for comfort, said, 'I don't have any sympathy for the rich. There's nothing I know about them.'

'The shopgirl and the poor bastard who worked in the Cock Hospital building weren't rich!'

'Yes, I heard about that.'

'They were *poor*!'

'They owned a company, that's all I know. The Royares brothers and Tolentino the Sentenciador: they were partners in a company – that's all I know.' Down below Felicidario was swinging his scoop preparatory to serving. Yun, still shaking his head at something, said firmly, 'I know that and that's all I know – they were partners in a company they'd formed and they drew money from it – *on which, I'm assured they paid tax* – and since it had very little to do with the gaming activities at the cockpit or anywhere else that's all I'm entitled to know!' He saw the look on Elizalde's face. 'And don't ask me what sort of a cop I am, because the sort of cop I am is a cop who is saddled with the debts of his family to a point – to a point of desperation – so crushing that I couldn't even take a bribe if it was a million pesos.'

'I didn't know it was that bad – '

'It's so bad that I'll never pay it off and it's so bad that if I take even one sick day off, the finance company and the bank – the bank here in Manila and in Hong Kong and in Penang and anywhere else my fucking father and my fucking grandfather and my fucking brother could draw money, will have me and

83

my children out on the streets and the clothes off my back!' He looked down at the mark he had made on the scratch pad. Yun said, 'My hobby is handicapping – at the moment you couldn't even *get* odds on me!'

'What about your –'

'They're all dead. My father and grandfather were murdered by the Triads in Hong Kong and my brother – my brother here in Manila – killed himself.' Yun said, looking directly into Elizalde's face, 'No, it's only me.' He took out a cigarette from a pack on the table – they were the cheapest Hope brand – and lit it with his hand shaking. 'I've got degrees in economics and accountancy, Felix – I could be earning big money in private practice, but, you see, if I'm a cop – even just a bureaucratic cop like this – the Triads won't want to touch me.' He said, kneading the cigarette between his fingers, 'I don't even carry a gun. If I carried a gun the Triads might think –' Yun said suddenly desperately, 'I can't afford to get into any more trouble from people with the power of life and death over me and my family!' He kept glancing around to check that no one was listening. Yun said, 'I heard what you did for the boy at the Cock Hospital. I know you. I know what sort of man you are. But I –'

'Are they powerful – the people behind Royares and Tolentino?'

'I didn't say there was anyone behind them!'

'If there wasn't you wouldn't be afraid.'

'I'm always afraid!' Yun said abruptly, 'Please, I come here before dawn. I work when there's no one around. I –' Yun said, 'I'm frightened to even go out on the streets!' He said for no apparent reason, perhaps for something he suddenly thought, or even because of something he could no longer bear, 'It's some sort of Swiss holding company or German or something – some sort of haven set-up – it's called Hipogrifo AG. It means "Winged Horse" – like the silver thing the jeepney drivers put on their decorated taxis, some sort of macho symbol – the AG means it's a company in Europe somewhere safe from scrutiny. The Royares brothers and Tolentino were part of it and I don't know who else was and even if I did I wouldn't tell you!'

'Where is this company? In Manila?'

'I don't know.'

'Is it in the phone book?'

'No.'

'What does it make?

'It doesn't *make* anything!' Yun said desperately, 'Leave me alone! Go through proper channels!'

'Ernesto – '

'Who cares? You can't win. Who cares? In the end the rich and the powerful will always destroy you!'

'They will if you let them.'

In the courts the practice had started again. The sound of the balls striking the wall like gunshots came up and rattled at the glass. Yun said softly, 'Oh Jesus . . .' Briefly, he put his hand to his face. Briefly, he thought of the relief of being dead. Yun said softly, 'You love all this, don't you? Like me, you could be something better, but you love it. It's a drug. It's a – ' Yun said, 'For God's sake, Felix, you haven't the faintest idea what you're playing with – these people aren't thugs and murderers or break-in men! These people aren't even organised crime! These people are – ' He said suddenly, 'I can't tell you. I don't know. I can't tell you any more.'

'Tell me what the company does.'

'It leases things.'

'Cars?'

Yun said, laughing bitterly, 'No.' He seemed on the edge. Something was happening in his eyes. He kept gritting them closed and then opening them again. Yun said, 'No, no, no . . .'

'Equipment? Plant?'

'No.' It was a game. Yun, grinning, said, 'You're not even close!' He no longer cared. His hands had stopped shaking. He stopped looking around. His voice was no longer low. He no longer cared. He had come to the final point. It was a little after dawn. It was early morning. Where he hid in the darkness – in the silence – someone was there beside him to listen. Yun said, 'No! They don't lease cars or trucks or plant or equipment – they lease – they lease – ' Yun said, 'Felix, look around you – see – everywhere – what's around you! Think! Think for a moment – just for a moment – just what it might be worth in sponsorship, in advertising, in – in the dreams of all the poor struggling slobs caught up in their little treadmills – in people's dreams and in – ' He didn't care anymore. His life was never going to change. He didn't even have that – the smallest dream of the most ordinary hopeless street vendor in Tondo, even that –

Yun, shouting, not caring who heard, finally, at last not caring what anyone did to him, said, 'Felix – Lieutenant god-damned Elizalde who loves this life so much – Hipogrifo AG – these people: the ones who have been killed, the millionaires – and God knows who else you don't know about – these people – this company *owns* Battling Mendez!' He said softly, 'God help you. Soon, when they know you know, you'll be exactly like me.'

He turned away to his scratch pad and his calculators and all the ruins of his life. He was a Christian Chinese. It was one of the reasons his family had fled the Revolution. He said something softly in Chinese that Elizalde could not understand.

Yun, turning to look at him with the strangest sad look on his face, said, translating it, 'God help you, because, now, no one else will.'

It was 7.32 a.m. He began silently gathering up his papers and his calculators and his pens to leave.

He hardly ever smoked in the mornings. There was a street vendor in Taft Avenue dodging his way between the cars and jeepneys and buses, selling from the tray he wore on a neck halter, trying to attract customers by making the kissing sound with his lips all the vendors used. Elizalde signalling him over, bought a single Marlboro cigarette from him for fifty centavos and waited while the vendor lit it for him with a chunky imitation Zippo lighter.

He was a thin-faced boy of no more than eighteen or nineteen. On his tray was written in his own hand – in a hand better than the hand that should have held a street vendor's tray – *MURA!*

It meant cheap.

Battling Mendez: he was the dream of every poor man in the

Philippines. He was everywhere. He was in all their eyes. Under his fawn safari shirt Elizalde carried his PPK in a soft leather belt holster. He wanted to touch at it to make sure it was still there but the boy had not gone back into the traffic, but was standing there watching him. He had seen something on his face.

The boy said softly, abruptly, 'Are you all right?'

'Yes.'

'Is the cigarette all right?'

Elizalde said, 'Yes.' He put his hand down and touched at his gun under his shirt, but to the boy it only looked as if he was in some sort of slight discomfort.

The boy, speaking English, said, 'Sir? Do you want a policeman or something?'

'No.' Elizalde, shaking his head, said as people passed around them in the street, 'No, no thanks very much. But thank you for asking.'

The cigarettes were not Marlboros at all. They were some sort of local copy packed carefully by someone, one by one, into real Marlboro packets and resealed with cellophane.

Reaching into his pocket for the money Elizalde bought an entire pack for a ten peso note.

As he took the cigarettes, without anyone noticing anything, he touched again at his gun.

In the darkened underground pistol range on Wainwright Street, Bald Head touched at his gun. It was a single shot Hammerli Model 150 Free Pistol made in Switzerland and as he held it lightly in his hand he put the faintest pressure on the trigger and felt it move back a hairsbreadth. It weighed over forty-three ounces loaded with an Eley Match .22 caliber cartridge: with the precision and balance the Swiss had worked into it like a watch, it weighed nothing. By him on the shooting bench there was a Bausch and Lomb tripod-mounted spotting scope pointed down range at the target.

Through the scope the little one and a half inch center ring of the twenty-five meter target looked the size of a dinner plate.

He had been at the range steadily practising for over an hour and a half. In that time he had fired eight shots. Every one of them was in the black center and every one of them had been fired with such care and accuracy that their holes cut through each other on the paper.

Slowly, meticulously, using the well-worn precision gun, he was shooting a perfect score. There was no one else in the range – he had his own key – and there was therefore no one to witness it.

It didn't matter. He did it for his own satisfaction. At the muzzle of the weapon as the trigger broke crisply under the pressure of his finger there was a crack and a puff of smoke. There was no recoil. Bald Head, lowering the gun slowly after having held it on target for a full held-breath count of twenty, cleared the mechanism with the Martini-style cocking lever on the side of the gun and placed it carefully on a rolled-up hand towel on the bench beside the scope.

Only the target area of the range was lit. In the darkness at the firing line, as he bent down to look through the scope, only his silhouette was visible.

It was another ten. It cut the other holes slightly high and to the right of the main group.

It was another perfect shot.

He had been up all night. He felt tired.

Loading the weapon carefully with a single lubricated round from a little wooden box near the scope, Bald Head, a silent, relentless shadow, an athlete training his muscles and his mind to stay sharp, cocked the weapon with a careful click and, drawing a breath, raised it up for another, slow timed, minutely accurate shot.

MENDEZ BEER!
MENDEZ BEER FOR VITALITY!
MANLINESS! MENDEZ!
MENDEZ! MACHO! MENDEZ!

It was everywhere, on all the signs and hoardings, on the bumper stickers of cars – it was everywhere.

Tread softly, for you tread on my dreams. Mendez! Macho! Mendez!

In his career he had been shot twice, once slightly in a raid on a house in Tondo and once, when he had least expected it, when he had been totally unarmed and unprepared, he had been shot in the stomach.

By his car in the parking lot of the Jai Alai fronton on Taft Street, Elizalde remembered.

He remembered, not what he had felt, but only the look on his wife's face when she had seen him in the hospital.

He felt his hand ache to touch at his gun and check it was still there.

He fought it. He fought the urge.

Rubbing hard at his face, he threw the second of his imitation, overpriced fake cigarettes away and went as briskly as he could manage to find a public telephone in the street to ring his brother-in-law Luis Lanternero at home before he left for work in the Taxation Department.

10

There must have been a quarantine warning on the fence of the Dinosaur Park, or maybe the gardener had taken up bell-ringing and walking the outer perimeter and was calling out, 'Unclean!' In either event the Dinosaur Park and all around it was still and deserted. Over the entire dog-leg six and a half acres there was silence and stillness.

No animal or bird moved in the trees. There was no movement of any kind anywhere. On the grass and at the feet of the dinosaurs and stegosauri, the mammoths, saber-toothed tigers and antediluvian hippos and ant-eaters there was a stillness. It was as if they were all carved in stone.

Behind trees even the moss had stopped growing. No earthworm disturbed a single clod of earth.

At 7.35 a.m. only the scent of the frangipani trees fell heavily to earth and filled the air with sweetness.

He was there. A Bontoc in the old primordial mould, he was there in the trees and stone itself, his own scent part of the falling scent of the trees – he was there. He was part of the earth, the trees, the stone itself.

He was there.

He was invisible.

He waited.

Search for him as you may: follow the walking track along bends and twists, past flowers and herb bushes and brush, he was nowhere to be seen. Glance up to the tree cover – to the dark branches of oak and elm – to unmoving leaves, to the stillness and eternity of growth and Nature – and he could not be seen. He was Oberon – a spirit, Pan, Intutungtso – he was a thought, an idea, a heavy presence . . . but wherever you looked he could not be seen.

Tiger stripe camo, nothing! An Episcopalian educated Bontoc who bought his axes in up-market antique shops *at a fair price* knew a thing or two.

Peer slyly into the stone lairs fearing he might erupt like a disturbed wildcat: he was not there. Sneak on tip toes or pad on carefully set-down bare feet and he was not there. Seek him here, seek him there – he was nowhere.

He was there.

In the little frog pond at the far western side of the park near one of the locked iron gates you would find, not him, but only the tadpoles.

The tadpoles knew he was there. They floated motionlessly on the top of the pond between stopped and waiting lily pads with hardly a ripple at their tails.

In the park Baptiste Bontoc waited, his hand unmoving on the haft of his axe.

If there had been worms brave enough to venture forth on such a day they would have turned. The grass had stopped growing. He was there with his eyes narrowed and half shut with no flickering behind the eyelids.

There was only the gentle bubbling sound of his breathing.

He was not in the tadpole pond, nor, this time, in a tree, nor, this time skulking in the stone lair of a stone saber-toothed tiger, nor anywhere to be seen.

He waited, silent, invisible, eternal, listening for the sounds of digging.

He listened.

He waited.

He had had a gutful. Someone was going to be in big trouble.

Unmoving, abstract, the presence of Doom awaiting a victim, he . . . awaited his victims.

*

In Roxas Boulevard the durian mugger had already been found.

It was too early for the shops so he had hit a cab carrying a tourist carrying duty free bags from his hotel to the airport. The tourist was a US Marine in full dress uniform. Half the dress uniform was hanging out of the open rear door of the cab. So was half the gasping US Marine. It could have been the top half. In the miasma of durian it was hard to tell. The Marine was shouting something about the state of his white hat after a jeepney, crashing into the back of a bus in the confusion, had run over it.

Ambrosio and Martinez had been one car away in the far lane. They were now no cars away in the far lane. The front of El Tigre, dodging the skidding jeepney as it went over the hat, had turned the car in front to a memory. The bomber was running. He was wearing grey slacks and a red and white striped T-shirt. He looked like a fleeing lizard. He was skipping through the traffic on the opposite side of the road going for Teodoro Kalaw Street carrying his rectangular package and the Marine's duty free plastic bags and Ambrosio was right behind him. He heard Martinez yell, 'My cab!' He heard the Marine yell, 'My God!' He heard himself yell, 'My *idea!*'

He had worked it out. SPROOG and IGLL had worked it out. He dodged a careering Mercedes dodging him, saw the bomber reach the sidewalk and explode into a crowd of people waiting for a bus and, Ambrosio, pulling on his POLICE baseball cap and missing a shrieking bicyclist by a fraction, yelled, 'UP! I'm on my way UP!'

He had worked it out. It had taken him all night. As he ran he grinned. He had worked out with all the irregular times the mugger had hit that there was only 7.30 to 8.00 a.m. left in which he hadn't hit. He had worked out the mugger had hit when no one had expected him. This time, he had been expected. He had worked out all the shops would be closed. He had worked out it would be someone on their way to the airport. He had worked out where the duty free shops in the hotels were. He had worked out the Manila Hotel was where the expensive people lived and where the airconditioned cabs waited and he had been there on the spot. He had worked it out.

He had worked out how to track him. He had worked out how – whatever the mugger did, whichever way he turned – he had worked out how, he, Ambrosio was going to get him.

He was going to smell him. He had spent the whole night working it out and blowing his nose and not smoking and deodorising himself after his soapless shower and he was going to smell him in his lair, collar him, and, with his proboscis and his great brain still quivering with hygiene; accept modestly the promotion a grateful Department –

The mugger turned into Corregidor Street. He smelled him. In the air, moving on invisible currents known only to the world's greatest Nose, he smelled him. He was running. For an instant Ambrosio saw him glance back and look terrified. Well he might. He was like a rat being chased by a bloodhound. A mongoose. A mongoose with a bloodhound's nose. He was afraid. He looked down at the two swinging yellow duty free bags and thought for a moment to drop them.

Ambrosio, shoving, pushing, weaving his way through knots of astonished, impressed people, said aloud, 'Heh, heh!'

The mugger dropped the bags. Rum and cigars spilled all over the corner of Nipa Street. Ambrosio said, 'Heh!' He was striding, letting his pace out, running the mugger down. He sniffed. He smelled. He got within three feet of the stink of the rum and the soggy cigars and, prepared for every eventuality, held his nose and kept the finely tuned instrument clear.

He turned into Nipa Street and the mugger was gone.

Sniff, sniff.

The mugger had turned from Nipa Street into Cavite Lane. He smelled him. He was still running, his stride unbroken. He saw him. He saw him look afraid. 'Heh! Heh!'

Success, ambition, *brainpower!*

He saw the mugger break into a frantic, panicked gallop. He smelled the durian.

People who threw glass durian bombs shouldn't – Enough.

He smelled him.

He ran.

He was winning.

93

SPROOG! IGLL!

Moment by moment, following his scent, unstoppably, wonderfully, career-wise, he was running him down like a dog.

'Dear Baptiste . . .'

In his mind Bontoc said, '*I can do it.*' He was invisible.

Uncle Apo Bontoc said, 'Huh, good. Good Bontoc.'

In his mind Bontoc said, '*I can do it.*' He thanked Miss Thomasina for the education. He said silently to Uncle Apo — even Uncle Apo could not find him and the sound of his voice in his mind kept coming and going as the poor old headhunter wandered the ether looking for him — '*Thanks for making me a Bontoc.*'

He heard digging.

He said in his mind, '*Thanks for teaching me how to use a head-axe.*'

He heard digging.

They had no idea he was there.

'Dear Baptiste . . . but are you sure you . . .'

'*I can do it.*'

'Huh. Good. Kill.'

'Are you so sure that to lurk unseen like the — '

'No lurk! Ambush!' Uncle Apo again.

'Miss Thomasina — ' Bontoc. Bontoc said in silence, 'A man has to do what a man has to do.'

'Huh. John Wayne! Good fellow!'

Miss Thomasina said, 'Shut up, you old fart!'

Bontoc's mind said —

His mind was wandering.

He heard digging.

He was invisible.

He was breathing in bubbles.

He fingered the axe.

Every muscle in his body was hard and coiled, like a spring.

All the voices in his head went silent.

His breathing came a little harder, faster.

He heard sounds, noises, movement. They were getting closer.

Bontoc, somewhere deep in his chest, working himself up, gathering strength, about to erupt said, 'GRrr . . . grrr . . . grrrr . . . grHHH . . .'

He heard digging.

He made it into the warren of streets around Parker Lane. The warren of streets around Parker Lane led into the warren of apartments in Parker Place, thousands of them, dozens of eight storey, rotting, paint-peeling Spanish colonial style buildings where you could hide and be safe from the Police.

From the ordinary Police. From the Security Police. From the Military Police. From the Thought Police.

But not from the Scent Police! Nowhere! Never!

Sniff!

He had him.

He lost him.

He smelled. He smelled, stank, reeked of durian from the bomb and he had him.

He saw him. He saw him go wide-eyed. He could never escape.

Ambrosio, running, yelling, laughing, shrieking in victory, shouted in final total mastery, '*Got you, you son of a bitch!*'

The long nose of the law was after him.

He didn't have a hope in Hell.

Ready . . .

Ready . . .

Ready to pounce . . .

The digging was there, less than . . .

The strength was flowing into his body, Uncle Apo's strength, Miss Thomasina's strength, all the strength of all the Bontocs of all time who, one way or another, had had the shit kicked out of them by headquarters, by gardeners, by life, by . . .

He was ready.

He tensed every muscle in his body and turned it to steel-tempered spring and sinew. His hand was on his axe. He felt its unyielding narra-wood handle. It wasn't so sharp, but by God, by Intutungtso, it was going to do the job.

He was God. He was going to send a few sinners to Perdition.

He was . . .

Bontoc, like a rocket launch, began counting it down.

Ten, nine, eight, seven, six . . .

He heard them digging.

Five . . .

Four . . .

They were there, inches from him. He was invisible. He was winged Death. He was . . .

Three . . .

Two . . .

He heard them.

He was gone. He was back. And then he was gone again. The mugger, darting from one tiny back lane to another was trying to shake him, running through all the smells of rotting garbage and peeling paint and the effluvium and crap of society in general and Parker Mansions in particular. Too late. The Stradivarius nose was resined to its finest pitch – it played only durian. It was one of those days when everything went right. It was one of those days when nothing would ever go wrong again. The mugger was running down some filthy stinking alley past corrugated iron sheds and slums and open sewers, through piles of trash, and there was nothing he could do to shake his own odor. The Stink Police had found him out and they were about to pounce.

He stopped, turned to see Ambrosio coming after him, glancing to his left to a graffiti covered mildewed doorway into one of the apartment blocks – into the caves – and Ambrosio shrieked, 'Go in! Get lost in there! I love it! I'll follow you to the ends of the Earth!' He had it in his mind to say something about the mark of Cain, but when he did his report it was all going to be professional, non-personal and the perfect bust. He would probably open up a new branch of scientific detection. They might even name a wing of the police college after him. He saw the mugger look down at the box under his arm, the thing he offered his victims to get them to open their windows and Ambrosio the Magnificent yelled, 'Yeah, go on, show me what it is! Whatever it is, I can surmount it!' To hell with non-personal. It was personal. Ambrosio yelled, 'You're not dealing with the rich now, you're dealing with the intelligent!'

The mugger reached into the box.

Ambrosio, fifty yards away, closing fast, unstoppably, yelled, 'Yeah, go on! What is it?'

It was a long-barrelled, gold-plated broom-handled Mauser automatic pistol.

Ambrosio said, 'Oh my God!' He couldn't stop running. His Walther PPK was in his ankle holster and trying to reach that would be like putting your hands in the spokes of a spinning bicycle wheel.

He saw the gun come up. He couldn't stop. Ambrosio, seeing the barrel of the giant weapon turn directly into him – between the eyes – yelled, 'Oh no! Oh, no!' His perfect bust! His career! His full ceremonial funeral. He reached down, touched at his leg, tripped himself up and, as the mugger stood there trying to decide where to shoot him, went over in a cartwheel into a mound of rotting bananas thrown away by some unsuccessful trader or banana-thief and, skidding out of them, crashed into a wall.

The mugger had the gun up. The gun was in his right hand, the box in his left. He was trying to decide. Ambrosio saw the weapon glitter. It was gold-plated. It was lethal. It looked about as big as a bazooka. He couldn't get at his PPK. His PPK in comparison was about the size of a cap pistol. He saw the mugger do something with the gun – he heard a click. He saw – He heard – He saw the mugger raise the gun up head high and then, grinning, making chuckling noises as Ambrosio, bouncing off the wall under his own volition and heading for the safety of the banana pile wrenched at his trousers for his Walther, the mugger carefully, happily, optimistically, confidently pointed the gun a little out from his own chest and, smiling broadly, looking victorious . . . shot himself.

There was no sound.

Burrowing into the bananas, his nose all clogged to hell, Ambrosio heard no sound at all as, presumably, supposedly – it must have been – the gun went off.

*

One!

It came from beneath the Sea. No, it didn't, it came from beneath the Earth. It came up in a single full-length resurrection from the bowels of Hell, it came up in a roar, in a shriek of bloodlust swing its axe. It came up in a single coiled effort of trained athlete's muscles from its grave six inches under a flower bed in a cascade of earth and reed breathing-tubes, stones, rocks, clods, fear-paralysed earth-worms, flowers, weeds, mire, mud and vengeance.

Bontoc appearing from nowhere, coming out from under the ground itself, buried during the night a handful at a time, shrieked, '*YAGGGH!*' He couldn't see a goddamned thing. He sought. He struck. He felt a neck in his hands and, swinging the axe to decapitate the head six inches above the place a head should be, he heard one of the bonehunters, one of his nemeses shriek in terror, 'Aaaggghhh!' It wasn't one of the nemeses, it was him. What he heard the nemesis say was, 'Urrp.' He had his hands around his throat. He couldn't see a goddamned thing. He felt the nemesis jerk out of his hand. He'd give them a bit of fake Japanese. Bontoc shrieked, '*Kore wa pen desu!* – this is a pen!' The nemesis, yanking away – boy, if you could have seen him you could bet the whites of *his* eyes were showing – howled in Philippino, 'No! No! No!'

He couldn't see a goddamned thing. He should have remembered to have covered his face with a handkerchief. Then he wouldn't have been able to get the reed in his mouth to breath. He should have asked Uncle Apo how to do it when he had had the chance. Uncle Apo, wandering around in the ether, hadn't been able to find him. He felt the bonehunter yank at him. Bontoc, his Bontoc experience (headhunting and massacres) increasing by the second, swinging his axe, yelled in Uncle Apo's voice, 'Now you die!' It was all coming together nicely for him. Bontoc shrieked as the bonehunter got his hands around him and reached for his ears to pull them off his head, 'NOBODY SAID LIFE WOULD BE EASY FOR YOU, BAPTISTE!'

The nemesis was going over. The mud man, his eyes black and unseeing, his axe flailing around in the air and making swishing noises, had his foot in his stomach. The living dead, the Zombie had –

98

He couldn't breathe.

He was going over.

He flailed at the headhunter's head with his hands. He tried for one of his ears and missed it for the mud.

He was going over, falling backwards against a tree. He reached for the tree to bash Bontoc's head in. It was an oak tree, non-portable. There were flowers and clods and bits of grass and reed, earth and earthworms falling all around them.

The gardener shrieked, 'YOU FUCKING GODDAMNED LUNATIC, LET ME GO!' The gardener, crashing down onto the roots of the trees and dislocating probably eight of his vertebrae for which, if he didn't get decapitated, someone was going to pay dearly in compensation, yelled, 'It's me! It's me!'

'WRONG FELLOW!'

'Oh, Baptiste, oh ... DEAR BAPTISTE, WHAT HAVE YOU ...'

He saw him. His eyes cleared. Hitting the ground, scraping the gardener all the way down the root, his face went into a clump of basil bushes and the leaves scraped his eyelids clear and he saw. He saw the axe. It was inches from the gardener's head. Bontoc said –

He saw them.

For an instant as he dropped the axe and simultaneously patting the gardener – too hard – on the face to try to make it up to him, he saw them.

All over the park, appearing from behind trees, from near the tadpole pool, from under and astern and forward of stegosauri and dinosauri and hippos, from the lairs, from everywhere, he saw the bonehunters with their hessian bags and their spades.

Bontoc shrieked, 'Look! Look!'

They were everywhere, running for the fences and the gates and the trees. He counted thirty, thirty-five – he counted them everywhere. Bontoc yelled, 'Halt! Halt in the name of the law!' He was the law of the jungle. Bontoc, pushing off the gardener, disentangling himself from legs and trees, bushes and flowers and mud, yelled in his best policeman's voice, 'Stop or die!' He reached for his PPK in its ankle holster under his trousers. He wasn't wearing his trousers. He was wearing a loin cloth. He wasn't even wearing that. He was wearing mud. Stark naked, the Mudman of Manila, Bontoc yelled − .

A second before the gardener hit him with it, he wondered where the devil he had dropped his axe.

He was gone.

There was no blood, no bone, no ejected empty cartridge case, no lingering smell of cordite − there had been no sound − and now, now everywhere he looked in the canyons of the apartment blocks, there was no mugger.

He was gone. He had evaporated. There was no smell of him or durians at all.

Ambrosio sniffed.

There was only the faintest lingering trace of what smelled like ships and the sea and salt air.

There was nothing.

His nose, his case − he had blown it.

There was nothing.

Ambrosio said, 'Oh . . . SHIT!'

There was that too. It was coming from a broken toilet somewhere in Parker Mansions. Parker Mansions was a broken toilet.

Ambrosio said −

SPROOG/IGLL . . . UP . . .

. . . OUT . . . DOWN . . .

His nose still hurt from all last night's blowing.

It was a little before 8 a.m. Ambrosio looked at his watch.

It had taken him less than two and a half minutes to run from El Tigre in Roxas Boulevard to El Catastrofe in Parker Place.

Picking banana peel from everywhere on his face and clothes, it was going to take him a lot longer to walk back.

The faintest glimmer of a tear in his eye, reluctantly, hopelessly, ruined beyond description, he took the first step.

The Hammerli pistol and its accoutrements had gone back into his safe at work. There, sitting at his desk and glancing only casually at the files and papers arranged neatly in his IN tray for the day's business, Bald Head looked at his watch and read the time.

7.58 a.m.

He was a little early and he waited out the last two minutes drumming at the top of his desk with his fingers.

He watched the clock, drumming at the desk with no rhythm or effort at melody. It was merely a regular, unceasing, dull percussion.

He watched the clock.

By the IN tray there was a package of expensive, imported American Pall Mall cigarettes. Stopping the noise for a moment he split open the pack with his fingernail and took a cigarette lighting it with his Zippo lighter.

7.59 a.m. exactly.

He watched the seconds elapse.

He thought things were going very well, in his favor.

He watched the clock.

Sure and confident, he leant back in his chair with the burning cigarette in his hand and smiled.

II

'Hipogrifo AG?' Sitting opposite Elizalde at one of the bayside tables on the apron of the Manila/Corregidor Hover Ferry Terminal that served as a café for waiting passengers, Luis Lanternero said, lighting a cigarette with a gold Dunhill lighter, 'You want me to fill you in over coffee on the affairs of a company registered in Vaduz, Liechtenstein, Europe, designed expressly to be secret and you'd like it all non-official and strictly on a personal basis.' By his coffee he had a folded copy of some sort of chess magazine. The article he had been reading while he had waited for Elizalde to come dealt with the Evans/Macdonnell game of 1826, a contest whose only single claim to remembrance was an opening gambit of total self-sacrifice whose value to this day had never been completely clear to chess-lovers. He was Elizalde's brother-in-law, something in the Ministry of Finance and Taxation that merited him the BMW 528i parked outside in the terminal carpark, but evidently did not merit him a waiting driver to go with it. Elizalde knew him hardly at all.

Elizalde said, 'Can you do it?'

Lanternero said, 'No.' He had a computer terminal in his house. He had already found out. Or, if he hadn't, he knew he would not be able to. Lanternero, shaking his head, glancing across the bay to the stone storm shelter jutting out from the Manila Yacht Club, shook his head. He looked briefly down at his chess problem and raised his eyebrows. He had an indelible pencil by the folded paper and where the notation read P-QN4 he added a small question mark.

They were well between sailings. The café was empty and, at the counter, there was only a T-shirted waiter cleaning up and restocking the glass cases with rice cakes. Elizalde said in Spanish, 'They own Battling Mendez.'

He knew Lanternero hardly at all. Elizalde looked at his expensive shirt – a wonderfully embroidered long sleeved barong tagalog and at his fingernails, long and clean and manicured. Five or six years older than Elizalde he was a man who had had money and respect and self esteem for a long time. For some reason she never discussed, Marguerita did not like him at all. They never went to his house and never asked him to theirs. Elizalde said, 'They lease Mendez out to Mendez Beer for the advertising.' He waited.

Lanternero said, 'Do they?' He looked again at the chess problem.

Elizalde said firmly, 'Yes.'

'And?' He glanced at the waiter to check if he could hear. The waiter had his radio on at low volume and was straining to hear some pop tune or other. Lanternero said, 'And?'

'And three of them are dead. Three people connected with the company. Francisco Royares, Paulo Royares and a Sentenciador from one of the local cockpits here called Tolentino.'

Lanternero said, 'I read about it in the papers.' He gazed for a moment out across the bay. It was calm and still. Lanternero said, 'Even assuming I could look any of these people up from their tax returns – '

Elizalde said, 'You already have.'

'Even assuming I could – assuming I have – all their returns might show would be overseas income or loans or wages or debts repaid from some company called Hipogrifo AG – it wouldn't prove what Hipogrifo was or, indeed, if it was anything at all.' It irked him. Lanternero said suddenly, 'Tax isn't like police work: you proceed slowly.' Lanternero asked, 'How's Marguerita?'

'Very well.'

'Hmm. I saw her in the street a few weeks ago. She – '
Lanternero asked, 'Has she ever told you why she and I don't get along?' He looked at his fingernails.

'No.'

'It's because I don't approve of you.'

He was getting nowhere. Elizalde, rising to go, said, 'No, it isn't.'

'Sit down.'

'Go to hell.'

Lanternero said, 'You're going to get yourself killed. Hipogrifo AG – all these sorts of companies – they're not some variety of alias for minor thugs and hold-up men – these sorts of companies are set up by people with *money*.' He saw Elizalde still standing. Lanternero said, soothing him, 'You're right. It's not you. Marguerita and I simply don't get along because – ' He saw Elizalde sit and look at him expectantly. Lanterno said, 'It's that she was our father's favorite. She was always the bright one and – and to me – to a Philippino of the male persuasion growing up in a male-oriented society – '

Elizalde said, 'Were the Royares brothers and Tolentino directors of this company?'

'They were recipients of its favors.' He saw Elizalde look blank. 'They were on its payroll. Whether that means it was their own money stashed away in a vault or invested in Switzerland or Liechtenstein or God knows where, God alone knows. The Philippines Ministry of Finance doesn't. But they paid their taxes on what they received and so we were grateful. And so we didn't ask. *Which is why people set up these sorts of companies in the first place.*' He asked, trying to moderate his tone, 'Do you see?'

'And what about the money the company gets paid for the various leases on Mendez? The beer company, all the super-market campaigns – everything?'

'That gets paid into another company called Mendez Holdings, which, in turn, gets paid into another company called something else and is converted into services or products on the commodities market and that, in turn – ' Lanternero said. 'And there, because it's all happened before and because we're grateful not to have to spend millions chasing up what in an accountant's stroke of a pen could turn instantly into mere hundreds, the Department gives up and says thank you for whatever people who are cleverer than it is are prepared to pay unbegrudgingly.' Lanternero said with a wintery smile. 'I'm a tax man, Felix – when I warn people they usually listen. I'm warning you now – for Marguerita's sake – you're courting trouble. You're dealing with people you're not used to – that nobody is used to – and they can crush you, me – the Department itself – like a bug!'

'How much were the Royares brothers and Tolentino worth?'

'I can't tell you that.'

'What other assets did they have apart from Mendez?'

'None. That I can see.'

'How long has Hipogrifo AG been in business?'

Lanternero said tightly, 'Ten years.'

'A fighting cock doesn't live ten years!'

'Then they had money before, didn't they? Or – ' Lanternero said, 'All I know is that Mendez Beer is looking for heavy re-investment on the US market at the moment in order to expand their production. Battling Mendez, as their logo, as their symbol, as their good luck piece figures heavily in their prospectus – '

'If Hipogrifo has been in existence ten years . . .' Elizalde said, 'I never even heard of Mendez Beer until a few years ago.'

'A few years ago they were a tiny family brewing company. When they leased Mendez as their logo things changed for them.' Lanternero said –

'And what's their current worth?'

'They're the eighth biggest company in the Philippines.'

'Because of Mendez?'

'Presumably.'

'Which Hipogrifo AG leases to them?'

'Yes.'

'Then where the hell did a Kristo, a cockdoctor and a Sentenciador get the money to set up a Liechtenstein company and pay themselves a fortune before they had Mendez to lease?'

Lanternero looked down at his chess problem. Lanternero

said, not looking up, 'Before they had Mendez it was only a small fortune.'

'Where did Mendez come from?'

'Why don't you ask the person who's got him?'

'No one knows where he is. He was passed from the brother Francisco to Paulo and then according to – ' He was going to say according to the boy Nitz – 'To someone else, he was taken away by Tolentino. Tolentino, like the Royares brothers, uses an address of convenience – in his case, the cockpit – and there's no further trace of him.'

'Presumably then there's a very opulent empty apartment somewhere in Manila going begging.'

'Presumably.' Elizalde asked, 'What address did he give on his tax return?'

'Care of the cockpit, care of his tax accountant, care of Hipogrifo AG, Vaduz.' He smiled thinly.

'Do you know who the other directors of the company are?'

'No.' Lanternero said, 'Felix, you're dealing with people who don't want to be dealt with . . .'

'Someone has killed seven people in the course of the last twelve hours!'

'People die all the time.'

'They don't get blown to pieces or shot in the head or have their throats cut!' He could see why Marguerita disliked him. It was like talking to a fish. The waiter was watching. He could not understand the Spanish. Elizalde demanded, 'Who are these people? What were they before they had Mendez? If they were rich enough to set up a company in Europe before they had anything to sell where did their money come from?'

'I don't know.'

'You do know!' Elizalde, leaning forward, said with his eyes narrowed, 'You punched it up. You sat there in your apartment after I telephoned you and you punched it all up on your terminal from the Ministry and, because you like chess, because your mind turns happily and merrily on problems exactly like this, you worked it out exactly and now, now as part of the game you've decided either, one, you're not going to tell me, or two, you are going to tell me, but it'll make you feel better about your sister being brighter than you if you can prove to yourself that you're brighter than her husband!' He saw the waiter watching. He made him turn away with a look. Elizalde, leaning forward across the table and nodding to the smooth, smug, unlined face, said, 'Fine. You've proved it. Now who were these people before they got hold of Mendez?'

'You are dealing with people who – '

'I am dealing with people who kill people!'

'Mendez Beer alone, is a fifty million dollar a year company! They employ over – ' Lanternero said, 'I don't want to see you get yourself killed!'

'Whether I get myself killed or not is not your concern!'

'It's my sister's concern!'

'It's not yours!'

'You can't subpoena me officially to give you any of this information because I shouldn't have had it in the first place!'

'But you do have it. You've got it all.'

'I haven't. That's where you're wrong. I know nothing about Mendez or where he came from or what the antecedents of the three people involved are – I know nothing at all because there isn't anything to know!'

'What the hell do you mean by that?'

'I mean – I mean, they pay tax. They paid tax. From the Ministry's point of view: the *end!*'

'Tax on what? On their income from Hipogrifo AG. And before that – what?'

'Before that, according to a note on each of their files, they were non-taxable, low income, subsistence level – ' His hand was resting on the chess column. The sacrifice of even a pawn at the beginning of a game could lead to results far and above the loss of the pawn itself. Lanternero said, 'They were fishermen. That's what it says on their files. They were uneconomic, low wage, small fishermen!'

'What?'

'That's what it says on their files.' Lanternero said, 'Hipogrifo – flying horse.' He saw Elizalde shake his head. 'Horse. Flying Horse.' Lanternero said, 'We leave them alone and they pay their tax, people like that – '

'Tolentino, the Royares brothers . . .'

Lanternero said, 'Yes. Flying Horse. Companies in Liechtenstein, big money with no antecedents.' He looked out across the bay at the storm shelter. Sometimes there was no shelter to be had. Lanternero said, 'We think – there's a single notation on each of their files with a question mark on it – we think they were contrabandits, smugglers.' Lanternero said with the faintest twitch at the corner of his mouth, '*Heroin runners!*' Lanternero, pleading, begging, all his mask gone, afraid, said desperately, 'Felix, this is a poor country. We are a nation of – ' He said, 'They paid their taxes – the ones they thought fit to declare to us and we took them. Their influence turned a loss making brewery, for a start, into a multi-million dollar export earner! It all comes from the top! It's called – '

It wasn't the Ministry's BMW 528i outside in the carpark, it was his own. That was why there was no driver. It was called corruption.

Lanternero, the magazine in his hand being crushed as he held it, said fervently, importantly, 'Listen, after our father died, who do you think put Marguerita through university – how do you think, in those days when I was a minor official, it was paid for? *It was paid for by not asking the sort of questions you're asking me!* Nobody cares how they got Mendez! Nobody cares where they said they lived or what they said they did for a living – what solely, singly, only, anyone cared about – from the government down – was the money.' He said with sudden hatred in his eyes, 'You wouldn't understand that, would you? The Elizaldes have always had money. The Spanish. Marguerita and I are Philippino – the real thing – the people your people oppressed, the people your people forced to – '

Elizalde said, 'My people have one-quarter Spanish blood in them and the rest is pure Philippino Malay or American like most people in this country!'

'*You are going to get yourself killed!*'

'I am going to find out who – '

'Bald Head! Bald Head – that's what the papers call him! Is that what you're going to do – catch *him*? Cops and robbers? These people, the people you're dealing with – the real people behind all this – they aren't – ' It was hopeless. He had thought that he might have simply spoken to the man, told him

108

nothing, and somehow felt good about it. He felt dishonored. Without his sister, without his family, his clan – the unit that drew the seven thousand islands of the Philippines into a single country, the unit that drew people into warmth and belonging – he had only his chess problems and his computer.

He had nothing.

Lanternero said, 'Look. Listen – in the name of God, please, please, don't tell anyone what you're doing!'

Elizalde said, 'I haven't.' He asked, 'And Marguerita?'

'Tell her – tell her –' Lanternero said sadly, 'You and I, Elizalde, you and I –' He said, deciding, 'No, don't tell anybody.' He said brightly, 'Tell her – tell her I bought a new car.'

In his office, Bald Head, starting on his IN basket, began humming.

It was a sort of waltz in slow time called *Visayas Sunrise*. It was an arrangement of a traditional folk tune from the lovely islands between Luzon and Mindanao. It was meant to be soothing.

It soothed him.

From time to time as he worked, he stopped to gaze at the wall clock in front of him and smile.

'Man, a gold-plated broom-handled Mauser Model 1896 with a shoulder stock!' Martinez, by the remnants of his cab in a side street off Roxas Boulevard, said in a lather of undisguised waffen-lust, 'No wonder people wound down their windows for that! For that I would have wound down my trousers!' He said, drooling, 'Man!'

Ambrosio said evenly, 'It didn't have a shoulder stock. When he took it out of the box all it had was sudden death.' He still had bits and pieces of banana stuck in his hair. He was not going to use El Tigre's mirror to look at them. He picked them out sight unseen.

Nothing was going to stop him. Martinez, positively slavering, said in an orgy of macho. 'Man, no wonder people wanted to buy it! No wonder they wouldn't say what it was!' He said, 'Oh, man, oh man –' He was going to launch into a discussion of Palabas – the Philippino urge to go out in a ball of flame – 'Imagine the palabas, man, of shooting a mugger with a thing like that – a gold-plated Mauser broom-handle! Imagine shooting yourself! Imagine what the papers would say if they found your body with a flowery note to your girlfriend – '

Ambrosio said, 'They almost found me!'

'He didn't shoot at you. He shot at himself!' Palabas, palabas. Martinez said, 'Man, he didn't shoot at all. All he had to do was hold that thing up and you dived into the nearest banana skin pile and he disappeared into the night!'

He hadn't disappeared into the night, he had disappeared into Parker Mansions. Ambrosio said, 'He'll hit again.'

'Oh, yeah!' Martinez, still thinking about the gun, said, agreeing, 'Well, yes, he would.'

'He'll hit sometime again this morning!'

'Well, he would, man. Someone like that – ' Martinez said, 'Well it's like falling off a – ' He was going to say horse – 'Off a stallion. You have to get straight back on to prove you're a man.' He said, salivating, 'Man, oh man!' He asked, 'I don't suppose you happen to know what price he was asking for the gun, do you?'

'*He wasn't asking a price for the gun! What he was doing was pretending to ask a price for the gun and when the windows got wound down –* '

'Right! Right!' Martinez said, 'Right!' He could understand that. If he had a weapon like that he wouldn't really put it up for sale either. Martinez said, 'Right! Right! So what do we do now?'

'We go to a sari sari shop where they sell plastic carry bags urchins pick up off the street or out of the trash cans and the garbage – good stores, Tessoros, Tiffany's, Harrods of London if we can get some – and we fill the goddamned cab with them and lure him out!' Palabas worked both ways. Ambrosio said, 'We'll make it personal. We'll make it so personal that if he doesn't hit the cab with the big prize he'll never be able to live with himself!' All he needed was just the faintest modicum of luck. That didn't seem too much to ask. Ambrosio, asking, said, 'Where's a good sari sari shop where they sell things like that?'

'Um, Esmeralda's Sari Sari shop on Bicycle Street in Tondo.'
He thought about it for a moment. Martinez said, 'Yeah,
that'd be the place.'

It was.

Ambrosio, trying not to see the little broom-handle
Mauser-shaped pinpricks of light in Martinez's eyes as he got
into the rear seat of El Tigre said, 'Right, OK, what are you
waiting for? Get in and let's get on with it!'

Behind the shelter of a brontosaurus the gardener hosing down
walnut brain asked, 'Who's your superior officer?'

Bontoc said, 'Lieutenant Elizalde.' The mud had dried in the
sun and it came off only with the hardest blast of the garden
hose the gardener could set on the adjustable nozzle. He must
have had it all over his face because the gardener kept playing
it on his nose. Bontoc said, 'Why?'

'Is he a nice man?' Midget Mind turned his nose away and
the gardener got him on the loin cloth.

Bontoc said, 'Yes.' He said as the blast hit him squarely on
the back of the knee and almost collapsed him, 'Why?'

'I just wondered.' The gardener said, 'You got bilked on the
axe. It wouldn't cut butter.' The hosing, unfortunately, was
almost complete. The gardener said, 'Here.' He threw him a
rag to dry himself with. The madman's clothes were in a little
soft overnight bag on the grass. The gardener, ever helpful,
tossed them to him and hit him in the stomach with them. The
gardener said –

Bontoc said, 'I recognised one of them.'

The gardener said, 'Oh, yes.' He said, 'He must be a nice
man, Lieutenant Elizalde, to put up with you.' He turned off
the hose. He asked, 'Where's your gun? I'll get it for you.' For
the briefest of brief instants his eyes glittered. He dismissed the
thought.

Bontoc said, 'I recognised one of them. I think I know what
it's all about.'

'Where's your gun?' He shouldn't have asked twice. He
wasn't going to shoot him, he just wanted, for a moment, the
feeling in his hands, that if he *wanted* to shoot him, he could.

'*I know what it's all about!*'

For a man with a bashed-in skull, the gardener was amazed at his own patience. Maybe Lieutenant Elizalde was often amazed at his own patience. Maybe Lieutenant Elizalde, like him, was simply ground down to the bone. It was wrong to contemplate shooting a fellow human being.

Bontoc said, 'All I need is a long metal probe and I think I can solve this mystery!' He wasn't listening. Bontoc said, 'Are you listening?'

Unless, in law, someone like this didn't *count* as a fellow human being . . . No, if that was true, the nice man, Lieutenant Elizalde, long ago, would have . . . The gardener dismissed the thought completely from his mind. Oh, no he didn't. The gardener asked, smiling, 'Where's your gun?'

'I need a long metal probe!'

'Where's your gun?'

'I buried it!'

'*Where? Where's your gun?*'

'I –'

'You can't remember, can you? That's what you want the probe for, isn't it? You can't remember where you buried your gun!'

'No!'

'Then where is it?'

'It's –' Bontoc said, 'I recognised one of them! I know what it's about! It isn't about Japanese bonehunters at all! It's –' Bontoc looked at the gardener. The gardener looked around. Bontoc said 'I – I –' Bontoc said, 'It isn't the policy of the intelligent and responsible police officer to inform civilians of the location of his sidearm.'

'Accidents could happen?'

Bontoc said, 'Right!'

The gardener said, 'Too true.' Poor Elizalde, whoever he was, he had a larger cross to bear than most. The gardener said, 'I'll get you a metal probe.'

'Thank you.'

'Then you can find your gun, can't you?'

Bontoc said, 'Right.' He saw the look on the gardener's face. Bontoc said, caught, tricked, outwitted, 'Um –'

'*Melon head!*' The gardener said, 'GRRR!'

He went to get the probe.

In the cab, Ambrosio wondered at the gold-plated gun.

He wondered how, in an instant, it could shoot, not cops or muggers, but smells.

He wondered how the mugger made the smell of durian disappear the moment he drew it from the box.

Lanternero wouldn't have known who else was on the payroll of the company. He only knew it when he saw it on an individual tax return who received money from it.

Hipogrifo AG.

They owned Mendez.

They owned everything.

Hipo . . . grifo AG . . .

It meant, in American English, Flying Horse . . .

12

It meant, in plain English, Pegasus.

In the main glassed-in office area of the Pegasus Advertising Agency on the fourth floor of the PHILCOM Building on Ayala Street, Vargas, at his desk gazed at himself in a mirror and saw Mendez's ivory leg and malacca cane leg and, above them in the display case on the wall facing him, three of the hand-honed Philippines Razor Blade Company spurs and, to the right of them and above them, a selection of Mendez's gold medals, awards, presentations, testimonials and, framing it all, his presidential citation for export earnings.

MENDEZ BEER. *Sales Up 283% This Year Alone!*
Pegasus Advertising Agoncillo Associates Inc
– Philippines –

It was a mirror fixed to the wall as a backing to the display case: sitting at his desk with his head less than half a meter away from the managing director's own glassed-in office, all day in the mirror he could see Mendez's trophies and his own reflection.

It was intended that he should.

He saw the face of a fifty-three-year-old, ill, flabby failure sitting at a desk that had no work to do on it.

It was intended that he should.

He had no nameplate on his desk. It was intended that he should not. He sat midway between Agoncillo's secretary, a little out in the main area where the creative people worked – the artists and the copy writers and the boys and girls of twenty or twenty-five with their heads full of dreams of advancement – and Agoncillo in his office where the decisions were made. A to B. For Agoncillo to speak to the creative people or for them to speak to him, they had to pass Vargas's desk. It was known by the juniors that to stop and be seen speaking to him was to forgo the dream.

He stared at his own face in what, before Agoncillo had taken over, had been his own mirror. The mirror once, had read Navarro Light Industries. It had been his biggest account. It had failed. He had only the morning newspaper open on his desk and a pen with which to do – if he felt like it – the crossword. He never felt like it. Sitting silently, he stared at the mirror.

In Agoncillo's office – in the carpeted affluence of it – Agoncillo needed only to tap on the glass window if he wanted him and Vargas could obediently get up and enter the place to give his advice or explain some aspect of the agency he had run since he had been thirty years old.

Agoncillo never rapped on the window. He never looked at Vargas. Sometimes, as he passed on his way to the creative people, he might have smiled in recognition to Vargas, but he never did.

Everyone in the office knew that to be seen with failure in the ad world was to be seen with failure.

Not even the girl who made coffee made it for him. He had to make his own.

Agoncillo, in the four and a half years he had had the agency – in the four and a half years the agency had had the Mendez account which he had brought to them – had turned it around from a steady loss to a gigantic profit.

The agency could even pay Vargas a salary to keep him on as a sign to its employees of its heart and concern.

It was intended that it should.

Vargas, clearly, could have stayed at home and taken his sinecure.

He was never, never going to do that.

He looked. He listened. In the carpeted office, Agoncillo was on the phone and, in the gaps and silences and pauses between the chattering of typewriters and the talk and enthusiasm and youth of the creative people in the outer office Vargas, sometimes, could hear what was being said.

His hand rested on his open newspaper, at the front page where there was a headline about the man who had been killed in the chapel in Intramuros.

He strained. He listened. Agoncillo was, like him, a man in his fifties; like him, getting old; unlike him, fit and healthy and with a glow of prosperity.

He listened.

Agoncillo was standing up, pacing around the room carrying the telephone in his hands, stopping, glancing out the window, listening to the conversation then, abruptly, saying something and then, just as abruptly, being silenced by the person on the other end of the line, and then, his voice rising, the pacing starting again, saying something quick and desperate into the receiver.

The office was airconditioned, the temperature and humidity set at a comfortable, computerised mean for work.

Agoncillo was sweating. He touched his forehead with a long, manicured finger and then the sleeve of his embroidered, tailor-made shirt with its pearl buttons.

He spoke quickly into the phone, then stopped and listened, then, pacing, going towards the window and turning half-way as the person on the other end of the line said something, stopped dead and listened with his hand gripping the corner of his desk until his knuckles showed white.

In the mirror Vargas saw his own reflection. He saw his own eyes. Watching Agoncillo out of the corner of his eye, he saw the expression of hatred on his own face and the way he strained to hear.

In a pause from the main office outside – in that strange, unpredictable, coincidental moment that always came when, for some reason everyone fell silent, he had heard Agoncillo say a single word into the phone to the person on the other end of the line.

He listened hard to hear what was being said, but the silence had not come again and he could only see Agoncillo's back and hand on the phone as he paced and walked and talked desperately into the instrument.

At his desk Vargas touched at his newspaper, patting it lightly with the pads of his fingers.

He still had a few friends in the agency, people he had employed when the agency had been his, people he had insisted stayed on, like him, until they died. They, like him, could not be seen. They had been put away, out of sight. One of his friends was the aging unmarried woman on the switchboard, Miss Flores.

He listened, touching at the newspaper with his eyes burning in the reflection of the mirror.

Tolentino.

He had heard Agoncillo on the morning the newspapers were full of the death of a man in the chapel in Intramuros say a single word, his name: Tolentino.

He saw how Agoncillo sweated.

He listened.

He hated.

Rising, moving slowly so no one might notice him, as if he was nothing more than a relic kept on by the good offices of the new order as a symbol and warning to those who might flag in their ambition and their success – going, like some weak bladdered old man to nowhere more important than the toilets – Vargas made his way towards the closed little room out near the elevators to speak to Miss Flores.

'*Tolentino.*'

He had heard Agoncillo say the name of a man who had had his throat cut by a murderer.

He turned back to look.

Agoncillo was still on the phone, sweating hard.

Vargas, moving slowly, consumed by hatred and humiliation, on fire each day with a silent, unseen burning – a failure, a demonstrable failure (as he was intended to be) – went towards Miss Flores' switchboard near the elevators.

'Tolentino!'

He heard it. In a silence from all the machines and all the

success and all the things he hated, he heard it. He heard Agoncillo say the name of a man who was dead.

Without the mirror he could not see the look of triumph in his own eyes.

He hurried. He went quickly past all the people at all the desks who did not look up at him.

He went to speak with Miss Flores at the switch.

He knew her well. She, from all their days together when he had been the director and she his executive secretary, would do anything for him.

She would do this.

Tolentino. He had heard the name.

He went quickly to the switchboard room and closed the door behind him to tap into the line and listen carefully, and with burning hatred, to every word that Agoncillo said that – *that made him sweat.*

He was perspiring lightly. In his private office in the Ministry of Finance and Taxation, Luis Lanternero looked at his wall clock.

It was a little before 9 a.m. and before him, his IN basket was full.

His fingers were drumming on the side of the basket as he thought of Marguerita and wondered what to do.

His telephone was in front of him. It was a private, secure line and nobody could listen in to it through the switchboard.

He watched the clock and drummed his fingers on the side of the basket.

When she had found out where the money had come from for her education, she had wanted to throw it all away. It was too late. She had her degree, she was someone and, whatever else he might have done, he had done his duty to her as a brother – with their parents dead, as the head of the family – and there was nothing she could do to undo it.

She was all grown up and married. She had been married now for over ten years and she was no longer a little girl whose future and welfare he had worried about and thought about and counselled her in.

She was Felix Elizalde's wife.

With both their parents gone, she was his only living relative. She was a Lanternero, the only person on Earth with whom he could remember all the things of his childhood.

She was his sister.

She had not spoken to him or seen him once in the last ten years.

He drummed at the IN basket with his fingers and looked at the clock.

He knew her number. He knew, because he followed such things, that the examinations at the school where she taught history were over and she would be at home in Paranaque marking papers. He knew her number.

He could not think of what to say to her, but he ached to say something.

9.00 a.m. exactly.

In his office, he watched the clock and drummed faster and faster on the side of the basket.

There was no point in discussing things with the gardener any further. He just didn't have the interest.

> a good many
> failures are happy
> because they don't
> realize it –

It was from Don Marquis' *Archy's Life of Mehitabel*. He had read it while he was at college in America when, for a long while, before he had had Uncle Apo and Miss Thomasina, there had been no one for him to talk to.

It was free verse. He had never learned how to read it aloud and he had only ever read it in his mind.

> many a
> cockroach believes
> himself as beautiful
> as a butterfly
> have a heart o have
> a heart and
> let them dream on.

He was not dreaming. It was real. He had recognised one of them. He had seen him for an instant before the gardener had brained him and he knew who he was.

He was no Japanese bonehunter. He was a Philippino.

Still in his mind, silently, Bontoc said, 'Hmmm.'

Carrying the long metal probe, jabbing it hard into the ground as he walked, Bontoc, his eyes narrowing, went first to look for his gun.

Hipogrifo AG.

There was nothing.

He looked in the Manila phone book commercial and industrial listings for anything called any variation of the words Flying Horse, but there was nothing there.

Mendez Beer: perhaps they had nothing to do with it. Perhaps Mendez was exactly what he appeared to be, a logo, a trade mark, a symbol like MGM's lion or the Jolly Green Giant or the Michelin Man or –

Or nothing.

In the three phone books in the public telephone booth in Rizal Park, near the docks, the listings for Mendez Beer and all its offices and warehouses went on for pages.

Perhaps . . .

In the booth Elizalde, for a moment, put his hand to his face.

Perhaps . . .

In the booth, slowly, reluctantly Elizalde began dialling the number for Headquarters to tell them where he was.

The phone had been vandalised and it did not work.

He replaced the broken receiver on its cradle.

Leaving the booth Elizalde, walking back towards his car at the deaf and dumb café, took out his badge and ID card in his wallet and looked at it.

He glanced at his watch.

It was 9.02 a.m.

Reaching the car he unlocked it and, making an illegal U-turn in the street, began to drive slowly and thoughtfully back onto the main thoroughfare towards Roxas Boulevard.

Metro Manila –

The man who had rung Mang Paulo and then killed him

with a rifle grenade must have said, clearly, 'Metro Manila – '

Joining the traffic in the boulevard, he saw a clear lane going south and accelerated into it.

He wondered.

He wondered.

He wondered what the next, identifying departmental word had been.

On the phone in his office Ferdinand Agoncillo, still pacing, said in terror, 'He cut his throat from ear to ear! It's in all the papers! He threw some sort of explosive booby trap made out of two mousetraps at him and then, with what the papers say was probably a razor-sharp butterfly knife, he almost sliced him in two! The papers say it's subversives!'

The voice of the man on the other end of the line was calm. He was older, wiser. He had always been the man with the money. Speaking in Philippino, the man said definitely, 'It isn't subversives.'

'He killed Mang Paulo with a grenade and Francisco with a forty-five automatic!'

'What have you done about Tolentino's mistress?' The voice asked, 'Have you been to his apartment in Makati?'

'Yes,'

'And?'

'The Police haven't been there yet.'

The voice said, 'No. They don't know where it is.' He knew that the same way he knew it wasn't subversives. The voice said, 'I've got friends in the police and in the security forces. They don't know anything.' He asked again, 'What did you do about Tolentino's mistress?'

Agoncillo said, 'I put her on a plane to Hong Kong.'

'Good.' The voice asked, 'Did you search the apartment?'

There was a silence.

The voice said, 'Tolentino's mistress didn't know anything about his past so he wouldn't have left anything in the apartment for her to see.' He asked again, 'Did you search the apartment or did you agree with me?'

'I agree with you.' Agoncillo said quietly, 'I always agreed with you. That's why I'm ringing you now. You were always the one we looked to.'

'I took no risks.'

'You took the risk on us. We were all younger then.' Agoncillo, his voice low and intimate said, 'In those days we weren't afraid of anything. We had nothing so therefore we had nothing to lose. Only you had something to lose and – ' He hesitated. ' – and now, now I have money myself I can see that in those days all you had to lose was money.' Agoncillo, his voice rising, said, 'I gave you my friendship and loyalty without question.'

'I understand that.' He was safe. He had been wealthy for a very long time and he never raised his voice. The man on the other end of the line said, 'I understand the obligation. What is it you want me to do? I'll do it gladly.'

'What I want you to do is tell me to get on a plane myself and go!'

'No.'

'It's not like the old days! We can't see it out to the end! I haven't got the facilities anymore to see problems out to the end when this sort of thing is happening!' Agoncillo said, 'The only weapon I own is the paperknife on the desk in front of me! At my house all my protection is done by security guards I pay on a monthly basis! Men with shotguns who sit around on my front lawn deterring burglars!' Agoncillo said, 'I'm fifty-three years old! I'm turning into a rich soft man! I pay people to do things I can't do myself! I don't even have my breath anymore!'

'Are you afraid?'

'Yes!' On his desk by the paperknife was his desk diary open at today's date. Agoncillo, reaching down for it and taking it up in his hand, said, 'Yes! Yes, I'm afraid when all my old friends are being killed and yes, I'm afraid when I come into my place of work and I find a note like this written in my diary! Yes, I'm afraid!' Agoncillo said, 'I don't have to play the macho with you! You know what I am and what I was! What I am now is a middle-aged businessman with guards on my house to protect my prosperity!' He gave the man on the other end of the line no chance to reply. 'It says *At exactly 9.28 and 30 seconds ring 01018. Dial direct. Dial yourself.*' Agoncillo said, 'It isn't in my secretary's hand! It isn't in the hand of anyone I know! Someone got in and did it!'

'Would that have been difficult?'

'No! I run an advertising agency, not a bank! I – ' Agoncillo said, 'I'm fifty-three years old! My biggest concern these days is a good bowel movement!' He said with his voice suddenly unnaturally calm, 'Whoever did it left the pencil he used. It's a government issue pencil with the words Administration - Metro Manila stamped on it.' He said, 'There is no number 01018 – it doesn't exist.'

'You haven't tried it?'

'I know it doesn't exist because it's not a number that could exist!'

'You haven't tried it?' The man on the line asked, 'What time is it now?' He answered himself, 'It's three minutes after nine.' The man on the other end of the line said, 'Leave it to me. I'll try the number from here. I know someone in the telephone company. Don't try the number yourself yet. I'll find out what number it is.'

'And if we find out whose number it is?'

'Then we'll find out what he wants.'

'And then?' Agoncillo said, 'And then?'

'It depends.'

'On what?'

'On what he wants.'

'He wants to kill us!' Agoncillo said, 'What he wants – '

'Relax.' The man on the other end of the line said calmly, 'Take it easy. It's only a few minutes after nine. There's plenty of time and plenty of people owe me plenty of favors and everything can be taken care of.' The man on the other end of the line said, 'Relax. Wait. Just wait and I'll try the number and talk to people.' The man on the other end of the line said, 'Don't worry. Everything will be all right. We'll find out who it is and – long before you have to concern yourself about taking planes out of the country or losing everything you've worked for, I promise you, whoever it is, he'll be long dead.' He said quietly, confidently, 'Wait. Relax. Calm yourself and do nothing. I'll get back to you.'

'Elizalde. E-L-I-Z-A-L-D-E. Felix. Lieutenant. Metro Manila Police.' The khaki uniformed sentry at the big iron gates to the

Coast Guard Headquarters on Roxas Boulevard, still holding Elizalde's ID wallet and badge in his hand as he wrote it all down on his clipboard asked in English, 'Which division are you from, sir? It isn't on the ID.' He was a young, fit-looking boy of eighteen or nineteen who looked with the regular PT sessions and discipline to have been carved out of solid muscle. His webbing and white pistol holster were immaculate, the creases in his shirt, sharp. Leaning in a little through Elizalde's open car window and at the same time casting a quick eye over the back seat, he asked respectfully, 'Sir?'

'Western District. Detective Bureau.'

'*Detective* Lieutenant?'

'Yes.'

'Thank you, sir,' He made a change on his clipboard. He was writing it all down. 'To see – ' He ran his pencil over the blank space on his clipped down form. He thought about it for a moment, 'Commander Quintero, I think, sir.' He smiled. He was writing it all down. He asked, lowering his clipboard a fraction and staring hard at Elizalde's face, 'All right, sir?'

'Yes. Thank you.' The Coast Guard headquarters building was directly in front of him. Two storeyed and squat, it had more guards at its front entrance and, a little to the left, near the visitor's carpark. They all carried clipboards. Elizalde, nodding, asked, 'Which way?'

'Straight ahead, sir, to the visitors' carpark.' He had written everything down. He handed Elizalde a pass. 'Just ask the sentry and show him your pass. He'll take you inside to see the Commander.'

'Thank you.'

'Thank you, Lieutenant Elizalde.' Stepping back, he saluted. Everything, everything had been written down. The sentry, holding his clipboard hard as if it protected something of great value, still saluting, smiling, said pleasantly, 'Have a nice day.'

There was a click. The sentry's voice was meant to cover it, but as Elizalde started the car, behind the sentry's voice, he heard it.

It was the sound of a security camera taking his photograph.

In his office, gazing at the wall clock, Lanternero, twisting a pencil in his fingers, wondered what he should do about Marguerita.

He wondered, now, if there was anything that could be done.

9.05 a.m. He glanced at the work in his IN basket and screwed up his face.

The open chess magazine was in the top drawer of his desk and, opening the drawer, he gazed down at it and tried to settle his mind on the problem.

He could not. The drawer was full of stationery issued by the Ministry of Finance and Taxation and, clearing his throat, he dropped the pencil in on top of the problem and took out one of his own, good quality, biros.

The pencil had stamped on it *Administration – Metro Manila* to identify it.

9.06 a.m.

Shutting the drawer with a bang he leaned forward and started work on the IN basket.

'I'll get back to you.'

In the closed switchboard room, Vargas, with a headpiece pressed hard up against his ear, listened.

He listened.

Miss Flores was a little off to one side of the room, fat and dumpy and old, making coffee.

The line from Agoncillo to the man with the calm voice was still open. It was being held open as Agoncillo waited.

At the switchboard Vargas smiled.

He waited for his coffee.

He had nothing else to do with his time, no claim on it at all. *It was intended that he should not.*

He saw Miss Flores glance back at him to see if he was all right and, gazing at her, looking her up and down, he smiled at her and touched at the headpiece against his head to make sure it was secure.

9.06 a.m.

In the Manila Hotel, the man in Room 333, standing at the window gazed out at the bay.

Outside, in the corridor, the little cardboard sign on his doorknob read 'Do Not Disturb'. The maids and the day staff who might come to make up his bed or clean the room would think he was still asleep.

He had not slept properly for years.

All that, now, was coming to an end. It was, piece by piece, being brought to an end.

He looked down at the palm of his hand and saw that, in the airconditioned room, it was clammy with perspiration.

He did not go into the bathroom to wipe it: he was afraid to lose the feeling of the moment.

9.07 a.m. He looked at his watch.

He drew a long breath and, with his eyes narrowed, not looking at the bay at all, but to something long ago, dead and lost forever, patiently, silently, trying to control the urge to shriek in triumph, he merely . . . *waited*.

13

It wasn't called Bicycle Street at all, it was called Admiral Edafio Street. Admiral Edafio, in Tondo, the worst slum suburb in Manila, was long gone; the bicycles weren't. The entire unsewered street, baking in the sun, was lined with corrugated iron shacks, each the size of a dog-kennel holding families and the few possessions they had, and their food for the day on packing case tables behind their holes in the iron that served as doors. Up and down the street in all states of repair were bicycles. Not one of them was painted, each was dark with rust, and as Ambrosio looked, not one of them had an inflated tire or a chain. They were scrap. They were how the inhabitants of the shacks made their living. There was no living to be made in the sale of rusted black chainless and tireless ancient and discarded bicycles: it was how, if they could, they would have made their living.

In Esmeralda's Sari Sari shop at the end of Bicycle Street, Esmeralda was making a small living. Her living was on a *tingi*, a piece by piece basis – in her stall-like shop – you could buy anything in ones or twos from cloves and single pieces of writing paper to torn comics with no covers or backs to – if a child had had a sudden windfall – single sections of candy bars or, if the windfall had not been that great, single M&M chocolate covered peanuts or half a square of toffee candy cut into fifty. She sold the plastic carry bags shops gave rich people and rich people threw out in their garbage. They were set out on the back wall of the shop, pressed out flat, ironed and washed with their plastic carrying handles and where it was needed carefully repaired. Behind them, on the wall, there were pictures cut out of magazines showing houses and washing machines and boxes of soap powder, Porsches, pin-ups and prosperity: all the things that, if you lived in Tondo, you could never have.

Martinez said, 'Harrods.' It was a bag that had been thrown out by a rich tourist at the airport.

Esmeralda, looking not at Martinez, but at Ambrosio, said 'One peso.'

Martinez said, 'Twenty-five centavos.'

Ambrosio said, 'A peso is OK.'

'Tessoros.'

Martinez said, 'That's local.'

'Fifty centavos.'

Ambrosio nodded.

'Tiffany's!' She held the bag up against her ample chest and floral dress as if it was the latest fashion. In a way, it was.

Ambrosio said, 'All right.' He had been born in Malate. It was a suburb where you were warned never to go to Tondo. Ambrosio said, 'We'll take it.'

'It's three pesos!'

'The police department can afford it.'

Esmeralda said, 'It isn't stolen!'

'I know that. It's only a bag.'

'It's a three peso bag!' Esmeralda, gazing at his face as he looked down the street and shook his head said quickly, 'I've got two of them!'

'We'll take them.'

'What do you want to put in them?' She looked interested. She wondered how much money the police department had. It was incomputable.

Martinez, who had been born in Tondo said, 'Bricks.'

Ambrosio, who had not, said, 'Valuable things.'

Esmeralda said, 'The second bag because it means a lot to my customers to see it here is six pesos.'

He wanted to go. Ambrosio said, 'All right.'

He could smell it. He could smell the smell of poverty. Ambrosio said, 'We'll take them all.'

Esmeralda said, 'No.'

'Why not?'

'My customers like seeing them here.'

'I'll pay you double what you ask.' For the first time he looked at her. She was a woman in her late fifties, lined and ground down by a lifetime of nothing. She was selling her dreams. Ambrosio said, 'All right, triple.'

Esmeralda said, 'Quadruple.'

Ambrosio said, 'All right!'

Esmeralda said, 'No.'

Martinez said quietly, 'We'll pay you what they're worth.' His eyes too were on the cut-out pictures on the wall behind. He had reached the stage of dreaming about the Porsche. The other dreams were smaller. Martinez said, 'OK? All right. Total . . . ten pesos fifty. Right?' Martinez said quietly to Ambrosio in English, 'Any objections?'

'No.' Ambrosio, shaking his head said, 'No.' Everywhere pinned to the wall, were dreams. The bags, to the people who had thrown them away, were of no value whatsoever. She sold them to people who lived in the iron shacks so they could have something to think on.

She sold pictures of washing machines.

She sold pictures of cars.

She sold pictures of houses.

She sold pictures of all the pictures that they saw on the screen on television sets in shops and could never have this side of the screen or the window. She sold something they could have, something they could hold. She sold hope. In Tondo there was no hope.

She moved a bag.

She sold a picture of a gold-plated long-barrelled Model 1896 broom-handled German Mauser in a wooden box.

This time, with no haggling at all, instantly, selling hope, she made a sale.

The sign on his door read 'Commander Teo Quintero, Miscellaneous Seizures And Liaison'. It meant he was in charge of the Coast Guard's basement. The basement he was in charge of was not even a storeroom or a museum, it was just a basement. Below sea level, twenty feet from the wharves and piers where the cutters tied up and the rats scurried in sewers beneath and around it, it dripped water and smelled of neglect and decay. From one end of the sixty-foot grey painted room to the other on walls, in piles, on trestle tables and in mounds all around Quintero's desk, there were the things the Coast Guard had brought in from the sea: ships' nameplates, parts of wooden rudders and masts, barrels, bits and pieces of clothing, wicker baskets, here and there buried and twisted metal, sodden clothing and shoes, jettisoned and lost cargoes, Japanese fishermen's glass floats, lengths of line and hawser that stank and smelled of age and long gone men and watery, unrecorded death and loss.

At his desk, he looked no more than thirty-five years old. Quintero in his starched white uniform, bearded and with no grey in his hair, fit and tanned, said, 'We told the Coast Guard Intelligence what we knew about the Royares brothers and Tolentino. Coast Guard Intelligence told Naval Intelligence and, I presume, Naval Intelligence told Civil Security. No one, to my knowledge, told the cops.' There was no chair for Elizalde to sit on. There was only the single desk in the room. Quintero, standing up, said, 'All I can tell you is what Coast Guard Intelligence told me and because they told me very little that's all I can pass on.' He made a throat clearing sound, then coughed hard as if there was something wrong in his lungs. Quintero said, 'Coast Guard Intelligence thinks they were gun runners and subversives.' He coughed again. Quintero said, 'Coast Guard Intelligence is made up of young men in their early twenties who are just waiting to get to sea. Coast Guard Intelligence is shit.'

'Were they gun runners?'

'They were smugglers.' Quintero said, 'They need proof these days. They've got computers. If it isn't on the computer it isn't proof. They haven't been to sea yet, any of them, and even then, when they do they'll still – ' Quintero said, 'They were smugglers, the Royares and Tolentino. They smuggled every-thing and anything they could get away with.' It was almost as if he was not talking to Elizalde, but to the room itself. Each day, day after day, he must have been alone in that room. Quintero said, 'They were never arrested for it.'

'I see.'

'Do you?'

'Yes.' He looked at the man's face. He was still not looking directly at him. His uniform was stiff and white, cared for, with weapons and electronics-officer patches. Elizalde said, 'And you, do you use a computer?'

'I don't need a computer. I need – ' Quintero said, 'What I need – what the service wants – is for me to hand in my papers and go away quietly and die so they won't have to pay me a disability pension.' Quintero, shaking his head, starting to move Elizalde out, said firmly, dismissing him, 'I'm simply the janitor around here. I've been put on light shore duties which includes seeing people the computer people upstairs right down to the guard on the gate think we shouldn't see at all. Professional courtesy, that's what you've had. The Coast Guard have told the appropriate authorities what they know and what they know is nothing. They have a few suspicions, but since you can't program them into a computer they're of no consequence.'

Elizalde said sympathetically, 'Like you?' He was still not looking at Elizalde directly. Elizalde had seen it before. It was called *hiya*: shame – someone there, someone upstairs in the building above the rotting basement had done something that had struck the man with shame and withered him. Elizalde said, 'You were a sea-going officer, weren't you?'

'Once a long time ago.'

'How long have you been in a shore posting?'

Quintero answering not a stranger asking, but merely a question, said, 'Ten years. At first, they put me in Administration, the Public Relations, then – then, for the past two years, down here.' Quintero said, 'They think I'm physically unfit.' He looked up at Elizalde. He had stopped walking him out of the room. He was looking at him as if he was a sodden mass of clothing or material or bolt of cloth, something that had been brought in from the ocean outside, 'Hydragyrism. Do you know what that is?'

'I'm sorry, I don't.'

'Chronic mercury poisoning.' Quintero looking down at his highly polished shoes, going a little red, said, 'It means you've ingested mercury vapor and after you've recovered from it it means that the Coast Guard Medical Board feels you'll never be physically fit again and that your health can break down at any time and if they don't get rid of you, they'll be paying off medical benefits for the next twenty years.' Quintero said without force, as if he had said it many, many times before, 'It isn't true. I've read up on it. I've paid specialists to tell me all about it. Medical science isn't a science, it's an art. The specialists – not the computer-trained whizz kids here, but the men with real experience, older men – tell me that the incidence of the true classical progress of the condition – weakening of the heart and eventual total disability – happens in less than ten per cent of cases.' Quintero said, 'I was boarding vessels and chasing goddamned smugglers and being shot at and shooting back when half of the bastards upstairs were still pissing in their trousers or thinking about their first fuck!' He said suddenly looking up, apologising, perhaps for the word, 'I'm sorry.' He said briskly, 'The point is that the Coast Guard can't help you with any information about the Royares brothers and Tolentino.'

'Did you ever chase the Royares brothers and Tolentino?'

Quintero said, 'Whether I did or not – '

'Say, ten years ago when they were active?'

'If I did, I never caught them. If I had, if Coast Guard knew something, you wouldn't be talking to me.' He looked down at the concrete floor of the room.

'How were you poisoned by mercury?'

'A fishing boat blew up. Mercury smugglers. We boarded it and put a crew of two men and myself on it to bring it back to port – it had been abandoned when they saw our cutter coming on their radar and – and there must have been a leak in the petrol tank and it blew up.' Quintero said suddenly, harshly, 'The other two, two of my men, were killed. The mercury was being carried in ten kilo bottles, thirty of them. Mercury vaporises at 360 degrees Centigrade. When the tank went up it vaporised.' He had a package of American cigarettes on his desk with a duty free label stamped on it. He reached for it and took one out with his thumb and index finger. His hand was shaking. He was still looking down at the floor. 'I ingested the vapor. Hydragyrism. That's what it's called. Classically, in the ten per cent of classical exhibitions – the doctors' expression – it kills you by destroying your lungs and kidneys and liver.'

'You seem fit enough.'

'It was ten years ago! Classically, I would have been dead by now. I'm not dead.' Quintero, looking up for the first time, said, 'I was twenty-five years old! I had a career ahead of me. I was the best the Service had! If I was going to die I would have been dead by now! Now, it's too late for me and all the children with their computers are ahead of me!' He looked as if he was about to break down and cry. Perhaps, in that room, alone, forgotten, shunned, he sometimes did. Quintero said, 'But I know things! I know things!'

'Do you know anything about the Royares brothers and Tolentino?'

'The Service – '

'No, do *you* know anything?'

There was a silence. He was still looking into Elizalde's face. He was reading something that was there. Quintero said slowly, 'I know – ' He said abruptly, 'No, I don't.'

Elizalde said quietly, 'Help me. I'm out on my own. There's money and power involved and unless I get something quickly I'm going to be put to one side and be told to – '

Quintero said, 'Elizalde, is that your name?'

'Yes.'

Quintero said, 'The – the other thing with mercury poisoning is that – is that the medicos claim you go mad with it in the end.'

'Yes.'

'Mad as a hatter. Have you ever heard that expression?'

Elizalde waited.

'It's because hatters used to work with mercury in their hat-making. In the end, the fumes – ' Quintero said, 'I almost arrested Tolentino once. Him and the Royares brothers – all of them. It was down near Mindanao. We – ' He said, 'I haven't any proof!'

'Please tell me what you know.'

'I don't know anything! I'm a respiratory and renal cripple! I'm going crazy bit by bit so they won't trust me with a ship or a crew and they want me out of the Service so they won't have to pay me benefits.' Quintero said, 'If they wanted you to know anything you wouldn't be talking to me!'

'I *am* talking to you! You are all I've got!'

'They were goddamned smugglers and gun runners! We almost caught them down in Mindanao, but as usual, they got away because they had all their boats equipped with radar that someone with a lot of money – their backer – was paying to have installed in their wheelrooms! Like the mercury boat, like the – '

'It was them? The ones who did this to you?'

'There's no proof.'

'They were mercury smugglers?' Elizalde asked, 'Who? Who was backing them with money?'

'Someone in Forbes Park! Someone rich. Someone – ' Quintero said, 'I don't know!' He said desperately, 'I'm fit! While there's even a chance they might put me back onto active service I can't tell you anything! If I knew anything, I – ' He was not talking to Elizalde, he was, as he always was in that room, alone, and he was doing both sides of the conversation with himself. Quintero said, 'All I know is that there was a gang of them: the Royares brothers, Tolentino and another one – All I know is – ' He had both his hands out in front of him as if he was gripping hard onto some invisible wheel. The cigarette between his fingers was being crushed. 'All I know is – ' He threw the smoking cigarette to the ground and went back to the desk so Elizalde could not see his face. Quintero, suddenly turning, said, 'Look! Look! Does this look like a man about to die to you?' He was at the desk. He almost fell forward onto it, and, at the last moment, caught its edge with his open palms. He began, frantically, so fast it was almost impossible to follow, doing push ups. His eyes were blazing. He held Elizalde's eyes with them. Up and down, up and down, effortlessly, fast and hard, not even raising a sweat,

Quintero said in total, complete desperation, not this time to the empty, stinking room, but to a real human being — someone who might listen — 'Look! Look! Does this look like a man whose life is finished at thirty-five years old?' He was there and then gone again, the eyes looking away, into himself, seeing only that room.

Quintero, unstopping, unstoppable, almost shrieked in the awful, foul decay and dampness, 'Please! Please! For God's sake, someone *look!*'

The voice came back on Agoncillo's open line. In the switchboard room Vargas, listening intently, heard it. Miss Flores, drinking her coffee, was saying something to him as she put calls through on the board, but Vargas listened to her not at all. Agoncillo must have been waiting with the telephone against his ear: there was no delay in his answering.

'*At exactly 9.28 and 30 seconds ring 01018. Dial direct. Dial yourself.*' The man on the other end of the line asked curiously, 'I took it down exactly when you told me. Is that what it says?'

'Yes.'

The man on the other end of the line said definitely, 'There's no such number.' He asked, 'Is it an office extension?'

'No.' Agoncillo's voice was shaking. In the switchboard room, Vargas with a thin smile on his face, heard it quaver. He was a fifty-three-year-old man. He was afraid. Agoncillo with an effort at control, said, 'All the extension numbers here are in three digits. They start with either two or three. Zero is — '

'It isn't an access code. The person I spoke to in the telephone company — '

'*Then what the hell is it?*'

The man on the other end of the phone lost some of the softness in his voice. He asked briskly, 'What time is it now?'

'It's almost — '

'Exactly! By the electric clocks in your office!'

'Nine twenty-one and thirty seconds.'

'Dial it now. See if the numbers open a line and if they don't then he's waiting to cut into a line at the right time and it's possible I can get my contact at the telephone company to — '

'It's nine twenty-one! That doesn't – '

'Dial the number!'

Agoncillo said, 'I can get one of my – '

'Dial it yourself! He says dial it yourself, so that's what you'll do!'

'He killed Francisco and Paulo and Tolentino!'

'Dial the number!' The man on the other end of the line, giving an order, said, 'Dial the number. Dial it direct. Dial it yourself. Dial it now!'

In the cab Martinez said curiously, 'The where? The National Museum? *Why?*'

He was not going to get anything out of the cop on his way UP. The cop on his way UP had had a brainstorm, was on his way DOWN, and was sitting glazed-eyed in the back of the cab hiding the picture he had bought. Martinez said, 'It's a big place. It isn't even open yet. We'll have to go in one of the department entrances. Which one do you want?'

'The natural history department.' Ambrosio said curtly, 'Oological section.' He said before Martinez could ask, 'Quick! Hurry! I need urgently to see an oologist!'

He had stopped. Standing there, defiant, his body still shaking with effort, his eyes bright and glittering, his face ruddy with power and strength, Quintero said, 'I know things, Elizalde. I know things. I know things they think I don't know.'

'You said the Royares brothes and Tolentino and one other – '

'They were the ones who did this to me!'

'Who was the other one?'

'Maybe, if I wait, someone will kill him the way he killed the others!'

'He killed innocent people as well! In Pasig Street when he killed Mang Paulo he killed innocent people as well!'

'They killed *me!*'

'Tell me the other name. Have Coast Guard Intelligence got the other name?'

'Coast Guard Intelligence hasn't got shit! Coast Guard Intelligence took whatever they've got from my records and they didn't even ask me! Coast Guard Intelligence hasn't got the name of the other one because the name of the other one isn't in my records because – ' Quintero said, 'We never caught them, any of them and now, now they're all respectable and maybe Intelligence – for all I know – maybe these days Intelligence is in their pay! I'm down here! I don't know! All I know is the name of the other one on the boat they abandoned.' He said suddenly, 'Maybe I'm the one doing it, maybe I'm the one killing them.' He said with a twisted look on his face, 'No, I'm not fit enough, you've already worked that out, haven't you? You dismissed me from the list of suspects straight away, didn't you?'

'Yes,'

'*Why?* I could do it! I read how it was done in the papers! I could shoot a forty-five and I could toss in a grenade and – '

'It wasn't tossed in, it was fired from a rifle.'

'Then I could certainly have cut that bastard Tolentino's throat from ear to ear! I could have done that!'

'The man who is doing it is totally bald. You aren't. And he certainly doesn't have a beard.'

'I could have paid him to do it!'

'You wouldn't. You'd do it yourself.' In the room Elizalde looked at him.

There was silence.

Quintero said quietly, 'Yes, yes, I would. I can. I am fit.'

'Yes.'

'You can see it, can't you? And I'm lucid and – ' Quintero said, 'Elizalde?'

'Yes.'

Quintero said softly, 'Thank you, Lieutenant Elizalde.'

'Will you tell me the the name of the other man in their crew?'

He paused. Quintero, deciding, said softly, 'Yes.'

It was 9.22 a.m.

Quintero, certain, sure, said firmly, 'Yes, yes, I will.'

It was a recording. It was nothing but a recording of some sort of religious lunatic talking in English in a fruity Deep South American accent. Agoncillo, on the phone, said, 'Jesus,

Maria!' He had been caught by the oldest advertising trick in the book.

There was a click, then a whirring sound and then another click – it was an answering machine set up to the number – and then the voice said after a brief snatch of what sounded like gospel singing, '*Y'all will see the light. Y'all will . . .*' It sounded as if there the tape had been spliced. '*Try again. Try, try again.*' There was a buzzing as if again, the tape had been spliced and not well. '*For the answer, try again . . . try . . . this number . . . wait . . .*' The voice, recorded from either television or radio had a tinny quality to it, '*Again! Telephone . . . again! Too early! . . . I knew . . . Too . . . early!*'

In the switchroom Vargas said with his fist clenched in disappointment. 'Agoncillo . . . !'

Agoncillo said on the line in relief, 'God! God . . .!'

The fruity recorded voice said, a syllable at a time, recorded on the tape carefully, minutely, sound by sound . . . '*Ag-on-cil-lo . . .*'

Agoncillo said in a whisper, 'Oh my God!'

'*Ag-on-cil-lo . . . !*' The evangelist's voice, calling souls to Heaven or Hell, said in a deep, measured, patient tone, '*Try. Try again . . .*'

It was 9.23 precisely.

The line, with a sort of buzzing sound as the spool ran out or rewound itself, went dead.

In Room 333 at the Manila Hotel, he waited.

It was 9.24 precisely by his Patek Philippe watch.

He waited.

Standing, staring out of the window at the bay and the ships, the man in Room 333 waited.

He dialled. He dialled 01018. He dialled direct. He dialled himself. It was 9.25 a.m.

He listened. He heard the tape start with a whirr. Holding the phone hard against his head, Agoncillo listened. He heard a click. He heard a sort of hissing sound as the poor quality tape began playing whatever it was that had been recorded.

He heard it cut in and all the hissing stop.

He heard . . .

There was a silence and then, as Vargas in the switchboard room heard it too, he heard only, far off, the sound of two distant reports.

They sounded like gunshots, like firecrackers, like booby traps fitted with percussion caps, like . . . like nothing at all.

Bang, bang – they were nothing more. On the tape, there was nothing more.

It was 9.26 and thirty seconds.

Standing there at his desk with the phone hard up against his head, Agoncillo heard only the hissing on the tape as it wound itself out and then, stopping, hitting an automatic switch, cut out with a click.

It was gone, whatever it was. He heard another click and then, because the number was a non-existent one, he heard the phone itself take over and in his ear, he heard only an uninterrupted unobtainable signal.

He listened.

The sound went on and on.

He wondered. In his office Lanternero wondered if he should call someone. It was 9.27: he glanced at the bare, undecorated face of the electric wall clock that every office in every department was issued with, and then, to confirm it, at his own wristwatch.

He could not concentrate on his work.

Reaching into his desk, he took out one of the Metro Manila pencils and, putting its end into his mouth, chewed at it thoughtfully.

He waited.

There was only the unobtainable signal.

In his office Agoncillo put his fingers on the telephone cut-off buttons to ring the man with the soft voice to tell him it had all been nothing.

As he touched the two buttons to disconnect the line, oddly, he heard another, a closer click.

He felt pressure on the buttons. He felt too much pressure. He felt an additional spring. He felt . . . 'Oh, no!' In the switchboard room Vargas heard him. He heard him say in a sudden shriek, '*No!*'

'Agoncillo. His name was Ferdinand Sixtus Agoncillo.' Quintero said, 'He's now the head of Pegasus Advertising Agency in Makati that handles the Mendez Beer account.' He said, 'Pegasus. It's the English equivalent of the name of their boat in Spanish, the Hipogrifo. Pegasus. Flying Horse.' He said, nodding, determined, 'Ask him. Ask Agoncillo. He knows. Whatever's happening and why it's happening, ask him, he knows it all!'

9.28 exactly. Against his ear, as his fingers came off the cut-off buttons before he could stop them, there was a click and then, against his ear, pressed hard against his head, in a total, obliterating flash and blast of flame and power and smashed and splintering plastic, the one and a half ounce of carefully packed plastic explosive in the receiver went off and decapitated him where he stood.

He heard it. In the switchboard room, Vargas heard it. They all heard it. They heard in that awful millisecond as it happened – in a moment too brief to calculate – the beginning of his scream.

He was already dead. The scream was already the scream of a dead man. It was an echo.

In Vargas' ear on the line, even though it was gone and the line howling with the broken connection, it was there. It echoed. It rang in the building.

It was 9.28 and thirty seconds.

There was nothing, nothing in the world but the beginnings of that awful scream and, as it echoed and echoed and echoed, the smell, drifting at first, then heavy, of sudden death and things beginning to burn.

9.29 and thirty seconds precisely.

In the Manila Hotel, the man in Room 333 said softly. 'Good.'

He had a small colored postcard in his hand advertising Mendez Beer and showing its logo of a rampant Battling

Mendez in red across a picture of the factory. Crushing it in his fist, he tossed it into the bamboo wastepaper basket in the room and went to the telephone on the bedside table to put a call through to America.

14

He had seen his oologist at the National Museum, Oology Department. He came out of their little door at the side of the building clutching his folded up cut-out picture and what looked like a military-style knapsack full of, presumably, ools.

In the cab, scratching his head, Martinez said, 'What's an oologist?'

His eyes were gleaming. He wasn't even on the same planet. Ambrosio, stealing a glance, first at a corner of his folded-up picture and then in through a corner of his knapsack, said, 'An egg collector.' He got into the back of El Tigre and rustled at the collection of plastic bags. Ambrosio said as an order, 'Now, to a herbalist!' Martinez was still scratching his head. Ambrosio said helpfully – poor fool – 'A herbalist is someone who – '

'I know what a herbalist is!'

'And then for some bricks for the bags.' He said before Martinez could speak, 'No, no brick kilns, no brick makers, just the nearest building site.'

'They won't let you buy any bricks.'

'Buy?' Ambrosio, clutching his bag and his piece of paper and grinning happily, said in a voice they never taught him to use at SPROOG, IGLL or even at UP, 'Buy? *Buy?* Buy shit! Take me to the nearest building site and we'll *steal* them!'

You could tell, he had a plan. Ambrosio, leaning forward

142

forgetting everything and bashing Martinez hard on the head with his knapsack, said, 'Well? Well? *Well, get on with it!*'

He fixed him with his glittering eye. This morning, all over town, there was a lot of it going around. In the Dinosaur Park, Bontoc, anchoring the gardener to the spot with a gentle hand on his shoulder that felt like a vice, demanded, 'So what's the answer? If it takes six men six days to dig six holes, how long does it take one man to dig half a hole?'

Glitter. Gleam. There was something funny happening in the eyes. They looked like dark brown pools with fish swimming around in them in the mud. Bontoc said, 'Forty years.' He looked significantly at the gardener for agreement.

The gardener, looking into those eyes, agreed. The gardener said, nodding, 'Of course it does.' He squirmed. The hand held him as if it was nailed to him. It didn't matter what he told you, he was from the tribe that ate trees. The gardener trying to step back and not moving or moving Bontoc a millimeter, nodding, said happily, 'Of course. It's obvious. Why didn't I think of that? Forty years. Right! Too true.'

He was going to massacre him.

Bontoc said, 'They think that because I'm short that I'm stupid.'

The gardener said, 'Tall people can be stupid too.'

Bontoc said, 'You're not tall.'

The gardener said, 'I'm taller than you.'

'Everybody is taller than me!'

'No. No, the dwarves in the Hobbit House in Ermita –' What was he saying? The gardener said, 'You're not short! You may not be tall, but you're not – '

'I am short! I can face it! I'm short!' Bontoc said, 'If you prick me do I not bleed?'

The gardener said, 'Yes! Yes!' He was starting to drip sweat, and pure, unbridled terror. The gardener, regretting ever having got into the gardening business, said in a panic of agreement, 'So you are! Well, I never noticed before. Yes, I suppose you are. Yes, you're very short indeed.' He was nodding, sweating, quaking, trying to move away, held in the vice. The gardener, blabbering said, 'Good little fellow.'

'*But I'm not stupid!*'

It was another trick question. The gardener said, 'Forty years! Am I right?'

'I recognised one of them after you hit me with the axe.'

Oh God. The gardener said, 'Oh . . . um . . . oh, God.'

'He was one of the people who sent me here because he thought I was stupid and short!'

Was he still short? Maybe he had grown. The gardener said, 'Oh.' You couldn't go wrong with that.

'Don't say "Oh". That's what everybody wants to say about me! Baptiste Bontoc: him . . . oh. Detective Sergeant, is he . . . oh. What is he? He's an educated midget from one of the headhunting tribes – you know, one of the cultural minorities . . . *oh!*' Bontoc, quoting from memory said, 'With your cultural background and primitive life-way-experience (head-hunting and massacres) . . . The man I recognised was one of the people who sent me here because he thought I was stupid!' Bontoc, dropping his voice, said intensely, gleaming, 'But he goofed it this time. I'm not as stupid as he thinks. He's the stupid one. He thought I – ' The gardener was looking at him dumbly. Bontoc, shaking him to get his attention, said, 'Listen! Don't you understand? It isn't Japanese bonehunters taking bones out of the ground at all! It's people putting things back *into* the ground! Their sacks, when they ran away, were empty! They're putting back into the ground . . . the rest of the hole!' He let go of the gardener. He said happily, rubbing at his bruise, 'See?'

He could have run. He couldn't have run.

'The half a hole they didn't dig forty years ago! They're putting it back into the ground!'

He must have been mad. The gardener said mildly, 'You can't dig half a hole.'

'They did! He did! The one I recognised!' He asked, 'Who? Who closed this park in the first place?'

'The Assistant Minister of Works.' The gardener said, 'Oh, no – !'

'Oh, yes!'

'*The Assistant Minister of Works is digging half a hole in a dinosaur park in Luneta?*'

'Yes!' Maybe Manilans weren't that dumb. Maybe it was just the way they talked. Once you explained things to them, maybe they . . . Bontoc said, 'Yes! Exactly!' He patted the gardener on the shoulder. Bontoc said, 'Right!'

The gardener said, 'Oh, God!'

'Yes. He was the one who got me ordered here by Headquarters so he could have the park closed off to mask his evil deeds!' He sounded like Miss Thomasina. Screw Miss Thomasina. Sucks to Uncle Apo. Hail Bontoc. Bontoc said, 'But I beat him! I out-thought him! I'm educated!' He had something on the ground beside him. He bent down and picked it up. It was the entrenching tool he had used to inter himself in the flower beds. 'And now, now – not as stupid as he thinks – ' He tapped himself hard on the bruise. (It hurt.) '*As stupid as a fox*, I'm going to dig and find it and you, you're going to keep watch on the brontosaurus over there and – ' The eyes gleamed. Bontoc said, 'Aren't you!'

'Yes!'

'And I'm going to dig!' He was as happy as a cockroach. Falling to the ground with the tool in his hands, in an ecstasy of excavation, he began digging. He was looking in the hole he had begun to dig for half a hole. His eyes gleamed. He saw the gardener standing staring at him. There was a handy brontosaurus not ten feet away. Bontoc, glancing up at the gardener, ordered the man, 'And you, you're going to climb up onto the brontosaurus and keep watch! Aren't you?'

'Yes! Yes!'

He dug.

The gardener looked at those eyes.

He climbed.

'Your gold-plated broom-handled Mauser costs twenty-seven dollars and fifty cents new.' Bit by bit, as he came out of each of the places on his list, he was turning into someone else. He had come out of the National Museum and turned into El Mysterio. Now, outside the herbalist in General Gil Street he was The Man From Dale Carnegie. Even his voice was stronger, firmer, more direct. He didn't ask: he gave orders. In the back of the cab he had his hand in the knapsack making sticking plaster noises. In the back of the cab he had his eyes ahead on the future. Ambrosio said, 'Twenty-seven dollars and fifty cents. Well aren't you going to say anything?' He asked, 'Where the hell did these stones come from in the bags? I wanted to steal some bricks!'

'I used to be a cop myself.' Martinez, staring at the eyes, said gently, 'If you're caught stealing bricks your chances of ever making anything of yourself after you leave the police force are zero.'

'I don't intend to leave the police force!' He still had his hand in his bag. Ambrosio, leaning back, ready to give the man the benefit of his learning said firmly, 'SPROOG and IGLL teach you to face issues. I have faced this one. I've examined my own feelings about it and the role of this criminal perpetrator in the steady erosion of Society's fixed values and I have come to an infallible plan to ensure his due apprehension. For his assaults on peaceable persons about their lawful occasions he will be duly apprehended, tried and incarcerated.' He nodded to himself.

Martinez said, 'Good.' He tried to see the ad for the wonderful pistol at a discount price but Ambrosio folded it up and put it in his pocket.

Ambrosio said, 'And for his personal, humiliating assault on me . . .'

Ambrosio said, 'For that, *when I catch him, I'm going to kill the rotten, lousy, stinking, smart-arsed son of a bitch!*'

On the brontosaurus' neck, the gardener shouted down, 'There's no one out there! I can see right across all the parks and all there are are perfectly normal people going about their perfectly normal business, being sane and – ' He wanted to cry. He shouted down, 'There's nothing there!'

'Topsoil!' He had a hole the size of a grave dug. Bontoc going black with the earth, looking, if it was possible, even more demented, shouted, 'Topsoil!'

'What did you expect?'

'Under the clay?'

'It's good land!'

'It isn't that good!' He looked up and saw the gardener looking down at him. He should have been looking for the Assistant Minister. Bontoc said, 'The Assistant Minister, he did this, didn't he?'

'I've no idea!'

'You've no idea?' He reached a rock and tossed it out and then climbing out of the hole got it again. Bontoc, holding it up said, 'Shale! There isn't any shale in this area! This shale has been put here!' Two subjects at once were no problem to a man of the Miss Thomasina and Uncle Apo ilk. Bontoc said, 'You've no idea? What the hell do you think an Assistant Minister of Public Works starts out as – a brain surgeon? He starts out as a construction company!'

'There isn't anything under there! The Japanese bombed it during the war and then the Americans bombed it during the war and the only thing that's under there is – ' The gardener had decided. He was getting down. He was going to get down while the Lunatic was in the hole and, with a bit of luck, he could make it to the nearest policeman before . . . The Lunatic *was* a policeman. The gardener, whining, said desperately, 'There aren't any tunnels or air raid shelters or Nazi gold bunkers under there! You've been reading too many cheap novels and you . . .'

The voice from the hole stilled him. The voice from the hole said menacingly, 'I never read cheap novels!' The voice said, 'Don't you start having a go at me again!'

'There's nothing down there but earth!'

'More topsoil!'

'Topsoil *is* earth!'

'It doesn't come in secondary layers!'

'That's the – that's the – '

Bontoc said, 'Stratification?'

The gardener said, 'Yes.'

'These strata are made up of slate and bits and pieces of – ' Bontoc said, 'Road metal! Road metal and ripped up asphalt and – ' He had a glittering prize. Bontoc shouted in triumph, 'Three broken Coca-Cola bottles!' He shouted out, 'Stay up there! And a brick! A house brick and a length of twisted – a tin can and – ' He shouted up, 'Get down here!' He shouted up, 'See anything?' He shouted up as he saw the gardener start to slide down the spine of the stone beast to safety, 'Stay up there!' He made a crashing sound with his spade. He shouted up. 'Bamboo! I've found bamboo! Don't tell me bamboo grows six foot under the ground in cut lengths!' He made another crashing sound. He shouted, 'Get down here!' And another crashing sound, 'More bamboo! Stay there! I keep finding bamboo and lengths of rattan cord and – '

He saw them. Far off in the park, he saw suddenly getting out of two Public Works trucks, no fewer than thirty people. The gardener said, 'Oh, my God!'

He saw the Assistant Minister.

The gardener said, 'I see them!'

The voice shouted, 'I see it!' There was a crash. The voice shrieked out in triumph, 'I've found it! I was right! *I've found it!*'

He had found half a hole.

The gardener, clambering down, yelled, 'They're coming!' He saw them beginning to run. He wondered what, for a moment, had attracted their attention.

It was the brontosaurus. It was moving. He was digging, not straight down, but at an angle and the brontosaurus, losing purchase on the ground, being undermined, was beginning to fall.

They were coming. He saw them.

In the hole Bontoc yelled, 'Here! Look!' There was a crashing sound. He shouted out, 'My gun! I remember where I left it!' Everything at last was clear. Bontoc shouted, 'I left it in the saber-toothed tiger's den!' The brontosaurus was going. He heard the gardener say, 'Aa – yo . . .!'

Bontoc shouted, 'He was the construction firm that filled in all the bomb craters and the holes here after the war and in order to save money and because the park was only going to be used for a few flowers he only filled in half the holes!' He shouted, 'I'm actually standing on the bamboo platform he put across the hole forty years ago so he'd only have to fill in the top half of the hole!' The locals had to have a picture painted. They had never heard of Gestaltist insight or a logical mind.

148

'The half a hole! He's not taking out bones – he's putting the rest of the filling into the hole a sack at a time because of the extra weight of the dinosaurs!' Give the gardener credit: at least he had taken the time to listen. Bontoc, patronising him, shouted out, 'Doesn't that seem reasonable to you?'

Only too reasonable. The gardener sliding, falling, going off the brontosaurus' tail like a man on a roller-coaster, shouting, 'Whoooo-aah!' running for the gate as, out in the park thirty men with keys and spades and sacks and probably guns and knives and hatchets came for him, yelled back as he flew by, 'Yes! Yes! Well done!' He saw, for an instant, a black creature in a hole the size of a well. Give him credit. The gardener flying past, nodding hard, yelled down, 'Great! Wonderful! Well done!' The gardener, flying as the earth rumbled as the brontosaurus teetered, yelled in the best admiring voice he could manage at the moment, 'GOODBYE!'

In the cab, as they drove, he touched not at his gun, but at his knapsack.

Ambrosio said softly to himself, 'Hmm!'

They were going back towards Parker Lane.

Ambrosio, grinning, sure, said again, satisfied, 'Hmm!'

It went. It came down like a great shadow across the grass and darkened his hole and he looked up and it had gone. In the hole Bontoc said, 'Oh, no – !' He saw the brontosaurus coming down: he saw the long neck fall across the circle of the sky from the bottom of the pit and then, as the great swollen body followed it, he saw the sky turn, not dark, but black, and then he saw . . . He felt the ground rumble. He saw, for an instant, thirty faces looking down at him and then, as the thirty faces saw the face of the brontosaurus falling down on them, the thirty faces were gone. He saw . . . He heard. He ducked. He cowered. He heard. . .

In a single crash, cascading dirt and bits and pieces of fill and stone and earth and clay down around him, the brontosaurus came down and missed his hole by inches. He saw . . . He was stuck. His foot was stuck on the bamboo platform ten feet below the surface of the ground and below that, if his theory was right, there was another gigantic hole into which no one forty years ago had bothered to pour more fill and clay and earth and bits of tin cans and Coke bottles.

He was right.

He saw the Assistant Minister's face looking down at him. He saw the spade and the sack of fill in the Assistant Minister's hand. He saw another twenty-nine faces and another twenty-nine shovels and sacks and he saw –

He saw –

He heard –

The Assistant Minister said, 'Fill him in!'

Bontoc said, '*No!*'

The Minister said –

He saw them start to lift up their sacks to pour earth in on him. Bontoc said –

'*Freeze!* Hold it right there! Hands up!' Somewhere, far off, the gardener said, 'Reach for the sky!' He saw, at the edge of the hole, the face of the gardener. It was a nice face. The gardener said with the PPK pointed firmly at the face of the Assistant Minister, 'I found your gun.' He saw one of the Assistant Minister's hired men start to move and he stabbed him in the face with the weapon and said, 'Don't even think about it!' He said again to the little slime covered man in the little slime covered hole, 'It wasn't in the saber-toothed tiger's lair at all. It was in the marsupial lion's den!'

Bontoc said humbly, 'Sorry.' Bontoc, grinning, said, 'Thanks very much.' He said unboastingly to the Assistant Minister, 'I worked it out.' He called out to the gardener, 'Get them to pull me out now and – ' Bontoc said, 'I'm not really a headhunter. I've never taken a head in my life. I'm an intellectual.' He saw the Assistant Minister's face. He smiled. He saw the gardener's face. He didn't smile.

Bontoc said, 'Well? *Well, you're not going to leave me down here all day, are you?*'

There was something else about the gun on the scrap of paper he had paid for. It was a single line. It was a red rag to a bull. It was a banana skin to a Keystone cop. It was . . .

It was a single legend in large, bold print.

It was printed on the hammer of the gun in the picture.
Made In Taiwan.

In the back of the cab as Martinez turned into Taft Avenue for the Parker Mansions area, Ambrosio breathing deeply, sniffing to clear his nose ready for action, seething, said for the third time, 'Hmmm!'

15

Agoncillo's office on the fourth floor of the PHILCOM building on Ayala Street was full of foam. Using extinguishers, the Fire Brigade had done something about the fires burning in the room. They hadn't done anything about the blood. When the charge had gone off in his ear it had shattered his skull: the blood and brains and bone were all over the walls, directly above his desk where he had been standing, and on the ceiling. There was nothing on his desk but a blackened pulp of saturated papers and what looked like the spine of a desk diary – everything made of paper had burned. He had not. Only the collar and top section of his shirt had caught fire and the blood, coming out like a fountain had put that out. He lay a little to one side of the desk, twisted up, unrecognisable, a length of plastic telephone cord around his wrist like a bangle. One of his shoes was off. It lay next to his hand, upside down, moving back and forth like a little raft on a flat sea of gently bubbling foam.

Outside, in the main office, Elizalde could see Patrolmen Innocente and Pineda taking statements from the editorial staff and Agoncillo's secretary. They kept looking in towards the office and shaking their heads. Innocente and Pineda kept following their glances. They were not writing very much down. There was nothing to write down. They waited, taking the names and addresses of the witnesses, for Doctor

Watanabe and Scientific. He saw Innocente stop and say something to one of the firemen and the fireman shake his head. There was nothing else to be done. The fireman gave Innocente his name and badge number and Station and also waited.

They had come forward, Vargas and the switchboard operator, Miss Flores. Of all the people in the office who knew nothing, they had come into the office with him while all the others stayed outside.

It had been in the phone itself, the mechanism. In the blast, the telephone had been ripped open and he saw wires and what looked like some sort of electronic digital counter that should not have been there. Elizalde said, 'It was in the phone.' He looked at Miss Flores' face and then at Vargas. Elizalde said, 'The charge that killed him was hidden in the phone and when he – '

'It isn't one of our phones.' Miss Flores, shaking her head, said, 'Our phones all have the extension number written on a piece of tape on the bottom. That doesn't. It isn't one of our phones.' She was a lumpy woman in her sixties: one of the fixtures every office that had been in business for some time had. He hadn't asked, but her first name would be Charlotta or Adelmara or some name long, long out of date and from another time and way of life. Her life was the company. She served and was served by it. She knew and would know everything that had happened in the office for the past twenty-five years. She would know all the people who had come and gone and, in the tight-lipped world of ambition and back-stabbing and intrigue she was the one everyone came to with their troubles. She was no threat to them. She was the switchboard operator who was going no further – wanted to go no further – and they would confide in her, test their plans and dreams on her, and, probing for weaknesses in their competitors' characters – searching for the secrets their competitors had told her – use her. She believed the company could not run without her and when, at last, she retired she would be given a gift – glassware or a clock – shockingly smaller than she expected and then, in her retirement, waiting to be called back to explain some delicate nuance of procedure or filing to the New Guard, she would be totally and utterly . . . forgotten.

By her, the man Vargas stood silently gazing down. She was the one. Elizalde said, 'Who was he ringing?'

She wept for him. Maternally, tears were glistening on her face. She was dressed in a print dress. In the switchboard room, in her overlarge handbag, she would have a lace handkerchief.

Elizalde said again, 'Who was he ringing?'

Miss Flores shook her head.

'Who was he ringing!'

'Not one of our numbers!' Miss Flores, suddenly looking up at him, disapproving, said, 'He wasn't ringing one of our numbers!' That made it all right. 'He was ringing a zero prefix number that didn't go through the switchboard. He was ringing 01018!' She glanced at Vargas, 'Mr Vargas told me! It was written in Mr Agoncillo's diary. It told him to ring that number. It doesn't exist.' She shook her head. 'It isn't one of our numbers.'

Vargas said, 'It was an answering machine.' He looked down at Agoncillo and smiled. Vargas said, 'The note told him to ring the number and when he rang it he got an answering machine.' He was glad the man was dead. 'He was on the phone to a man asking him about the number and the man told him to ring it and he did.' He said before Elizalde could ask, 'The message on the answering machine told him nothing and when he hung up – '

Miss Flores said, 'He was a good man . . .'

Vargas, looking at her, said, 'Yes.'

'If he rang the number zero wouldn't he have got the switchboard?'

'No.' It was a point of pride with her. Miss Flores said, 'Nine. You have to ring nine in this office to get the switch. If he rang zero – ' She said quickly, safely, 'The system was changed when we got International Subscriber Dialling. Some of the phones are direct lines and the Telephone Company suggested that if we kept the zero as the switch call digit then people would keep getting mixed up on their international dialling and so we changed it to nine.' She said, 'When we started off, years ago, before even Mr Vargas took over, we were a small firm with only old Mr Ver and two of his sons and in those days when you had to get the operator to get you any number at all it was all right, but as we got bigger, and especially when Mr Agoncillo took over, we, the Telephone Company – ' She said suddenly, 'He wasn't married. He was all alone.' Miss Flores said, 'He was nice to me. Sometimes – not as often as old Mr Ver used to – he used to come by the switchboard room and talk for a while . . .' She asked Vargas, 'Didn't he?' She asked, 'Mr Vargas?'

Vargas said, 'Did he?'

'Yes, he did!' Miss Flores, rounding on him, said, 'I didn't hate him! You were the one who hated him because he took over from you, but he was good to the people who worked here and he kept the firm going and he paid bonuses!' Miss Flores said, 'He knew you hated him! He knew you listened in to his calls! He told me once! He was a good man – he said it didn't matter to him!'

'Nothing mattered to him!'

'You listened in to all his calls!'

'I – '

Miss Flores said, 'You did! You're glad he's dead!' Miss Flores said, 'The only place the answering machine could be is in the junction box by the elevators, by the windows!' She looked hard at Vargas' face and saw there something she could not understand from a lifetime of office life: something that had nothing to do with the things she knew from the office. Miss Flores said, 'You listened in to all his calls and I let you because you were once my boss and I – '

'You did what you were told because you're just the switchboard operator!'

'He knew! He knew you listened in because I told him!' Miss Flores said, 'And now he's dead!' She looked down at the body, 'He's dead!' She saw Elizalde gazing at her, listening. Miss Flores said with vehemence, 'He listened in! He knew everything that poor man did! *He listened in to all his calls!*'

In the cab Ambrosio said, 'Don't talk!' They had found a relatively pollution-free spot at the intersection of Parker Lane and Taft Street and Ambrosio, sniffing, shaking his head, was clearing his lungs and his brain for the final conflict. He was armed for the struggle. He had done a course in SPROOG in Human Interface Behaviour Prediction (Reference Amerasian/Latin Male, Philippines) and he needed only God's good clear sinuses, a steady hand, a resolute heart, his MANILA POLICE baseball cap, his ools and his honed brain and Good would inevitably triumph. Ambrosio said, 'He'll come. He'll come because it is in the nature of the Amerasian male not not to come and he'll come.' It wasn't exactly the terms the course instructor had put it in, but the course instructor hadn't been breathing and sniffing deeply at the time. Ambrosio said, 'He'll come out from his rat hole in Parker Mansions thinking he'll do another hit on Roxas Boulevard and he'll see us here with all our bags full of – he'll presume – riches he won't be able to pass up and, even if he thinks he should pass up such riches – he'll hit us as a point of honor.' He nodded. He sniffed. He said, nodding and sniffing, 'The average Philippino, once he gets an idea fixed in his head, will pursue it to the bitter end, even if it means his destruction and the destruction of all those around him.'

Martinez said nervously, 'Right.' That was exactly what he was worried about.

Ambrosio said, 'Don't talk!' He sniffed. He peered out from behind a Tiffany bag full of stones and scanned the street. It was empty. Ambrosio said, 'Just sit still and I'll take it from here.' He was trained. Ambrosio said, 'Just watch for a man wearing grey slacks and a red and white striped T-shirt carrying what looks like a wooden box and –' He said expansively as his nose cleared, 'If you don't want to watch, don't bother. This matter is now in the hands of the police. In my estimation, having estimated the time lapse between recovery from flight, thoughtful consideration of his future, rising annoyance and humiliation at almost being caught –'

Martinez said under his breath, 'Ha!'

' – and determination to play out an ego restoring role by hitting another cab, he'll be along in a fixed time.' He sniffed. The fixed time was a little hazy in his mind, but it felt about right. ' – and then – and then, in exactly thirty-two minutes or so he'll – ' He peered out the window. There was no man in grey slacks and striped T-shirt anywhere around. That was all right. Obviously he was still at the pre-ego restoration stage, 'And then – And then I'll arrest him.' And maybe beat him senseless. Ambrosio said, 'You're my witness. I want you to make it clear in your statement that I used all the principles I was taught to apprehend him.'

Martinez said, 'I'll – '

Ambrosio said, 'Don't talk!'

'One thing – '

Ambrosio said, 'Don't talk!' He sniffed. He waited. There was a fat man wearing an Hawaiian shirt coming up the street and for an instant, fearing the clash about to take place, Ambrosio thought of winding down his window to warn him off. He decided against it. In the all-out fight against crime, civilians had to take their chances too. There was a statistic about acceptable casualty rates, but he could not recall what it was. Ambrosio, seeing Martinez's face in the rear vision mirror looking worried, said to soothe him, 'I'm a trained man. All the bases have been covered. You won't be one of the acceptable casualties.'

'Surely he would have – '

'Don't talk!' He was a leader. He had to be resolute. He had to be silent. Every syllable – a little more – destroyed the fine tuning of his nose. Ambrosio, sniffing the syllables back, said, 'Thin man, grey slacks, laterally striped T-shirt, box under arm – ' He saw the fat man waddle up towards the taxi and he muttered, 'Acceptable casualty. Be on your guard ever!' He saw the man look over into the cab and touch at his paunch. Poor, out of training slob. He touched at his flowered shirt. With no taste. Ambrosio said as Martinez opened his mouth to speak, 'Ever vigilant. Ever – thirty-one minutes to go!' The man in the Hawaiian shirt, smiling, rapped on his window to ask him something. Dumb, fat, stupid, tasteless and lost. Ambrosio winding down the window said sweetly, 'Yes?' He saw Martinez's face in the rearview mirror. He saw the fat man become a thin man. He saw the gun box come out from under his shirt. He saw it open. He saw the gold glint. He saw the bomber see his MANILA POLICE baseball cap on the seat next to him. Amerasian male ego restoration: where was it when you needed it.

He saw –

He saw the bomber's face change and the box of gun become, in his hand, a vial of vile. He saw – Scrabbling, gasping not for air, but for a shriek in the back of his throat as the vial sailed through the open window and turned Martinez's windscreen and driver's seat into the San Quentin gas chamber, Ambrosio kicking open the door and splintering it into a shower of wire, fiberglass, buckled tin and total destruction, shouted, 'You're early! You're too goddamned early! And you changed your goddamned clothes!'

He saw the man reel back.

He saw fear in his eyes.

Ego restoration: it washed over him in a single, wonderful floodgate-opening surge. He was virgin, untouched. He sniffed. His nose was clear.

The mugger was running. He was fleeing, his box tucked hard under his arm. He was afraid.

Professionalism, training, competency, efficiency, method, that was what he had learned in Police College.

Revenge: that was what he had learned in life.

Ambrosio, crouching on the pavement, reaching into his knapsack, decided to give the little bastard a good head start.

Oh no, he didn't. He let him get ten feet and then, squarely, throwing it with all his might, crowing in delirious joy, he hit him in the back of the head with the first ool.

The answering machine wired to the unused internal zero connection in the junction box by the windows of the fourth floor was an old plastic Hanimex, made in Australia and, unavailable in the Philippines, probably untraceable.

'*Y'all will see the light. Y'all will* . . .' There was a click in the tape. '*Try again. Try, try again.*' There was a buzzing. The fireman and Innocente and Pineda were in the main office and, with the elevators all on other floors, there was no sound in the corridor by the windows, '*For the answer, try again . . . try . . . this number . . . wait . . . Again! Telephone . . . again! Too early! . . . I knew . . . Too . . . early!*'

158

There were tears on Miss Flores' face. Vargas had heard it all before.

'*Agoncillo . . .!*'

'*Ag-on-cil-lo . . .*'

'*Ag-on-cil-lo . . .*'

'*Try. Try again . . .*'

Dimly, after a long pause, there was the sound of two distant reports, like cannon shots.

He listened. The tape went silent, and he ran it back a little to listen to the two far-off sounds.

He had gone a little too far back.

'*Ag-on-cil-lo . . .*' It sounded like the voice of a man long dead, of a ghost.

'*Ag-on-cil-lo . . .*'

In the corridor, in the terrible, hushed silence, Elizalde looked hard at Vargas' face and tried to read what was there.

'*Ag-on-cil-lo . . .*'

He saw Miss Flores, with tears rolling down her cheeks, put her hands to her face to shut out the sound.

The bomber stopped. He staggered. He stank.

The ool was a duck egg filled with durian essence from the health food shop. The mugger was running towards the safety of Parker Mansions. The gold-plated broom-handled Mauser 1896 automatic pistol in a box was a plastic man's aftershave dispenser that dispensed at a water pistol-like squirt, a jet of man's pine-scented aftershave that killed the smell of durian.

The mugger, squirting, yelled, 'Ha Ha!' Ego restoration.

Ambrosio, hurling an ool and hitting him in the face with it, yelled, 'Ho! Ho!' Durian restoration.

The mugger said, '*Shit!*'

SPROOG/IGLL, clean sinuses and a fine mind – by God, it taught you how to behave. Ambrosio yelled back, 'Fuck you!'

The mugger squirted his gun.

Ambrosio threw an ool.

The mugger ran.

Ambrosio chased him. He sniffed. He smelled. He smelled durian.

He saw the mugger make for a paling fence over the back of

a disused building and, the man of the future, with an arm like a Dodgers' pitcher, caught him square in the back of the head with a curve ool and, shrieking in joy and expectation, went unerringly over the fence after him.

In his office, Luis Lanternero decided.

Leaving the Ministry building by a back door, he went to find a call box to make a private, untappable call.

Power. It was all he ever craved. They were in the courtyard of Parker Mansions, surrounded on all four sides by high rise buildings. The mugger was making for the south entrance, breathing hard. If he got in there with his pine fragrance gun he would be lost.

Power!

He wasn't lost.

He didn't get in.

Ambrosio hit him with an ool and turned him from a daisy into sewage. *Power*. Power was an ool. Ambrosio, hopping up and down, pulling another egg from his knapsack, winding himself up, crouching down, feigning curve balls, high balls, low balls and straight-to-the-head balls, yelled, 'Strike one!' The taped-up egg detonated two solid ounces of pure, undistilled, herbal quality durian juice over his arm and against the doorway. He wasn't going in that doorway.

Ambrosio sniffed. He could smell it. So could half the Western World. All along the verandas and balconies of the buildings people were coming out to look. They looked. They sniffed. They gasped. Ambrosio shrieked, 'I can smell you! There's no escape! I'll track you down wherever you go!' He hit the Mauser toting mugger with an ool that caught him on the ankle and sent him back like a pinball from a northerly direction to a southerly.

The mugger squirting his gun at himself, tried west.

He caught a lob square on the top of his head.

He staggered. He gasped. Up in the balconies people said, 'Ohhh!' There was a ripple of applause.

Ambrosio should have yelled, 'Police!'

Ambrosio yelled, 'How was that?'

The mugger staggered. He shot himself in the head with his squirt gun.

The crowd yelled, 'Ahhh!' (There wasn't much else to do on a Monday morning in Parker Mansions if you weren't out stealing hub caps or mugging people yourself.) The crowd yelled, 'Yay!'

Ambrosio, enthused, crouched down as the mugger, trying a direct frontal approach, charged at him like a tank, let him have a gentle, almost cool ool in the chest underarm. The mugger, like a tank hit by a missile, ran out of the steam, shuddered, and went backwards. *Shoot again*. Ambrosio, hurling hard, hit the mugger square in the groin and doubled him up.

The mugger had a glass durian bomb out. He drew it back.

Ambrosio hit him with an egg on the hand.

It was the wrong hand. The durian bomb came back and hit Ambrosio and turned him from Audie Murphy at the breech into Beetle Bailey at the septic tank. The crowd yelled, 'Aggh!' (They caught the double smell in one terrible whiff.)

Ambrosio said, 'Yaggh!' He hit the mugger with a double ool.

The mugger stood his ground and fended off a flying egg with the Mauser. He almost fended off the second.

The mugger shot back with a glass durian bomb.

Ambrosio hit him with an egg.

The mugger squirted and everywhere there was the pure clean smell of pine. Well, not quite everywhere. Up on the balconies with the thermals rising there was the sound of gagging and fainting.

The mugger yelled, 'Cop!' He threw a bomb.

It missed.

Ambrosio yelled, 'Criminal anti-social element!'

He threw an egg.

It didn't miss.

The mugger aimed his Mauser and squirted himself from head to toe. He wasn't going anywhere smelling nice. It was a reflex. He smelled like shit. Up on the balconies people were beginning to call the police.

No one sent him into a mountain of rotting banana skins and lived.

The mugger was about to give up. Ambrosio saw him open his mouth to surrender.

Ambrosio let him have an ool in the face and the mouth closed again.

Ambrosio, in his best voice for the balconies, yelled, 'Won't give up, eh?' He threw another egg and then another and, grasping in his mighty hand, three at once, bracketed the mugger and turned his face not red from exertion, but a bright blue from asphyxiation.

'I GIVE UP!'

Ambrosio shouted, 'What? I can't hear you!'

He had two ools left. He needed one for the Police Museum. He let the mugger have the other one.

The mugger yelled, 'I GIVE UP! I GIVE UP!' He came forward, gasping, coughing, reeling, staggering, pathetically holding out his gun, butt first.

Maybe he didn't need one for the Police Museum. Maybe he could – He saw the crowd watching. In all the apartments and rat holes people were calling the cops.

Ambrosio said, 'All right.' He had it all worked out. He, the trained mind, had it all – all worked out.

He was a man of mercy. He took the Mauser and feeling its slight weight in his hand, nodding benevolently, said, 'And now we clean you up with a smell that will not offend respectable law abiding people as you walk by them on your way to the slammer.'

He took the Mauser and, squirting thoughtfully, working his way up from the mugger's shoes to his head, going carefully and systematically over each stinking inch he sprayed the fragrance until, at last, gratefully, the mugger said, 'Thank you . . .'

What a mighty man was Ambrosio.

Ambrosio said quietly to the mugger, 'I'm on my way UP.'

He smiled.

It had all worked out.

He stank like hell.

Everything planned, calculated, reckoned to the fraction.

He turned the gun on himself and squeezed the trigger.

The gun, instead of *squirt* went *pzzt . . .*

The mugger, smiling, said, 'Thanks very much for cleaning me up.' He asked with an evil grin, 'Empty, is it?'

Ambrosio said, '*Neeeyagh!*'

He had the single usable ool left for the museum.

In a wonderful, joyous, liberating example of good old veteran, vintage, non-sociological, basic, primeval, police brutality that, for the first time in a long time, thrilled him to the soul, Ambrosio, at point blank range, used it.

In the corridor near the elevator Elizalde, looking hard at the man's face, asked Vargas quietly, 'Now he's gone will you get your company back?'

Miss Flores had gone back to her switchboard. She had said everything she had wanted to say and now she had wanted to be alone.

Vargas, shaking his head, said, 'No.'

'He kept you on.'

'He kept me on for people like her.' Vargas, with a strange, bitter smile on his face, said simply, 'He crushed me. Now the Board will appoint someone new to take over and there'll be no reason for me to stay on.' Vargas said, 'I'm glad. He crushed me, but I'm still alive and he isn't.' He looked at the tape recorder and shook his head. 'The note on his diary was written by someone with a Metro Manila issue pencil. I heard him say it to the other party on the line: the man with the soft voice.' He said, 'I have photostat copies of all his papers and everything that went across his desk – everything. Everything about Mendez and his business.' Vargas said, 'He crushed me.'

'Can I have them?'

'Yes.' Vargas said, 'Yes, I can get him.'

Elizalde said curiously, 'But he's dead now . . .'

Vargas said, 'Yes.' He was a man who had spent a very long time seeing himself in a mirror. For a very long time he had hated what he saw.

Vargas said, 'Yes. But I'm not. I can still get him.' He wasn't talking to Elizalde at all: it was to someone else, something else, something awful and intangible, something that had

163

grown inside and fed from him. Vargas said again, 'Yes, he's dead.' He looked up and held Elizalde's eyes.

Vargas said in a voice that chilled Elizalde to the bone, 'But I'm not and my hate for that man – for what he did – my hate for him is immortal!'

He said quickly, 'Wait here. I've got all the copies hidden away in my desk where no one could ever find them.' He ordered Elizalde, 'Wait. I just want to see his dead body one more time and then I'll get them for you.'

It was 1.38 exactly.

On his desk, Bald Head's phone rang and, after the caller identified himself, he lit a cigarette and checking that no one was around to overhear him, sat back comfortably and interestedly in his chair to listen.

16

It was impossible to stop. Sometimes, during the early part of the process, he had wanted it to stop, but it was impossible. He had wanted to tell her. There was no way to tell her. It was impossible to say when he had ceased taking money to see her through University and to secure her future and when, when there was more money than it took, when he had started taking the money for himself.

That he had taken was indisputable.

In his new BMW 528i, Luis Lanternero, parked across the street from Elizalde's apartment block, lit a cigarette with his gold Dunhill lighter. He had been waiting there all afternoon to see his sister. He had hoped to see her on the street.

It had been his duty after their parents had died, as the elder brother, to take over their role. It was family, a duty rooted in something stronger than the Catholic duty the Spanish had imposed in their five hundred year domination of the Philippines, something stronger than the old Malay sense of belonging – it was a combination of the two: the huddling together of the tribes in a harsh world and the intimacy, the haven of belonging in a country run by strangers.

Children, at their adulthood, kissed their parents' hands in gratitude for all that had been done for them. With the death of parents, the younger children kissed the hand of the elder brother or sister who had given up all his opportunities in life to ensure their own.

Marguerita would never have wanted him to give up all his own opportunities.

In a way – in a way he understood without words and he feared was unforgivable – she had never forgiven him for not giving up those opportunities.

The first time he had done a favor for someone the man had given him a small, second-hand Volkswagen motor car. Its acquisition had been easily explained. The man who had given it to him drove a BMW. Now, in his own BMW, Lanternero had reached a position in the world where he did not have to explain anything.

He had moved up. The big fish for whom you did favors turned little fish into bigger fish. You became one of them, adopted their class and, below you, none of the little fish on their way up, dared ask you questions.

It was *Pakikisama* – the sense of fellowship to your own. You went along with, not your own, but the people you wanted to be your own – the people who had the BMW's. *Utang Na Loob*: that was the other side of it. It meant 'To Oblige', to pay your debt of honor.

It meant once you had begun you could never stop. It meant, without mitigation, you were corrupt.

It meant, like the man who ran Hipogrifo AG you had loyalty, you were loyal, you did and had done for you – it meant, you were owned.

She had not wanted him to give up his future for her and he, even now, did not want her to kiss his hand in gratitude.

All he wanted now was to see her.

By him, on the passenger seat of his car, he had a folded computer print-out. It was his excuse. He could give that to her and she would have to stop and see him.

She had not seen him.

She had not come.

He had rung the number like a schoolboy, ready to put the receiver down the moment he heard her voice, but the phone had rung and rung and rung and there had been no one there.

He thought he might see her on the street.

He had never married and with both his parents dead, he was alone.

When he had been poor – the first time when he had taken the old, easily explained, second-hand little car, he had thought that that was all there was to life.

He was forty-four years old and nobody, nobody in the world other than the people he did favors for or the people who owed him favors gave a damn whether he lived or died.

He glanced down at the folded computer print-out on the seat next to him.

He had been waiting there, alone, all afternoon hoping to see her and she had not come.

It was almost five o'clock in the evening. In an hour, it would be dark.

He did not want her to kiss his hand in gratitude. He merely wished –

He merely wanted.

He was alone.

He was always alone.

Starting the car, he stubbed out the cigarette in the ashtray and, glancing one last time down the street and not seeing her, not knowing what he thought, he began to drive carefully back towards the city.

According to the American astronomer Carl Sagan, before the sun finally went supernova a million years from now, the world would see one last, perfect sunset.

The next day the bottom would definitely fall out of the Manila tourist business.

Far across the bay, behind the grey mists and coast of Bataan, as the tourists on the Sunset Cruises ferries clicked away with their cameras to the strains of *Amazing Grace* piped through amplifiers from the engine rooms, the day was ending.

Far across the bay, as Elizalde watched from his parked car in Reclamation Road on the shoreline, it was sinking as a great suffused ball of yellow fire, its light and rays spreading across the grey water and lighting it with phosphorescence and shadows, silver darts and flashes of light, lines and mosaics and patterns of shade and color and stillness.

It was ending. The heat of the long, long tropical day was ending and soon there would be the cool fragrance of night. Moving behind the hills and mountains, as if it touched the sea, the light exploded out into an aurora borealis and, then, in layers, shimmering in a sudden pyrotechnic display, it broke loose and cascaded light and fire across the entire horizon and turned it deep purple.

Out beyond Bataan, far out where the sun sank, there was the South China Sea. There was the darkness of night, Laos, Thailand, Burma: there was the continuity of a million sunsets and a million years – there was the end of the day.

All over the bay, the tourist boats and ferries were beginning to turn on their lights. There was no sound but the gentle throbbing of their engines. The sun, striking the sea far beyond the mountains, cascaded last light into the sky.

Agoncillo, Tolentino, the two Royares brothers, Nitz of the Cock Hospital and the girl at the window of the jeweller's shop – he realised he did not even know her name – there would be no more days for them.

The light was going. In his car, all of Vargas' photostated copies of Agoncillo's papers on his knee, Elizalde put his hands to his face and drew a breath.

Newcomer to Wall Street, Mendez Beer Holdings (Philippines) is offering a major challenge to the confidence of US investors with the announcement of a share issue of 10.3 million dollars to expand into the South American and Caribbean markets.

It was a photostat of a clipping from the financial pages of *The New York Times*.

It was nothing. It was about Mendez Beer. There was a drawing of the Mendez logo to one side of the article, but it was all full of sharebrokers' projections and advice to investors and there was nothing there in it for him.

Agoncillo, Tolentino, the two Royares brothers: they had been fishermen. They had been smugglers. They owned Mendez. Mendez was merely leased to Mendez Beer through Hipogrifo AG or some invisible holding company and there was nothing there in it for him.

Question: What do Charles de Caserne Sidi-bel-Abbes, Charles de Caserne Casablanc et Hanoi, Charles de Caserne II, III, IV, Terrible Tran of Saigon Rex and Battling Mendez (Juan Carlos de Manila) all have in common?

It was the lead-in to a story from *Fortune* magazine called 'Mendez Beer – Giving Us US Investors A Solid Leg To Stand On?'

Answer: They were all fighting cocks, they all had one leg, and, if Macklin, Abrahams and deSoto, sharebrokers of this city, get their way, they will raise for the present lessee of their descendant, Battling Mendez of Philippines cockfighting fame, a cool 10.3 million dollars of welcome expansion capital.

They had all been smugglers and drug runners a long time ago when they had been young. It was too long ago. They had been respectable for years. They drove Mercedes and they spoke to men with quiet voices.

Elizalde, in the last dying light, turned through the photostated pages. He had extracted only the ones that dealt with Mendez. They were all of the same style, all planted and probably paid for articles in small investors' journals or rare large stories in prestigious magazines like *Fortune* or newspapers like *The Times* and there was nothing about Hipogrifo AG or any of the dead men in any of them.

There was nothing.

In 1980 Mendez Beer celebrated its fourth full profit making year in a row. From a small, loss making brewery in the seventies, the expanded and revamped company, riding on the back of perhaps the most famous avian Philippino the country had ever produced, Battling Mendez, has turned a loss of Pesos three million to a stunning profit of US dollars 16 million a year with an annual turnover of some US dollars 50 million . . .

It was from *The Times* of Manila.

There was nothing, not a word, about any one of the dead men or Hipogrifo AG.

There was a wad of clippings, rough drafts from ads and planted stories, there were pictures and drawings of Mendez, there was part of the US prospectus Agoncillo must have had a hand in writing, letters from Macklin, Abrahams and deSoto concerning the listing of Mendez Beer on the US stock exchange, but about all the things he wanted, there was nothing.

The light was going. Behind the mountains of Bataan, the sky was darkening and all the silhouettes of the ferries and boats on the bay, twinkling with light. Along the shoreline around the crescent of the bay all the street lights in the parks and buildings were coming on.

They had been fishermen.

They had been drug smugglers and probably gun runners.

. . . a congenital hereditary feature of unknown origin, all the birds back to their great progenitor Le Capitaine Danjou de Camerone, 1863, have fought with one wooden or ivory leg or, in the case of the latest in the line, the company's logo, Battling Mendez, sometimes with a leg of solid eighteen carat gold . . .

It was a handout from Pegasus Advertising marked US Distribution Only. It had probably been written by Agoncillo. He knew his market. At the bottom of the article he had pencilled in with a question mark: *'The beer for rednecks? Cockfighting illegal in US. Forbidden fruits line?'* Wall Street knew its customers. They would have raised the millions in record time. The next move would be the US market itself.

The bay had darkened. He had to turn on the light in the car to see. He read on. There were no more letters from the sharebrokers and, done out as a poster, as an appendix or an insert to the prospectus, pictures of Mendez opening supermarkets and buildings, a photograph of Mendez at a levee with the President being held carefully by a uniformed *aide de camp*, projections of Mendez's earnings potential as an advertising personality and, almost as an afterthought, a list of his championship wins over the last five years he had been fighting.

The light on the bay was gone.

Elizalde turned back a page and then another. Mendez had been fighting five years.

He reread the story on Mendez Beer.

The beer company had had its losses turned around four years ago.

They had been smugglers, drug runners ten years ago.

Ten years ago, Mendez would not have even been born.

He turned back a page. He felt something tingle in his back. He turned back, looking through the photostats.

Danjou.

He had heard the name somewhere else, before.

Capitaine Danjou de Camerone, 1863. The gushing story gave the impression – had meant to give the impression – that the line of gamebirds, like some royal European house, stretched back through Mendez in an unbroken succession to 1863 and the mists of time. He looked through the article and even found that phrase. He knew the name. Going back, he began tracing the names of all the birds through the disorganised story with his finger. The photostat in the poor light was yellow. It was as if his finger traced back through old, cracked handwritten documents for news of a treasure ship.

It did. That was exactly what he was doing.

Mendez, Juan Carlos de Manila (Battling Mendez) – he began at the present . . .

Terrible Tran (Tran of Saigon Rex) . . .

It was the wrong way. He was going backwards. He felt his mouth go dry. Out on the bay there was only the gentle throbbing of the ferries' engines and, somewhere out there, like Sagan's dying sun, there was the echo of ten years ago and men who had had only a boat and, suddenly, suddenly with the acquisition of Mendez, had had a fortune.

Le Capitaine Danjou de Camerone, 1863. It was the name of Mendez's ancestor, the first name of his pedigree. He counted. Between him and the present bird, the story – complete, no doubt worked out exactly and planted and verified by Agoncillo himself – listed six other birds.

Fighting cocks lived only ten years at the most. They were bred at age five.

Danjou 1863. It referred to a bird, not born in 1863, but

probably born in, at most 1949. It, like all the birds that followed it, had only one leg.

Elizalde said suddenly, 'Oh my God!'

Le Capitaine Danjou de Camerone, 1863 had had only one hand. He knew who he was.

Charles de Caserne, Sidi-bel-Abbes.

He estimated. He worked out the year. 19 . . . 54 . . .

They bred them at five years old because, in the ring, they died early.

Charles de Caserne . . . it meant *barracks* . . . Casablanc et Hanoi . . . 1959 . . .

And the next, Charles de Caserne, number II . . . 19 . . . 64 . . .

Charles de Caserne, IV . . . 1967 . . . Charles V . . . 1971 and then . . .

He knew who Danjou had been. He knew what the name commemorated.

. . . and then . . .

. . . and then Tran of Saigon Rex (Terrible Tran) . . . 1973 . . . it had to be. And then . . .

. . . and then, suddenly after generations of Charles and a single Tran of Saigon there had been . . .

There had been Mendez.

Elizalde said softly, 'Oh my God!'

He looked out into the darkness of the bay.

Danjou had been the hero of the Mexican campaign. He had been a soldier during the time of Maximilian, a soldier for the French who had held off an Army of Mexican revolutionaries with only a small band of soldiers and died in the process.

All his own people had ever found of him after the battle had been his wooden hand.

His own people . . .

His own people, to this day, kept the hand in a place of honor in a Museum in France.

His own people were the French Foreign Legion. Before him, on his knees in the pedigree, that was what Mendez' progenitors had been. Casablanca, Hanoi, Saigon, it was a history of the Legion.

Hanoi, Charles de Caserne III and IV and V, Charles de Caserne, Sidi-bel-Abbes, Terrible Tran of Saigon Rex . . . it was a history.

It was a history of the French. It was a history of French colonialism.

Then suddenly, in 1973, the name had changed to Tran, to an Asian name, to . . .

To Tran of Saigon.

It was a history of Viet Nam.

Elizalde said softly in Spanish, 'Madre . . .'

Agoncillo, Tolentino, the two Royares brothers . . . ten, eight years ago, Mendez had not even been born. Ten, eight years ago, they had not had Mendez.

What they had had been Terrible Tran of Saigon.

What they had had was treasure.

What they had had when he bred and they could give his descendant a Philippino-Spanish name had been . . . Mendez.

He knew how they had got him.

Agoncillo, Tolentino, the two Royares brothers, he knew, ten years ago on their boat, what they had been.

He knew who they were and who it was who was murdering them.

He sat in the faint light in his car gazing out across the darkness of the bay.

Agoncillo, Tolentino, the Royares brothers . . .

What they had been, on their little boat, had been . . .

Pirates.

'Tomorrow.'

In Room 333, on the phone to America, he waited.

There was a silence on the line.

Softly, he heard a woman sobbing.

The man in Room 333 said again in a whisper, 'Tomorrow.'

He put his hand to his face and listened.

Through the window of his room, he could see the bay and, beyond it, there was the sea.

At the phone, with the sun going down, he felt the coldness.

He listened.

He could not speak for the tightness in his chest.

173

His hand shook.

He felt tears on his face.

He stood for a long time with the telephone in his hand saying nothing until, at last, the hotel switchboard operator came on the line and asked him if his call had been successful.

The man in Room 333 said in a voice so faint she had to strain to hear him, 'Yes,' and, at his request, the operator disconnected him and the phone in his hand went suddenly dead.

The man in Room 333, putting the receiver back gently into its cradle, looked out through the window at the sea.

It was almost, for him, final, terrible night.

Out there, out there in the darkness, in one awful moment on a phantom-filled sea, amid the shrieks and cries of their victims, they had taken one of the boats of the boatpeople escaping from the Communists after the fall of Saigon.

They had expected gold and money and perhaps ivory and jewellery.

They had found instead – or perhaps as well – Terrible Tran of Saigon.

They would have killed anyway, but they had killed for it. They had found its pedigree. One of them, Agoncillo perhaps – or the man with the quiet voice who had financed them – had realised what they had found.

The Vietnamese boatpeople, some of them anyway, had had relatives in America.

The prospectus had reached America and one of them, one of the relatives, seeing the pictures, reading the pedigree . . .

Out there, in the darkness, after the fall of Viet Nam, the pirates had turned the South China Sea into a liquid Auschwitz.

It was pitch black where he sat in his car on Reclamation Road. None of the street lamps had been connected. It was a newly filled-in area of the bay. He sat in darkness.

Out there, whole families had died in darkness.

They had been pirates.

They had been torturers.

They had been . . .

They had been stupid.

They had – if you knew how to read it – written down everything they had done in newspapers where some of the lucky ones on the boats had escaped to and now, somewhere, somewhere in the city, there was someone who had come back, who had never known what had happened to his relatives – *but who knew now* –

There was someone out there who had come back from the dead, from the sea, from safety – there was someone out there who, like the Israelis with memories that never faded – had come back from the dead or the near dead to kill the killers of his family.

The night was dark.

Somewhere, somewhere in the city, piece by piece, without haste, burning with terrible vengeance, that person planned his next move.

17

'Yes, sir.'

In his office the General, his elbow on his desk, his hand to his forehead, said with his eyes closed, 'I understand that, Minister, yes, sir. I'm sorry you walked in through the main entrance of Headquarters at the very moment that he – ' He said, 'Yes, sir. Ambrosio, Detective Sergeant, that's right, yes, sir.' He had been the Commanding Officer of the Western Police District for less than a year. Each day, at his desk, he still wore his Army uniform and ribbons. He had been a transport officer. 'No, sir, I do not approve of my men entering by the main entrance in that condition as the Minister For Security drives up in his car with his advisers, no, sir. No, sir, and certainly not in that condition.'

He listened.

'Yes, sir, I would say that "vile, stinking wretch" described his appearance adequately.' He listened again. 'No, sir, a baseball hat with the words MANILA POLICE on it is not recommended half uniform for our detectives. Yes, sir, I know Security has taken over the subversive killings and I have Lieutenant Elizalde waiting downstairs to be disciplined for failure to check in.' He said quickly, 'Yes, sir, yes sir.'

He said desperately, 'He's a cultural minority. I'm sure he didn't really mean to handcuff the Assistant Minister of Works and shove him roughly into a police van with thirty of his common workmen!' He said, 'Yes, sir. No, I didn't see Detective Sergeant Bontoc myself, but I am certain he was filthy and disgusting with unwashed earth!' He said, 'Yes, sir, yes, sir – yes, they're all part of the same team.' He said, 'I believe, in fact, the stench on Detective Sergeant Ambrosio was of durian – '

He said again, 'Yes, sir.'

It was 8.51 a.m. by his wall clock. Elizalde and Bontoc and Ambrosio had been waiting downstairs in the library conference room over an hour. He was going to have their heads.

The General, sweating in his tight uniform in the dark, heavy room, said again, 'Yes, sir. Yes, sir, I understand the situation perfectly – '

' "Forty-six Legionnaires fought the Battle of Camerone in Mexico on April 30th, 1863. The date is still considered sacred by the Legion and observed every year. It was even observed during the Legion's bloody defense of Dien Bien Phu when its position was overrun by the forces of General Giap during the Indo-China War in 1954." ' Elizalde, reading from a page in his notebook said, 'I roused someone from the French Embassy late last night and he read it to me from some sort of comic book called *l'Histoire Illustré* from which, apparently the French all learn their history.' He was pacing in the library conference room, glancing at the rows of leather bound books bought by the yard by the Department or some interior decorator that, from their titles, would tell him nothing. ' "The legionnaires withstood assault after assault by the two thousand Mexicans besieging them until only six were still alive. Out of ammunition, they then made a final bayonet charge against the enemy. Of that six, three survived and three were taken prisoner." ' Elizalde said, ' "Of the others, the garrison, like the Spartans at the pass, they were not conquered, merely killed. The officer in charge, Capitaine Danjou lost his wooden hand in the battle. It now rests in a place of honor in the Legion's Hall of Fame in Aubagne near Marseilles in France." ' He looked over at Ambrosio and Bontoc sitting at the long conference table in the room.

Ambrosio was not listening. He was looking down at the tabletop, feeling suicidal.

Elizalde said, 'The first bird on the list was named after Danjou. Each of the birds, in line, had a congenital defect. Each of them, like Danjou, had a wooden limb.'

Ambrosio said, 'Then why the hell didn't it fall over at birth?' In everyone's case, in the long run, if you stank and you were seen by a couple of hundred people assaulting prisoners, it would have been the kindest thing to happen.

Elizalde said, 'The legs were withered.' He looked at Bontoc. Bontoc had troubles of his own. 'The legs were withered at birth, they were probably enough to get around on – probably enough to give the birds the spunk and edge to fight – and then when they began to fight, the withered leg was probably lopped off surgically and replaced.' Elizalde said, 'The line of birds travelled with the Legion backwards and forwards between its bases in Morocco and Viet Nam probably two or three times and then, when the French were heavily involved in the first Indo-China War, stayed there with them until they were defeated, then probably fell into the hands of a local French ex-legionnaire *Colon* who – '

Bontoc said as a matter of fact, 'The French don't go in for cockfighting.'

'The Belgians do.'

'The French Foreign Legion is French.'

'The French Foreign Legion is foreign.' Elizalde said, 'And then, after the Americans evacuated Saigon before the Communists took over, the bird, with its name changed to Tran – probably the name of the handler or someone local who had taken it over – then the bird – ' He looked hard at them. They were defeated. Elizalde said roughly, 'And then it was put on a boat and ten or twenty or thirty people including the bird's owner, tried to make the voyage to the Philippines.' He said before Bontoc could comment, 'The Philippinos do go in for cockfighting.' It was 8.45 a.m. They had been waiting for the General for over an hour. Elizalde, still pacing, said, 'Between the years 1975 and 1980 the total number of people who tried to escape from Viet Nam by sea totalled over three hundred thousand. God alone knows how many tried to make it here, but so far, only ten thousand have been taken ashore alive.'

Bontoc said softly, 'Felix – '

'The rest either drowned or were killed by pirates!' Elizalde said softly, 'I saw them. Last night, late, I walked back from the Embassy along the shoreline and I saw them out there in the darkness.' He looked hard into Bontoc's face. 'I heard them. I heard the children and the gunshots and the screams.' He saw Ambrosio look up, 'I heard the rats on the sand where the bodies had floated in and I heard the lapping of the water as their raped and mutilated shadows rolled over and over with the tide. I heard them. I saw them.' His hands were shaking. Elizalde said, 'Out there, in that terrible darkness – out there, lost, hopeless, running in leaking, sinking boats, I saw them.' He said, 'The two Royares brothers, Tolentino, Agoncillo: they were pirates. They came across them – they found them on their radar on their warm, comfortable bridge – they saw the huddled rags of people and heard their cries for help – they saw dead, starved old men and women, children with scurvy and scabs and death in their faces – and they machine-gunned them, killed them, raped them, looted them and then, leaving no trace, leaving their lives hanging and unrecorded, in that moment sentencing their relatives who had escaped on other boats and been successful, to an eternity of suffering and sorrow, they sank the boats where they found them!' In Quintero's storeroom in the basement of the Coast Guard there had been mounds and bundles of clothing, shoes, debris and bits and pieces of rotting wood, nameplates and numbers. They had been the flotsam the Coast Guard had picked up from the sea. Elizalde said, 'They fell on them like vultures. They picked them clean. They took everything they had and then, if there were any survivors, they took all their dignity and their hope and then they killed them.'

There was a silence.

Elizalde said, 'One of them – one of the survivors from another boat – someone now rich and successful, *someone who can afford it* – now, someone has come back to kill them!'

There was no sound in the room.

'Someone rich who saw the prospectus for Mendez Beer –

who saw Mendez, who read his history – someone who knew – and one by one he is killing all the people who killed his family!' Elizalde said, 'He's a Vietnamese. He's here.'

Bontoc said, 'Bald Head?'

'He's Philippino.' Ambrosio, shaking his head, said, 'No, if you had that sort of money you'd employ someone.' He looked at Elizalde, 'If he's Vietnamese – ' He asked, 'How do you know he came here from America?'

'Because that was the only place the prospectus was issued!'

' – then he wouldn't know Manila. Then he'd employ Bald Head.' Ambrosio, wrinkling his forehead said, 'Hipogrifo. You said the company they formed was called Hipogrifo AG. If the Vietnamese was from America, how would he know about a company formed in Switzerland or Liechtenstein or somewhere?' He asked, 'How would he know the names of the pirates? The cockfighting people maybe, but he got that man Agoncillo in an advertising agency.' He was thinking fast. It didn't make sense. It was all questions. Ambrosio asked, 'If he just hired some sort of local killer, how come the local killer can get his hands on, not only pistols, but rifle grenades and – '

Bontoc said, 'And plastic explosives and wire them up to a telephone and splice tape and – ' Bontoc said, 'Whoever it is, he isn't some sort of stupid, uneducated dumbo.' Neither was he. Bontoc said, 'They want to send me back to Bontoc!' He was on his feet. 'I like Bontoc! At least I can understand what people say!' Bontoc, tapping his mouth with his knuckles, said quickly, 'How? If all you say is true, Felix, how did he find out all their names?'

'I don't know.'

'Are there more? Who was Agoncillo talking to on the phone?'

'I don't know.'

Ambrosio said, 'There must have been more. If these people were all, in theory, only fishermen then there must have been someone directing them, financing them, organising them – ' SPROOG/IGLL. It taught you you needed leadership. He, obviously, didn't have it. He, obviously, at the end of his career, didn't care. There was always the taxi-driving business. Ambrosio, looking to Bontoc, said, 'Baptiste, who? Who directed them? And *how*? How did the Vietnamese find out about any of them?'

'He asked someone?' Bontoc said, 'Felix?'

Elizalde said, 'Yes.'

'Who?' Ambrosio said, 'Who did he ask who would know? He came here – he got off the plane at Manila International Airport – and he – if he reads prospectuses he's a businessman for the love of God, not a professional killer – and, like a businessman, like someone with a trained business mind, someone who's done courses, he located someone who would know – he went to the kernel of the problem – and he – ' He looked at Bontoc. Bontoc was staring hard at Elizalde. Ambrosio said impatiently, 'Who? Do you know? Who did he ask?'

Bontoc said, 'Yes.' He looked at Elizalde. Elizalde was waiting.

Ambrosio said, 'Who? Who did he ask?' He hadn't failed SPROOG and IGLL: he had passed. What he had failed was life. Well, that was life. Ambrosio, realising, said suddenly, 'Felix! Felix! Who did *you* ask?'

He had asked Quintero.

Elizalde said softly, 'Quintero. I asked Quintero.' He saw them waiting. Elizalde said, 'I asked a man whose life they had ruined.' It was so simple. It was the way it had been done. Elizalde said, 'I asked the people who were professionals about it all. I asked Commander Teo Quintero at the Metro Manila – ' He said suddenly, 'Oh, my God!' He heard for an instant, Nitz's voice. He said again, 'Oh my God! I asked Commander Teo Quintero of the Metro Manila Headquarters of the Coast Guard!' He had had qualifying patches on his uniform. 'I asked an electronics and weapons officer of the Metro Manila Coast Guard who knew all their names and who had followed their progress day by day because they had ruined his life!' He said, aghast, 'I asked *Quintero!*'

'Yes, sir, I know it concerns Mendez Beer! Yes, sir, I realise – '

In his office, the General sweating heavily, said desperately, 'Yes, sir, I do know whose influence got me this posting! Yes, sir, I know my military career was at an end. Yes, sir, I – ' He was going red in the face. There was a limit. The General said suddenly, 'Yes. I wrote the memo to Sergeant Bontoc explaining line by line that he was in the park merely to – ' The General said, 'Yes, he can read! He's got a better education than you have! I wrote it because I was told to write it by – ' The General said, 'I think Elizalde is a good man and I – ' The General said, 'Yes, I realise the situation!' The General, nodding, exploding, holding himself in check, not succeeding, his voice rising, said over and over again, 'Yes! Yes! *Yes, Minister – !*'

Elizalde said, 'Bald Head! Quintero arranged Bald Head and turned him loose for money! He was the source. Somehow, he must have known, or must have suspected that they – that they were the ones. Maybe he even had the actual ship's nameplate there among all his rubbish in the basement. He must have known there was no way it could be proven in a court of law because there was no way he had been able to prove what they had done to him in a court of law and he – '

Ambrosio said, 'What had they done to him?'

'They set off a bomb on one of their boats as he and two of his ratings sailed it back to Manila. It was carrying stolen mercury from the mines here probably to Borneo for transhipment to Europe or America. It killed both the ratings and nearly killed him.' Elizalde said, 'He was the source. When the Vietnamese came to him he had all the information, all the weapons, the hatred, the need for money. He must have seen his chance and he took it, and he arranged Bald Head. The untraceable .45 automatic, the military ball cartridges, the Lee Enfield rifle from the Malayan Emergency and a French rifle grenade, the plastic explosive: they're all things he would have had pass through his storeroom from captured smuggling boats or smugglers – all he had to do was lose them in the paperwork!' Elizalde said, 'He's going nowhere. The Coast Guard is trying to get rid of him without a pension. He arranged a little pension for himself! *He arranged Bald Head!*'

Ambrosio said, 'What are the two bangs? The firecrackers and the mousetrap percussion thing and the – '

'It's a devil scaring ceremony.' Bontoc, his eyes narrowed,

said tightly, 'They have it in Bontoc animistic religion. It's probably Annamese. It probably goes back a long time.' He looked a little embarrassed. Bontoc said, 'As each of the men who killed his family was himself killed, the bangs were to frighten his soul off the path to Heaven and take it straight to Hell.' He went red.

Vargas had said, 'My hatred for him is immortal.' The hatred of the Vietnamese for the killers of his family had run deeper. With the two explosions moments before they had been killed and their souls had fled from their bodies, he had consigned them to everlasting fire, to Hell, to perdition, to limbo. Ballistics had said the mousetrap detonator had been a terrorist weapon. Quintero, like all serving officers in the Armed Forces, had been trained in counter-terrorism. He had been trained to know how the terrorist devices worked.

Bontoc, still embarrassed, said to no one, 'I read it in *The Golden Bough*. I don't know if they still do it in Bontoc these days. I read it as part of my Anthropology major . . .'

Ambrosio said, 'Why can't it be him? If he's so good – if he's got all this equipment – why can't it be Quintero himself?'

'He rang Royares at the Cock Hospital.' Elizalde was not listening. 'He rang Mang Paulo at the Cock Hospital and told him who he was. He told him he was from the Metro Manila Headquarters of the Coast Guard. That was why Paulo was so frightened. He didn't give his name. He probably only spoke to him for a second because Paulo thought I was him. He probably told Paulo he had proof of their activities years ago and that unless Paulo came up with some bribe money – ' Elizalde said, marvelling, 'It was him. It was all so simple and so neat for him and it suited his own purposes as if it had been tailored for them. It was him. When the Vietnamese told him what he had come for he must have thought God had answered his prayers! And then Bald Head – '

'What are you talking about?'

Ambrosio's eyes were on Bontoc. Ambrosio said, 'There's no Bald Head. *He's* Bald Head. Quintero.'

'He can't be.'

'He can.' He was smiling. He felt sorry for Bontoc. He was short and ugly, but in his own way he wasn't such a bad fellow.

He was bright red. He could get embarrassed too. He wasn't Superman either. He, like Ambrosio and Elizalde, when the General came down, was also for the chop. Ambrosio said, 'I did a course too. Unlike either of you highly educated people, I was a patrolman. I had to learn how to scrape people off the sidewalk and what to do in typhoons and floods and landslips and, and – and when disaster struck.' He had been, like every other patrolman in the world, the poor schmuck who had had to know everything. Ambrosio said, 'I did a course in civil defence. I did a course in demonstrator pacification. I did a course in dealing with the anti-pollution lobby. I did a course in – ' Ambrosio said, 'Chemhaz, I know exactly what happens if trucks carrying dangerous chemicals explode in the street.' No one looked at him with loathing. They were listening. He had never thought tertiary education taught people to do that. The university demonstrators he had had to club in anti-Government demonstrations had never listened to him. Ambrosio said, 'Mercury poisoning. The ingestion of toxic mercury vapor.' He was quoting. It was how he hoped to succeed: by learning all the words and hoping to God they fitted the situation, 'Mercury Vapor Ingestion: compare with the effects of radiation or chemotherapy. Symptoms: renal failure, general disability, weakening of the heart and lung tissue, possible brain cell degeneration and – ' He looked at Elizalde. He asked, 'What does Quintero look like? Is he heavily bearded and young-looking, no grey in his hair?'

Elizalde said, 'Yes.' He listened. It was Ambrosio's finest moment. Felix Elizalde, who he had always wanted to be like, listened. Elizalde said curiously, 'Jesus-Vincente?'

Ambrosio said, still quoting, 'And alopecia.' He saw Bontoc look at him. Ambrosio said, 'Baldness. *Baldness!* It takes time, years maybe, but finally after all the hair on the affected part of the body has come out in tufts what you're left with is complete, utter, total alopecia – hair loss – baldness!' Ambrosio said, 'It's a wig.' He was almost going to tell Elizalde he should have noticed from the lack of grey in the man's hair. Elizalde was an educated man. He knew he should have noticed. He saw in Elizalde's eyes, admiration. He would die rather than tell him he should have noticed. Ambrosio said,

'Baldness. Total, utter, complete baldness.' He said, 'In Ermita there's a prosthetic surgical supplier. It's the only one in town. I used to patrol by there each day. Ring them. Ask them.' SPROOG/IGLL, professional ruin and failure – it all meant nothing. It was his moment, the culmination of his life. Ambrosio, pointing to the phone books and the telephone on a small Spanish table near the bookshelves full of learning, said as an order to them both, 'Ring and find out. Ask them!' He said, grinning in terrible triumph, 'It's him! It's Quintero! *It's a wig!*'

It was a wig. Like the beard, it came off. In the front cab of the white Coast Guard van, Quintero in full battle dress, said with his eyes staring ahead towards the hill that led to Forbes Park and the rich, 'He's there. He lives up there. It's where the rich live in Manila. It's closed off – the entire suburb – and you need a pass to get through.' The Vietnamese from Room 333 in the Manila Hotel was dressed in an expensive tailored grey suit. He was not a young man. Only his eyes looked young and they burned with light. Quintero said, 'They'll let us through though. They're only private security guards and when they see the van and the uniform they won't dare stop us.' He said, smiling thinly, 'And you. They'll see the way you're dressed and they'll think you're from Forbes Park and they won't dare even speak to you.' He had a fully automatic M16 A1 rifle clipped to the dashboard. He touched at it and the spare magazines taped to it. Quintero asked, 'All right?'

He had rung his family in America before he had left the hotel. He had told them it was today. Gathered together in the house of the senior member of the family in San Diego – in his father's house – they would be waiting. The Vietnamese said quietly, 'And Mendez. "Battling Mendez" – I want that killed too.'

'OK.'

'It's important!'

The Vietnamese had a cigarette in his hand. He put it to his lips and drew in deeply on it. His hand was shaking. The Vietnamese said, 'I want it all, *all*, wiped out forever!'

'Yes.' Quintero had his hand on the key in the ignition. He

took it away and rubbed at his bald head. It was glistening lightly with sweat. Quintero said, 'Our aims are the same.'

There was a silence in the cab. It was, as if, briefly, the Vietnamese was praying. The Vietnamese said, not to Quintero, but to whoever he spoke to, 'We waited, we hoped, almost ten years. There is now so little left of what we were in Saigon.' He looked suddenly at Quintero with a bitter smile, 'All we have now is money.' He said, somehow to distance himself from it, 'You are being paid!' He looked hard at Quintero's face. He could read nothing there. The man merely waited.

The Vietnamese, shaking his head, his eyes full of tears, said, 'But, thank you. *Thank you!*'

In his office, Lanternero, sitting forward in his chair, took up the red striped file from his desk and opened it at the first page. He glanced up at the wall clock in front of him. It was exactly 9 a.m. He had spent the night alone at home, reading the contents of the file over and over.

The file had stamped across its red stripe 'INVESTIGATIVE SECTION MINISTRY OF FINANCE AND TAXATION. DEPUTY COMMISSIONER'S OFFICE NOT TO BE REMOVED'. He had mortgaged his soul to get it. He had got it easily. Maybe the Deputy Commissioner, once, had mortgaged his soul to Lanternero and it was merely a payback.

Lanternero, at 9 a.m., didn't know.

He didn't care.

The title page in the file, also red lined, had stamped across it 'RESTRICTED INFORMATION. NOT TO BE ACTED UPON'.

The file contained only three foolscap typed pages.

On each page there was a stamp reading 'UNREVIEWABLE. NOT TO BE USED'.

It was a list of names and addresses.

It was a list of names and addresses of the directors of Hipogrifo AG.

On the last page there was a single typed line.

It read 'CROSS REFERENCE MENDEZ BEER

COMPANY (PHILIPPINES)'.

It had stamped across it, across the words themselves, 'DO NOT UNDER ANY CIRCUMSTANCES COMPROMISE'.

In his office Lanternero glanced at the clock.

9.01 a.m.

Closing the file, he picked up his telephone to ring the Western District Police Headquarters to locate Elizalde.

In his office, the General shouted down the line, 'I think you're missing the essential point! The essential point is that, whether it happened to be real or not, people who offered to buy it thought that what the mugger was selling was an illegal concealable firearm!' The General said, 'I would have thought, from my limited experience as a serving soldier, not making little notes in dossiers about illegal concealable firearms, but trying to avoid having my soldiers shot dead by them, that that was a serious offence that might excuse someone inconveniencing the grand entrance of a civil servant into a government building – however grand that civil servant might be or however elevated his position!' He barely paused for breath, 'And as for Bontoc, the Assistant Minister of Works ordered his thirty men – thirty men, I might remind you who were not on the staff of the Ministry of Works, but vagrants and scum he picked up on the streets of Tondo – he ordered his men to bury my officer alive!' He had had enough. He glanced at the wall clock. 9.03. He had been on the phone for almost an hour. The General, not listening to what the man said on the other end of the line, said clearly, 'Fuck Security.' There was no anger in his voice.

The General said quietly and calmly, 'Fuck you.' The General said, 'Do what you like.' He still had his Army pension. The General, going ice cold, said, 'I don't have shares in Mendez Beer the way you do so maybe I'm not so anxious to protect their interests.'

The General said, suddenly shouting again, 'No, sir! No, sir! No, Minister – what *I* have . . . I EARNED!'

It was 9.03.

It was time.

In the van, drawing a breath, the Vietnamese, nodding to Quintero as the man waited with his hand on the ignition key, said decisively, 'Do it! Let's go!' He ordered the man, 'Now, Go! Let's do it! *GO!*'

18

He slammed the phone down.

The General, shaking with anger, shouted to the walls, 'You go to Hell! You get the reports, you get the disciplinary action, you get the case through channels! You and Security, you and the whole fucking system – *you go to Hell!*'

He had heard the sounds on Agoncillo's telephone before: the two explosions. They were the sounds of a Bofors gun. It was the sort of gun the Coast Guard used to fire ceremonial salutes to naval ships or dignitaries entering or leaving port. Quintero had been an electronics and weapons officer: he had recorded the sounds or, like the tape of the evangelist, gotten hold of a recording of them. In the background, behind the Duty Officer's voice at Coast Guard Headquarters he could hear sirens and the sound of men running. There was a sort of drill or ceremony on. Elizalde, shouting to make himself heard to the man, demanded, 'Quintero! Commander Teo Quintero.'

'Not here.' The man was young with a clipped, practised American accent. He sounded like the sort of career officer who, if like all Philippinos, he had not been a Catholic, would have been a born-again Baptist. The Duty Officer, wanting to dismiss him, said smartly, 'Sorry. We've got an Entering Harbor alert drill on here this morning. All the lines to the offices are closed except for emergencies.'

'What do you mean, he's not there?'

'Gone. Not here.' The Duty Officer said, sighing, 'This is Lieutenant Navarro, Duty Officer, I'm empowered to speak for the Service. We've got a drill on.'

'Get me your Commanding Officer.'

'I can't do that, sir.'

'Then his assistant.'

'His assistant is supervising the drill.' Navarro, holding the phone away from his mouth for a moment, said to someone, 'Yes, sir, thirty seconds.' He said to get rid of Elizalde, 'We've got an Entering Harbor alert drill on from Command. I have to clear this line.'

'Tell me where Quintero is!' He was a shore officer. He ran a basement full of debris. He was never alerted. Elizalde said as an order, 'Put me through to Quintero's office.'

'He's not here. He isn't here. He isn't in the building.' There was a pause as if Navarro, quickly, irritably, glanced at the orders of the day. 'Commander Quintero is no longer with the Service.' He sounded surprised himself, 'Commander Quintero put in his papers last night.' He was quoting, 'No ceremony will be held.' Navarro said, 'I've never heard of Commander Quintero.'

'He, like Phlebas the Phoenician, was once as handsome and as tall as you!'

'What?'

'Where the hell is he?'

'He's put in his papers. He resigned last night. He finished service at midnight last night.' He was still reading, 'For health reasons, Commander Quintero has resigned and intends to fly to the United States Pan Am flight number – ' Navarro said, 'Today. Noon today.' He said to Elizalde as if he had the answer, 'Was he sick? What was wrong with him?'

'Nothing.' Elizalde saw Bontoc and Ambrosio waiting. Elizalde said, 'You must know him!'

'I don't.' Navarro said, 'I've got problems of my own. I've got an alert on and I'm Duty Officer and I've got a Coast Guard vehicle missing and I – '

'What sort of vehicle?'

'A van. A Coast Guard van complete with weaponry.' He

was talking to the Police. Maybe they could – Navarro said, 'Do you want a description? It's – '

Elizalde said to Bontoc quickly, 'It's him. He's on the move. He's got a white Coast Guard van. It's today!' He saw Ambrosio staring at him. Elizalde said, 'Get out an APB now!' He ordered Bontoc, 'Armoury! I want some automatic weapons! Now!' He ordered Bontoc, '*Go!*' Elizalde turning back to the phone demanded, 'What rank are you?'

'Lieutenant I told – '

He tried it. Elizalde said, '*Quintero is the officer with the wig!*'

Navarro said, 'Him? Is that his name – Quintero?' He said as an epitaph to Quintero's last ten years, 'I never knew what his name was. The only name I ever heard anyone call him was Sinatra.' He said, embarrassed, 'I thought – ' He said, appalled, 'I even called him that once to his face myself. I thought it was his real name!'

It was him. It was today. It was happening now.

Navarro, all the efficiency and the accent gone from his voice, said abruptly, sounding as he no doubt was about twenty-two years old and a boy, said in horror, 'Sinatra – the wig . . . he was a brother officer! I – ' He said in terrible humiliation, 'I didn't know! I thought – '

The line had gone dead.

With the sirens howling in his ear Navarro, at his desk in the duty office, hoping no one had heard, said, 'Hullo! Hullo? Lieutenant Elizalde, are you still there?'

The phone rang. It was Lanternero. Lanternero said tightly, 'Felix? Listen . . . *listen!*'

Azcarraga Street, number eighteen, Forbes Park.

They had gone through the security cordon on the perimeter of the suburb with the sirens blaring. They had not been stopped. The guards had taken one look at the vehicle and the uniform of the man driving it and they had opened the barrier. They had seen the way the Vietnamese was dressed in the passenger seat as the van had swept by and then, to protect it, doing their jobs, they had closed the barrier behind them. In the van, Quintero, pointing, turning the vehicle at high speed in the middle of the street, said, 'There!' It was a high wall with a gateway set back a little from the sidewalk. The gate, blackened iron with devices of spears and chevrons cast into it, was wide open. Beyond it, through trees and stands of bamboo and high grass, was a driveway. He turned into it, switching off the siren, not slowing down. Quintero said, 'Here. He's here. There aren't any guards. He lives here alone. Just him. Just him and the bird.' His eyes were narrow, his hands, on the wheel, twisting and flexing themselves, 'I traced him. I traced him a little at a time over years and everything, everything leads to this house!' He glanced quickly at the Vietnamese next to him. Quintero said with hate. 'Fifteen acres. He has fifteen acres in the middle of Forbes Park with no guards – no nothing – and he doesn't even live here. He just comes here every day to make all his phone calls and he –' Quintero said, 'There's nothing, no security – nothing! All there is is one unlisted telephone line.' He was shaking his head, his breath coming in shallow gasps. Quintero said, 'I traced him. Bit by bit, a little at a time, I traced him here!' The driveway was overgrown, untended. Everywhere there seemed to be darkness and tall trees. Quintero, racing down the driveway in the four-wheel drive van, not talking to the Vietnamese, talking only to his ten years of pain and humiliation and failure and hatred, said, nodding ahead towards the house, 'There! The man we're both looking for and that damned, filthy, stinking, fucking bird Mendez, they're both in there now, waiting for us to kill them!'

'Hipogrifo AG.' On the phone Lanternero, reading tonelessly, said clearly, 'Directors Royares, P., Royares, F., Tolentino, E., Agoncillo, F. –' He paused for a long while, 'Silvero, L.' Lanternero said, 'It's from a file from the Investigative Section. It isn't in any of the computers, and it isn't listed under any of the directors' names. It's listed as a back-up file to Mendez Beer.' He paused. Lanternero said, 'Silvero, Leon Benedicto. The others are listed as directors, but Silvero is the one who runs it, the one who set it up.' There was a pause.

Elizalde said, 'Luis?'

'Silvero, Leon Benedicto.' His voice was strained. It was as if he had gone over it, rehearsed it and, whatever was said or done, he was going to say his lines and have them heard. Lanternero said, 'Background: marine; specialty: marine radar design and installation; hypothesis: drug smuggler and –'

Elizalde said, 'Pirate.'

' – pirate. Associates: Royares, F., Royares, P., Tolentino, E., Agoncillo, F.; reason for non action: *Mendez Beer*.

Elizalde said, 'Address?'

Lanternero said, 'Azcarraga Street, number eighteen, Forbes Park, Manila.' He sounded tight, controlled, on the edge. Lanternero said, 'I'm probably finished, Felix. I don't know. I've lost track of who owes what and who I protect and who protects me.' He said, again tightly, 'I don't know.' He said, 'Tell Marguerita . . . don't tell her anything.' He said, 'Royares, P., Royares, F., Tolentino, E., Agoncillo, F., Silvero, L. – and there's one more.' He asked, 'What did they do?'

'They hit the Vietnamese boatpeople. They hit a boat carrying people and they killed them.' He glanced around for Bontoc and Ambrosio coming back, but there was no one else in the room. Elizalde, dropping his voice, said, 'Luis . . .'

'And one other,' Lanternero, drawing a breath, said, 'And one other, with a question mark against it – one other name –'

'Luis –'

'Listen! Listen! One other name!' Lanternero, shouting down the line, the head of his wife's family, someone, someone important, someone to be listened to at least once – *at least once* – said in a shriek, '*Listen!*'

He was out there. He was out there at the side of the house, running. From the side of the van, the Vietnamese saw him running the length of the side of the house looking for the telephone and power lines. He saw him stop, look up, find the lines, he saw the gun come up and the sound of the safety being clicked forward and then – then he heard the firing.

There was no one about at the house. It was silent, like the grounds, dark and still. There was no one at the windows.

No one came.

They were inside.

No one came.

He saw Quintero, his eyes blazing, look up at the twisted and shot-through wires on the side of the wall.

No one came.

It was 9.21 a.m. and, in the whole world, there was no one but them, no time but this time and, somewhere out at sea, in memory, there was only a burned and ruined hulk floating on a bloody, vast ocean, with all his family lying like slaughtered animals in their own blood on the decks.

He saw Quintero come towards him with the Armalite in his hands.

He looked up at the house.

There was nothing, no movement, *nothing*.

They were waiting.

It was their time and they were waiting.

No one came.

He looked across to the front door. It was open. Inside, inside the big, dark, still house, he could see only darkness and stillness.

It was ordained, right.

It was time.

He saw Quintero pause, turn towards the front door and, with the rifle up, start to go in.

At the van, the Vietnamese had changed his clothes. He wore now a long saffron robe, the garb of a monk, a believer, a man dressed to talk with the gods and do their work.

He had a sealed bottle of clear liquid in his hands. It was purified water.

Breaking the seal and carefully rinsing his hands in the water and spreading it on his bare head, the Vietnamese closed his eyes for a moment in prayer.

He looked across to the temple, to the house.

There, inside, was the last of the evil.

Putting the empty water bottle onto the front seat of the van, the Vietnamese, folding his hands inside the sleeves of his robe to protect them, went slowly and carefully a single step at a time towards the house.

With his saffron robe moving gently with his step, he was like an apparition, a ghost.

He was someone come back.

He had come a very long way to keep an appointment.

He was keeping it a step at a time.

He felt no feelings at all: he merely was.

He was there.

He walked.

He was, at last, after a very, very long time . . .

He was Death.

'Where the hell are you going with those weapons?' In the corridor, the General, dazzling in his uniform, shouted at Ambrosio and Bontoc, 'You two! Where the hell do you think you're going?' He saw their faces. They had him. Whoever it was, they had him. The General, his heart pounding, demanded, 'Have you got him? Bald Head? Have you got him?'

'Yes sir!' Ambrosio, carrying an Uzi, going forward quickly, said, 'Yes, General, we –' He glanced quickly to Bontoc.

Bontoc also had a submachine gun. It was some sort of Swedish weapon. In his hands it looked huge. Bontoc said, 'Sir, we –'

They saw him, for the briefest of brief instants, smile. The General, halting Ambrosio with his hand, said, nodding, 'Jesus-Vincente . . . ' He looked hard at Bontoc and grinned, 'Baptiste . . .'

The General, shaking his head, said to move them, 'No, no, later, later!' He said as an order, 'Go! Go!'

He said softly under his breath, 'Thank God . . .!'

He saw them staring at him in disbelief.

He gave them an order.

The General, waving them off hard, said as a command, 'Go! Go! Take him! *Go!*'

On the phone Elizalde said in disbelief, 'What? What name? What was the name of the last one?' He had thought, perhaps, maybe, if the opportunity had presented itself, he might have let the Vietnamese, whoever he was, get away with his part in it.

He had thought maybe, perhaps, what was happening was, if not law, then . . .

Then justice.

He listened as Lanternero, this time, spelling it, gave him the last name on the list, the final name, the name with the question mark, the name that, indisputably, owned Battling Mendez, the name that indisputably . . .

He listened, shaking his head.

He had heard the name before.

He knew what it meant.

He saw Ambrosio and Bontoc come quickly into the room and, without taking the receiver from his ear, Elizalde ordered them, 'Car! Get a car! I'll meet you in the garage!' He said into the phone, still shaking his head, 'Luis . . .'

The line had gone dead. He had given the name and he was done. There was no more to say.

Justice . . .

It was not justice, not with that name.

What it was . . . was mass, wholesale, calculating *murder*.

19

'Ayo! Look at it!' In the car, Ambrosio, driving, said, 'Look at it, Felix!' It was not how the rich lived, it was how houses died. On the radio there were calls going out to patrols all over Manila and cars answering. In the front seat, cocking his PPK, Elizalde heard Patrolman Innocente's voice. He and Gil and Pineda were in Makati, coming fast. The SWAT team was being called up. On the radio, as the cars answered, there was the sound of sirens. The house was ruined, rotting, falling to pieces. Two storeyed, here and there the roof had collapsed and tiles and rafters hung down through smashed and filthy windows. Ambrosio, gunning the motor, not stopping, bumping and careering down the long overgrown driveway, said, 'Azcarraga Street, number eighteen – are you sure it's the right address?' He saw Bontoc pointing at something from the rear seat. It was a white Coast Guard van. He heard Bontoc cock his machine gun. Ambrosio, looking to Elizalde, demanded, 'Where? Where do we go in?'

He had been shot before. He felt the wound in his stomach paining in a long, terrible anticipating ache. 'There! Behind the truck!' The telephone and electricity lines were down. All around them were expended .223 brass Armalite cartridge cases. The front door was open, hanging loose on its hinges. He saw only darkness behind it. Elizalde, glancing up to the house, said shaking his head, 'It's too big! There are too many entrances and windows!' The car came to a halt behind the Coast Guard van. The van was empty. Elizalde getting out, gun in hand, ordered them, 'Stay together! Back-up's on the way! We'll stay together!'

The house had been let fall down, the steps to the long tiled veranda had rotted and sunk; the Federal style architecture collapsing at its weakest points into the soft earth. It was like some sort of ancient Southern antebellum mansion in the tropics, the creepers and lichen and moss taking over and swallowing it.

It was dead. The house had died and it was going back to its constituent parts and decomposing. The smell overpowered them. It came from the pores of the stone and the moss and the thick, heavy, wet air: it was the smell of putrefaction. There were insects; borers, white ants and termites. From the side of the house as they ran for the front door, clouds of mosquitos rose from stagnant pools by holes and smashed drainpipes. The insects were taking over and eating into the fabric of the house from inside the walls and honeycombing it like cancer. There were bird droppings everywhere: in the rusted and rotting drainpipes, on the veranda, in every crack and crevice in the roof and on the house itself.

They reached the door and the darkness. They smelled the damp, the running, oozing rust and filth and millions of insect eggs. There was no light. Once there had been a chandelier in the great entrance lobby to the house, but its supports had rotted in the heat and the decay and it hung down crazily from the ruined plaster. There was a stink, a vile smell of rotting paper. Everywhere in the gloom there were mounds of newspapers, rags, tins and bits and pieces of debris being devoured by cockroaches. There was the sound of scuttling everywhere.

It was the wrong house. No human being could live there. He was rich, the man who lived there. No one lived there. There was no man. There was a flash by one of the smashed windows and the light streamed in as Bontoc pushed over a pile of newspapers and sent them spilling out across the floor. The entire floor was moving with insects and slime. He had exhumed a smell from years back. In the light Elizalde saw one of the headlines on the newspaper, before as he watched, it seemed to melt and turn into ooze. It was years old. Elizalde losing Ambrosio as the light hit his eyes, yelled, 'Jesus-Vincente – !'

'Stairs! There are stairs here!' He was to one side of the chandelier, pushing at papers and mounds of what looked like vile, dripping fabric. There were pictures on the walls and everywhere in the room, the mounds of material were not mounds of material at all, but furniture. The pictures were portraits of a family, Spanish, Philippino, American done in oils, hanging, rotting, the faces torn and ragged, the paint melting and running, all the features, the eyes, the clothing dripping from the faces and bodies as if they melted. The furniture was all dark narra-wood in the Spanish style. Ambrosio, pushing at what looked like a sideboard to get to the stairs, said, 'Ayo!' as the sideboard, rotted and tunnelled with borers, turned to sawdust in his hands. He saw light at the top of the stairs, up there in the darkness. Ambrosio, kicking something aside at the bottom of the stairs, said, 'Here! Bald Head's gone up here! I can see where he walked in the damp!' He shouted to Bontoc, 'Baptiste! Here! Help me! It's fallen across the stairs! Here, help me push this cupboard aside!' He shouted to Elizalde coming towards him, 'Mother of God, what is this place?' He looked up. He saw a light. He saw a flash of movement. The whole place seemed to be moving, creaking, falling apart. He heard a sound: a movement. He saw, in the darkness at the top of the stairs, a long corridor. He heard, down the corridor –

He heard a burst of gunfire. Ambrosio, taking the strain against the cupboard and going down with it as it turned to sawdust, yelled, 'Felix! Felix! *Where the hell are you?*'

He couldn't find him. He had only seen the estate from the road. He had never been inside. He had had no idea it would be like this. Bald Head, kicking doors open as he went down the long, dark corridor, yelled back at the Vietnamese, 'Up here! He's got to be up here!' The doors had no resistance. They crashed and splintered like balsa. He kicked open another door, fired off a short burst into the darkness, and crouching, went in. It was like all the others. There was nothing but darkness and decay. There was nothing. He saw, for a moment, through a smashed window, the trees surrounding the estate. They were almost at the window, growing in, taking over. Bald Head, turning, seeing the Vietnamese at the door in his long yellow robe, yelled, 'He's here! I know he's here! I tracked him for eight years! This is where he is!'

The Vietnamese was watching him. He was blank faced. Bald Head, shoving past him, getting the gun up to port for the next door, shouted, 'He's here! He's in one of the rooms here!'

He lashed at the door with his foot and it came down in a cloud of dust and powder. There were more doors: down the long corridor that had once served all the bedrooms in the huge house, there was door after door.

Bald Head, turning, twisting in the corridor, shooting the door facing him to pieces with a long, uncontrolled burst of fire that lit up the corridor and sent cases pinging and bouncing down the uncarpeted floor, yelled, 'I'm right! I'm right! *He's here!*'

'*Police! Throw down your weapon!*' He was on the landing at the far end of the corridor. He had come up what had once been the servants' stairs at the corner of the entrance lobby through a small service door that led down to the basement and up to the top floor. Elizalde, pushing his way through piled-up furniture in the stink and decay, feeling his skin crawl as insects from the floor and the walls attacked him, yelled into the gloom, 'Ambrosio! Bontoc! Stay down there! Don't come up!' He could not get through, the furniture and newspapers piled up in the corridor were stuck, glued to the floor, bound there by nests and cobwebs and millions of tiny dead and alive creatures living in them. Elizalde, pushing, shoving, trying to get past, shouted down. 'Stay there! You've got the only other way down covered!' He heard Ambrosio and Bontoc pushing aside furniture. He could not see anything of the floor below. He heard a crash. He heard movement. He ordered them. '*Stay there!*'

'Goddam! Goddam! Goddam!' He was running, snapping a

fresh magazine into the Armalite as he went. He saw the Vietnamese's eyes from the light from one of the holed and smashed windows in one of the open rooms. Bald Head, running, not stopping, going for the staircase, yelled, 'I can do it! I can do it!' He saw the Vietnamese hesitate and he caught him by the shoulder and spun him around with the gun barrel an inch from his face. Bald Head, shrieking, spittle on his mouth, yelled, 'I can do it all! I can take them all! *I can do it!*'

He saw him. At the top of the stairs he saw him. He was a shape, a flash of light. He saw bright metal on the Armalite flash. Half-way up the stairs, Bontoc shrieked, 'Stop! Halt!' By Uncle Apo Bontoc and Miss Thomasina Landsborough, he wasn't going to do it wrong twice. Bontoc, bringing his gun up, yelled at the top of his voice, 'This is the Police! I am giving you a legal order! Drop that weapon or I'll fire!' He heard Ambrosio and Elizalde yell at him simultaneously and he yelled back as the Armalite was cocked with a sudden hard click, 'I'll fire a warning shot first. I'll – ' He looked down for the change lever on the submachine gun to put it to single shot. Bontoc, not looking up, balancing precariously on the rotting stairs, shifting his feet to find a steady spot from which, like Archimedes, to move the world, yelled –

He saw him. He was some sort of midget, some sort of monkey with a giant gun in his hand. He was half-way up the stairs. He had stopped. He was doing something. He had not seen him. There were more of them. He heard a voice from somewhere on his left shout, 'Baptiste!' and then another voice, lower, on the first floor, order him, 'No! Get back! No!' and Bald Head, shooting into the shadows, emptied an entire magazine down at him and set the stairs on fire. He heard crashing, creaking. Bits and pieces were flying up everywhere from the stairs. There was dust. The entire stairs were giving way. He got another magazine from his pocket and fired into the flames. He saw the stairs burn. For an instant he thought he saw a dark, ugly face looking up at him and then the stairs went and the house seemed to shake as they collapsed in a single giant explosion of dust and wood and smoke. He saw the Vietnamese in his yellow robe running towards him. He was shouting, yelling. He had found a locked door. He had heard a voice behind it, pleading, shrieking. Bald Head running back through the corridor, loading the Armalite, yelled in triumph, 'I did it! I can do it! I can do it!' The door was at the end of the corridor. It was locked. It was hard wood. It had been varnished against the insects. Standing back, shouting, his eyes blazing, Bald Head firing a long, raking burst, turned it to flying spinning matchwood.

Behind the door, he saw a light.

His gun had gone. He was hanging onto the stair-rail like an acrobat and his gun had gone. He was choking, suffocating in the dust and smoke. Bontoc, falling, losing his grip, shouted, 'Intutungtso – help me!' He was shouting in Bontoc. He was shouting to all the old Bontoc gods. He was going. He felt himself slip. It was a nightmare. There was nothing left of the stairs, but in the darkness he was hanging on to some part of the stairs and they were going. His gun was gone. He could see nothing through the smoke. He heard noises, sounds, creaking, all the wood on whatever he was hanging onto falling to pieces in his hands and turning into pulp.

'Intutungtso – !'

He heard shouting. He heard gunfire. He felt something hard get him by the hand and take him in an iron grip and he shouted at whatever it was, 'No! *No!*' He saw a gun glint, dull metal against his shoulder and face. He saw, for an instant, Ambrosio's face. Bontoc, kicking, pushing, scrabbling, to find purchase as Ambrosio lifted and yelled at him to push, *pushed.* Bontoc, changing to Philippino, trying to do the Manila dialect, failing, doing his best, tears of dust and grime flowing down his face, yelled at the top of his voice to the man's face only inches from his mouth, 'Thank you! Thank you! THANK YOU!'

'*No!*' He heard the scream. Elizalde, getting the muck aside on the landing, seeing the light at the far end of the corridor, shouted, 'Baptiste! Jesus-Vincente!' The sound of the gun was still ringing in his ears. He shook his head to try to clear the ringing. His clothes were alive with insects. '*Bontoc!*

Ambrosio!' He heard someone yell back in English, 'Yes! We're all right!'

'*No!*'

He heard someone scream from the room at the far end of the corridor. Pushing, shoving the furniture aside, getting towards the light, for an instant Elizalde saw someone in a long saffron robe. He was entering the room at the far end of the corridor.

He knew who he was.

He knew what he was going to do.

He could not get through. Some huge piece of furniture was stuck across the corridor and he could not move it. He saw the light at the far end of the corridor, in the room there. He saw only the Vietnamese framed in the doorway.

He saw him looking inside.

'*No!*'

He heard whoever was in that room – Silvero – scream.

He saw the Vietnamese, from his long, flowing, yellow robe, slowly, drag a long, killing butcher's knife.

He was through. He had got the last piece of furniture on its side and it had pivoted for a moment, one of its legs snapping, and then toppled against the railing and crashed over the side through a railing to the floor below. He heard the chandelier swing, tinkling, glass breaking, and then with a crash that raised dust and insects and the stink of decay, it came down. On the stairs Bontoc and Ambrosio had the fire under control. They were beating at it with sodden newspapers. It flared up, then died, then flared up again. He was through. Far down the end of the corridor he saw the light. He heard voices. He heard someone shriek in terror. Down there, in that room, there was Silvero, the bird, everything. He saw Quintero outlined in his battle dress at the doorway. He was fitting a magazine into his gun. He was shouting at someone, urging them to do something. He heard the Vietnamese shout, 'Cover me!' He was not going to take Quintero's orders. He was not going to do something in a hurry. He heard him shout, 'Cover me! Go back and cover me! If you want to go to America *go back and cover me!*' He saw him come. He saw Quintero, outlined clearly at the door, draw back the cocking handle on the Armalite and begin running back down the corridor.

Elizalde had his gun out. He felt his stomach pain in a long, terrible spasm of agony that doubled him up. He felt his grip harden on the butt of his pistol. He could not get it up. He felt himself sinking, going, being paralysed with fear.

'It's out!' On the stairs, Ambrosio, beating at the fire, shouted, 'It's out!' With the fire gone so was the light. He took a step higher and felt the riser give way and collapse. The stairs were rotten. He turned back to Bontoc, still beating at the last sparks and yelled at him, 'My gun! Get my gun! It's behind you! I put it down on the floor!' He heard someone running in the darkness, heavy footsteps, like someone wearing military boots. He heard the echo of the gun being cocked. Ambrosio, stuck on the stairs, his foot caught in the rotten riser, twisting back to see Bontoc, yelled, 'Gun! Get my gun!' He could not see Elizalde. He shouted, 'Felix!' He looked up. He saw Bald Head's silhouette at the top of the stairs. He saw, he sensed, he felt –

He saw, in the last glint of the fire behind him, the man's eyes.

He was stuck, unarmed. He couldn't move. He heard Bontoc on his hands and knees scrabbling for the gun in the darkness and broken wood, coughing at the smoke.

He saw the gun come up. He saw the man and gun turn into a single shadow. He saw –

Ambrosio yelled at the top of his voice, 'FELIX!'

It was a stark, unpainted room with nothing in it but a desk and a computer link and a telephone. It was his office. It was where he worked, where he planned, where he slaved like a dog over his victories and his profits, where he had planned the taking of a boat.

It was where he would die.

In the room, advancing on him, the Vietnamese, the long knife shaking in his hand, said in a whisper, 'Ghosts. All the ghosts have come back . . . They've come back for you.'

He was a man of the Vietnamese's own age. They were

linked to the same time, to the same world. They were linked to the same lives. They were inextricably linked to the same time and memories and blood. His name was Silvero. He was a man like the Vietnamese. Like soldiers, strangers meeting on a battlefield, they were bound together. The Vietnamese said softly, 'I've come a very, very long way . . .'

He came forward in his saffron robe, the knife shaking in his hand.

His eyes were blank and staring. He was Death. He came forward.

Silvero, his face collapsing, becoming featureless, staring, shrieked, 'NO!' He shrieked, 'WHO ARE YOU?'

'Quintero!' He had the gun up. In the corridor he was at the head of the stairs with the gun ready and cocked. In the darkness, somewhere there was Bontoc and Ambrosio. Elizalde, standing away from the fallen and smashed furniture, his pistol held out in two hands, yelled with all his strength, 'Quintero!' He saw the man turn – he saw him as a shadow – he saw the gun move, turn onto him. He felt the awful, tearing wound in his stomach again and again. He felt again what it was like to be shot. The gun was coming around to him. He saw, in the light from the far room, Quintero's face turn to see him. He heard Quintero say in a gasp, 'You!' He had been shot before. He felt again the feeling. Elizalde, trying to hold himself upright, trying to keep the pistol out in front of him, said, 'Stop. Stop . . . Stop . . . !'

'FELIX!'

He saw the shadow at the top of the stairs turning away. Somewhere, somewhere in the darkness, Bontoc could hear Elizalde's voice. It was soft, almost pleading. He could not find Ambrosio's gun! His own PPK was in its ankle holster. He reached for it but it was gone. He could not find Ambrosio's gun on the floor. Bontoc, scrabbling, reaching for anything and everything in the darkness with mad grasping fingers, yelled, 'I can't find it! I can't find the gun!'

'NO!' He heard Silvero scream. At the top of the stairs

Quintero said, 'I'm fit. I can do it . . . They ruined all my life and now . . .'

He shot him. In an instant, pulling once at the trigger of his PPK, Elizalde shot him. He had never shot anyone before in his life, but he shot someone now. He shot him in the chest. He saw him stagger and he shot him again. He saw the Armalite waver, he saw it seem to move in a wide arc down towards the stairs, and standing there, in full view of the man as he looked at him, Elizalde shot him again and again until he fell.

He shot him. He seemed, somehow, not to be there: he was shooting in the darkness, watching the flames light up the corridor and he was shooting over and over until the gun clicked empty and then, somehow he was still shooting him with no sound and the man was standing there looking at him, then going over, then somehow pausing, getting hold of himself, being arrested in mid-air, and he was shooting the pistol at him again, over and over – the same moment of the first bullet being run and re-run over and over – and he was shooting him again.

He had thought the worst thing in the world – the thing of all his nightmares – was the terrible, awful moment when he had been shot himself in the stomach, when, in that moment, he had thought that he was dying and that everything he had done had been wrong and selfish and for himself alone. He had never taken life seriously until the instant when it was fading for him and he thought –

It was not the worst thing in the world. The worst thing in the world was not to be killed, but to kill someone else.

He was firing, the scene was running over and over and he was still firing; he was shooting the life out of a human being, the bullets beating his humanity, his shape to pulp and he was –

'NO!' He heard Silvero shriek.

'FELIX!' It was Ambrosio. He was there with Bontoc at the top of the stairs, reaching for Quintero's Armalite. Quintero was dead, he had been dead for seconds.

'NO!' He heard Silvero shriek as the long butcher's knife drew back to slaughter him.

Elizalde, running, wrenching at Ambrosio and Bontoc as he went by them to the room at the end of the corridor, yelled to the killing, to both the killings, to all the killings, 'No! It's all wrong!' He heard Silvero shriek like an animal. It was his last moment on Earth.

Elizalde, running, crashing down the rotted wooden corridor to the last room, shouted to the Vietnamese to stop him, 'No! It isn't him! It's all wrong! There's someone else! IT ISN'T HIM!'

20

It was the end. In the other room at the end of the corridor, the owner of Mendez, the owner of the house, closed his eyes and putting his hands softly to his face, listened to the sounds.

It was the end. He knew it would come.

There was no furniture in the room, nothing on the walls. Squatting, he sat on bare unpainted floorboards and stared first at Mendez in his wickerwork cage and then at the polished sleeper-like planks of wood resting one on top of the other against the far wall where the uncurtained window was. There was a brocaded box on top of the stack. He put his hands together in an attitude of prayer and gazed first at it, and then at the window.

The trees, inch by inch, were making their way to the glass of the window. Soon, they would push in and smash it and begin to take over.

He looked at Mendez. The bird was still recovering from its wounds. It was still drugged with sedatives from Mang Paulo's Cock Hospital. Without its wooden leg it lay quietly on one side watching him from its one good eye.

He looked at the window and saw the trees.

He knew it would come.

He knew the trees would take over and he knew what he heard outside, like the trees, was inevitable.

It had been a very long time.

The house around him had rotted.

He had rotted.

He felt a scream bursting in his lungs. He looked at first the trees and then the room, the box, then at Mendez and finally at his hands in front of his face and he felt a scream bursting in his lungs.

'*SILVERO – !*'

He heard the man outside, the Vietnamese, the scream in his lungs bursting free, shrill in triumph.

He had him. At last, he had him. In the room, he had Silvero, the last of them, the leader of them, on the floor in front of him with the knife against his throat. He had his head pulled back by the hair. Yanking, jerking, making the man mew in terror, he was pulling his head back further and further and pressing with the knife. It was sharpened to a razor's edge. He only had to draw it a fraction across the man's throat and it would slice into him and open him up like a pig.

The Vietnamese, his breath coming in gasps, pulling, yanking, pressing with the knife, could not bring himself to speak. He had ceased to be human. He had come to the point where his dreams and reality crossed and the moment was going on and on. He was grunting, snarling. He felt the knife as part of his hand. He pressed. He ached to draw it across the throat but the moment was all he had dreamed of for years and he could not bring himself to finish it.

The man had wet himself on the floor. He was shaking, jerking, terrified to move, but moving in spasms. He was not a man but a creature. He was the way the Vietnamese's family had been when the pirates had come on the boat and killed them. He was at the moment they had been at when they had realised that there was nowhere to go, nothing more to do, nowhere to escape and that they would die.

He was going to die.

The Vietnamese, the sounds in his throat reaching a crescendo, put all the force in his hand in a single shaking surge of strength to draw the knife deep across the man's throat.

He heard noises. He saw them running towards them. He saw their guns. It was the end. It didn't matter. He had told his family in America he was prepared to die to see the killers killed. He had thought before the killing started, before he had turned Quintero loose, before he came to an arrangement, that he might be able to get back home, but it was too late now.

He would not get home.

He had told his family.

He was prepared to die. He began, slowly, drawing the knife across Silvero's throat.

He felt the man in his grasp jerk.

They were coming, Innocente, Gil, Pineda, the SWAT team. He heard the sirens. At the end of the corridor, Elizalde running, Bontoc and Ambrosio running with him, yelled to the Vietnamese. 'It isn't him! You've got the wrong man! *It isn't him!*' He saw the Vietnamese's face. Above the saffron robe, above Silvero's yanked back head, above the thin line of blood starting at the neck, once started, unstoppable, the Vietnamese was no longer human. Elizalde pushed Bontoc and Ambrosio back as they came in ready to shoot, shrieked, '*It isn't him!*'

'Quintero – !'

'He's dead! Everything he told you is a lie!'

He was grunting, pulling on the knife. The Vietnamese, his eyes rolling, shouted to someone listening, not to Elizalde or Bontoc or Ambrosio, not to the fear of their guns, but to the gods, 'They were pirates! They killed all my brother's family! They took everything that was his and they killed them in the sea and raped them and destroyed them like vermin!' His hand was shaking. He was looking to the gods for the word to slice deeply, finally, into the neck, 'Quintero told me! He knew them! He said he had seen the wreckage of my brother's boat. He saw the nameplate. He had it once in his storeroom! He knew who they were! He had all their names! Tolentino, the two Royares brothers, Agoncillo – Silvero!'

'No!'

'They had Mendez! They had the last in the line of the birds my family got from the Legion in Indo-China! They even published its lineage! They cared so little, considered the deaths, the rapes, the murder of my brother's family to be of so little importance in the entire world, that they advertised what they had done!' The knife was hard against Silvero's throat. Silvero's nose was running. In front of him was the pool of urine. He could no longer speak. His eyes were going white, ready for death: he was dead already — his mind had shut down, refused the horror and his arm hung limply down at his sides waiting for the knife.

'They were mercury smugglers! They were mercury smugglers and gun runners and for all I know narcotic smugglers, but they didn't — '

'They had the bird!'

'No!' Elizalde saw Bontoc with Ambrosio's Uzi start to try to get around behind the Vietnamese. Elizalde, stopping him, said, 'No.' He saw all the life going out of Silvero's eyes. Elizalde, shouting at him to bring him back, demanded, 'Tell him! Tell him! Tell him why you weren't pirates! Tell him the truth! Tell him where Mendez came from!' He saw nothing in Silvero's eyes but growing death. Elizalde, shouting, ordered him, 'TELL HIM! Tell him who the other one is!'

He had laid out all the low, polished lengths of wood around him in a semi-circle and placed the brocade box in front of him where he squatted on his heels.

In the adjoining room at the end of the corridor, staring hard at Mendez and the trees, the man there took off his shirt and, folding it carefully, put it to one side and reached out for the box.

The first thing he touched inside the box was a little book of matches.

He took them out and checked to see that they were dry.

He was beyond tears.

He merely looked hard at the matches to make sure they were dry.

'Tell him!'

'No . . . money . . . in it!' It came out as a gasp, as the truth, as a jerk of his head. Silvero, trying to mew, trying to plead, the light coming back into his eyes, whining, making sounds, said, 'No . . . money in it!'

'He's Hipogrifo! Quintero tracked them for years! They had

got him too! He was their victim too! He had his own reasons for – '

'*He lied to you! They did nothing to your family! What they did they did to him!*'

'They had the bird!'

'They bought the bird!'

'They took its father from the boat!'

'They took nothing! They're smugglers! Hipogrifo means Flying Horse! It was the name of their boat! They were drug runners! It's a slang word for heroin! Hipogrifo was in operation before they got the bird! I've checked! I've had it checked! They got the bird from someone who *sold* it to them!' He saw the knife move. Elizalde shouted, 'Don't kill him!' Outside, he heard Innocente and Gil and Pineda and the SWAT team getting through the broken furniture and debris on the ground floor. If the SWAT team got up to the room they would kill the Vietnamese without hesitation. There had been enough killing already. Elizalde, going forward, his hand out to stop the knife, said clearly, 'Your name is Tran, like the bird's.'

'My family's name is Tran! All one side of the Tran family is dead! All one side of the Tran family is bones on the bottom of the ocean! There were women, children, old men – they killed them! They raped them and they killed them and then they disposed of them like vermin, like cockroaches, like – '

'*Where is he?*' He actually had his hand on Silvero's shoulder. Elizalde, pressing down on the man, trying to bring the eyes back, ordered him, 'Tell him! Tell him!'

'This isn't my house! It's his!' Twisting, trying to turn, feeling the knife bite, feeling blood starting in his mouth, yelling before he drowned in it, Silvero shrieked, 'I work for him! It's his house! It was his bird! We formed a syndicate! It was always him! And then, then when he – We ran it for him because he – '

'WHERE IS HE?'

'There! He's in there!' There was a door in the darkness, a single unpainted entrance to another adjoining room gone mouldy and stained with neglect. Bontoc, seeing it, said, 'There!'

'Kick it down!' Elizalde, holding the Vietnamese's eyes with his own, his hand actually on the knife, pulling it away said, 'Tran! Your name is Tran. The name of the original bird they bred. Mendez was from Tran – *and so is the name of the man in there!*' He heard a crash as simultaneously, Ambrosio and Bontoc put their shoulders to the door and brought it down in splinters. Elizalde, shrieking at both the Vietnamese and Silvero, demanded, '*Who? Who is he?*'

It was his own brother. On the boat, to save himself during that awful voyage, he had killed every one of them. Out there, on that terrible sea, in that terrible darkness, he had taken a gun and, one by one, while they slept, he had killed every one of his own family. Perhaps it had been within sight of the Philippines, perhaps it had been because, like all the boat-people, he had heard stories of the boats being sent on, being towed out to sea to sail on in a ghastly, unending voyage or perhaps it had been merely that he had become afraid or mad or both, but out there, before he swam ashore with his only possession, with the great fighting bird, he had methodically killed every one of them and scuttled the boat.

It was there in his eyes.

Behind the semi-circle of lit candles, behind the little altar, the defence the low polished blocks of wood made, it was in his face. He could have been no more than forty years old. His face was the face of an old, old man. He had rotted. He had come ashore with the bird, found everything he had hoped for and, once he had it and there was time to think – time not merely to survive, but to live in ease – from the inside, he had begun, like his house to rot. There was the awful smell of an opened tomb in the room. In the room, the corpse, behind his candles, looked at them.

Bontoc said softly, 'God in Heaven . . .' He heard Ambrosio suck in his breath.

Elizalde said to the Vietnamese, 'Let him go.' He saw the knife come away from Silvero's throat and he reached out for it. It came away of its own accord and fell to the floor.

It was his own brother. The Vietnamese, going forward, said softly, 'You . . .'

By the candles Mendez was in his wickerwork cage. In the warmth of the candles with his wounds healing, he slept. The Vietnamese said softly, 'You . . .' He put out his hand as Bontoc reached out for him, 'You . . .'

He was already dead. The thing squatting behind the candles was already dead. It had a long-barrelled revolver in its hands, the metal of the cylinder glowing in the candlelight, but it was already dead.

He heard them coming, the rest of the police and the men with guns. The Vietnamese screamed, 'YOU? YOU?'

There were no words.

'Aaaaaiiiiyahhh!' It came from his mouth as a shriek from the soul. It came from the ocean and that terrible night. It came from Hell. The creature behind the candles, his mouth open and gaping, a dark, bottomless hole, screamed from the depths of his being, '*AAAAAIIIYAHHH!*' He had the gun to his head. His eyes were not looking at his brother, at any of them. He heard nothing as the SWAT team, running, came up the hall. He saw nothing of Elizalde or Bontoc or Ambrosio or Silvero on the floor, or his brother at the door. He saw only the light and the candles, he saw only that he had been seen. He saw only that – The man behind the candles, begging, entreating, pleading, cried out to the darkness, to anyone who might listen, '*Don't* – don't frighten my soul as it leaves! Let it –' He shrieked out in his final, hopeless words, deserving nothing, only hoping, 'Let it go to my family! Let me ask their forgiveness through eternity! *Don't – !*'

He had the gun to his head, cocked.

He looked, one last time, at the bird, at Capitaine Danjou de Camerone, 1863, to Charles de Caserne, Sidi-bel-Abbes, to all the Charles de Caserne, to Tran of Saigon Rex, to Mendez, to –

MENDEZ BEER FOR HOPE.

MENDEZ BEER FOR VITALITY.

MENDEZ! MACHO! MENDEZ!

He was already dead. He had been dead for a long time.

In that awful, candlelit room, in the unspeakable place where he lived, looking up into the darkness, afraid of what, through eternity, he would find there, having no other place left anywhere to go, in a thundering blast that lit up the room with the muzzle flash and toppled him over into the burning candles, he pulled once, firmly, on the trigger.

They had never seen it close up before, something of so much value.

In the little room, in the faint light from the window and the last of the burning candles, the SWAT team, shaking their heads, stared at Mendez, at the wonderful fighting bird in total and utter silent admiration and awe.

Battling Mendez of Manila.

It was said, because of the riches he had earned for his owners, he had a leg for every occasion.

In the wickerwork cage, like the spirit, like the history itself of the entire Philippine islands and people, he slept only briefly, temporarily, recovering for the next time, from his wounds . . .

Bestselling Crime

☐ Moonspender	Jonathan Gash	£2.50
☐ Shake Hands For Ever	Ruth Rendell	£2.50
☐ A Guilty Thing Surprised	Ruth Rendell	£2.50
☐ The Tree of Hands	Ruth Rendell	£2.50
☐ Wexford: An Omnibus	Ruth Rendell	£5.95
☐ Evidence to Destroy	Margaret Yorke	£2.50
☐ No One Rides For Free	Larry Beinhart	£2.95
☐ In La La Land We Trust	Robert Campbell	£2.50
☐ Suspects	William J. Caunitz	£2.95
☐ Blood on the Moon	James Ellroy	£2.50
☐ Roses Are Dead	Loren D. Estleman	£2.50
☐ The Body in the Billiard Room	H.R.F. Keating	£2.50
☐ Rough Cider	Peter Lovesey	£2.50

Prices and other details are liable to change

ARROW BOOKS, BOOKSERVICE BY POST, PO BOX 29, DOUGLAS, ISLE OF MAN, BRITISH ISLES

NAME...

ADDRESS...

....

....

Please enclose a cheque or postal order made out to Arrow Books Ltd. for the amount due and allow the following for postage and packing.

U.K. CUSTOMERS: Please allow 22p per book to a maximum of £3.00.

B.F.P.O. & EIRE: Please allow 22p per book to a maximum of £3.00

OVERSEAS CUSTOMERS: Please allow 22p per book.

Whilst every effort is made to keep prices low it is sometimes necessary to increase cover prices at short notice. Arrow Books reserve the right to show new retail prices on covers which may differ from those previously advertised in the text or elsewhere.

Bestselling Thriller/Suspense

☐ Hell is Always Today	Jack Higgins	£2.50
☐ Brought in Dead	Harry Patterson	£1.99
☐ Russian Spring	Dennis Jones	£2.50
☐ Fletch	Gregory Mcdonald	£1.95
☐ Black Ice	Colin Dunne	£2.50
☐ Blind Run	Brian Freemantle	£2.50
☐ The Proteus Operation	James P. Hogan	£3.50
☐ Miami One Way	Mike Winters	£2.50
☐ Skydancer	Geoffrey Archer	£2.50
☐ Hour of the Lily	John Kruse	£3.50
☐ The Tunnel	Stanley Johnson	£2.50
☐ The Albatross Run	Douglas Scott	£2.50
☐ Dragonfire	Andrew Kaplan	£2.99

Prices and other details are liable to change

ARROW BOOKS, BOOKSERVICE BY POST, PO BOX 29, DOUGLAS, ISLE OF MAN, BRITISH ISLES

NAME . . . .

ADDRESS . . . .

. . . .

. . . .

Please enclose a cheque or postal order made out to Arrow Books Ltd. for the amount due and allow the following for postage and packing.

U.K. CUSTOMERS: Please allow 22p per book to a maximum of £3.00.

B.F.P.O. & EIRE: Please allow 22p per book to a maximum of £3.00

OVERSEAS CUSTOMERS: Please allow 22p per book.

Whilst every effort is made to keep prices low it is sometimes necessary to increase cover prices at short notice. Arrow Books reserve the right to show new retail prices on covers which may differ from those previously advertised in the text or elsewhere.

Bestselling Fiction

☐ Hiroshmia Joe	Martin Booth	£2.95
☐ The Pianoplayers	Anthony Burgess	£2.50
☐ Queen's Play	Dorothy Dunnett	£3.95
☐ Colours Aloft	Alexander Kent	£2.95
☐ Contact	Carl Sagan	£3.50
☐ Talking to Strange Men	Ruth Rendell	£5.95
☐ Heartstones	Ruth Rendell	£2.50
☐ The Ladies of Missalonghi	Colleen McCullough	£2.50
☐ No Enemy But Time	Evelyn Anthony	£2.95
☐ The Heart of the Country	Fay Weldon	£2.50
☐ The Stationmaster's Daughter	Pamela Oldfield	£2.95
☐ Erin's Child	Sheelagh Kelly	£3.99
☐ The Lilac Bus	Maeve Binchy	£2.50

Prices and other details are liable to change

ARROW BOOKS, BOOKSERVICE BY POST, PO BOX 29, DOUGLAS, ISLE OF MAN, BRITISH ISLES

NAME...

ADDRESS..

....

....

Please enclose a cheque or postal order made out to Arrow Books Ltd. for the amount due and allow the following for postage and packing.

U.K. CUSTOMERS: Please allow 22p per book to a maximum of £3.00.

B.F.P.O. & EIRE: Please allow 22p per book to a maximum of £3.00

OVERSEAS CUSTOMERS: Please allow 22p per book.

Whilst every effort is made to keep prices low it is sometimes necessary to increase cover prices at short notice. Arrow Books reserve the right to show new retail prices on covers which may differ from those previously advertised in the text or elsewhere.